IN THE HANDS
OF THE
LIVING GOD

IN THE HANDS
OF THE
LIVING GOD

Lillian Bouzane

SUMMERSDALE

First published by Turnstone Press in 1999.

This edition published in 2002 by Summersdale Publishers Ltd.

This edition copyright © Lillian Bouzane 2002.

Summersdale Publishers Ltd
46 West Street
Chichester
West Sussex
PO19 1RP
UK

www.summersdale.com

Printed and bound in Great Britain.

ISBN 1 84024 216 7

Cover design by Blue Lemon Design Consultancy
www.bluelemondesign.co.uk

About the Author

Lillian Bouzane is an award-winning writer and poet. She lives in Newfoundland, Canada. *In the Hands of the Living God* is her first novel.

Acknowlededgments

I wish to thank the following people who read this novel from beginning to end: Joan Tubrett who twice read what I now know to be notes for the novel; Linda Renaud who kept saying 'tell me more'; my agent, Karen O'Reilly, who did a brilliant analysis of the first draft, and sold the second; Georgina Queller who contributed her special brand of criticism; my niece, Regina Smart, who was my music advisor; and Mark Morton, the editor wisely provided by Turnstone Press, who raised questions, pointed out flaws. Any errors are mine.

I also want to thank all those associated with the good ship *Matthew* (*Mathye*), especially my fellow crew-members who sailed her from Penzance to Bristol.

I gratefully acknowledge the assistance of the Year of the Arts Committee.

A number of books helped in researching the fifteenth century, in particular *The Cabot Voyages and Bristol Discovery under Henry VII*, edited by J. A. Williamson; *The Portuguese Columbus* by Mascarenhas Barreto, translated by Reginald A. Brown; *Venice: A Documentary History, 1450–1630*, edited by David Chambers and Brian Pullan with Jennifer Fletcher; and *Venetian Narrative Painting in the Age of Carpaccio* by Patricia Fortini Brown.

Contents

Introduction 13

Chapter One 15

Chapter Two 46

Chapter Three 82

Chapter Four 137

Chapter Five 188

Chapter Six 223

Chapter Seven 284

Epilogue 303

Glossary 312

List of Characters

All characters listed live in fifteenth-century Venice and are recorded in history. Exceptions in time and place are noted.

Americ, Richard Merchant and chief backer of Giovanni Caboto, Bristol.

Barbarigo, Agostino Doge of the Republic of Venice.

Bellini, Gentile Painter, brother of painter Giovanni Bellini.

Bianco, Andrea Cartographer.

Buonarroti, Michelangelo Tuscan sculptor and painter, 1475–1564.

Caboto, Giovanni Navigator in search of a short route to the spices of the East.

Caboto, Lodovico Eldest son of Mathye and Giovanni.

Caboto, Mathye Wife of Giovanni. Composer and choir director at San Zan Degolla.

Caboto, Sancio Youngest son.

Caboto, Sebastian Middle son.

Canynges, Thomas Bristol merchant, one of Giovanni Caboto's backers.

Carmeliano, Pietro Friar and Latin secretary to Henry VII, Brescia.

Carpaccio, Vittore Painter.

Carpini (John de Plano) Monk who, with a brother monk, William de Rubruquis, was sent by Pope Innocent IV as envoy to the Great Kahn in the thirteenth century.

Catherine of Aragon Daughter of Isabella of Castile and Ferdinand of Aragon.

Charles VIII King of France.

Columbus (Colon/Zarco), Christopher Navigator in the employ of Queen Isabella of Castile.

Cornaro, Zorzi Knight and senator in the Government of Venice, brother of the Queen of Cyprus.

Count Giovanni Pico della Mirandola Intellectual and friend of Friar Savonarola, Florence.

Count Ugolino Pisa, died 1289.

d'Ailly, Pierre French cartographer and cardinal, 1350–1420.

de Carbonariis, Giovanni Antonio Friar and royal messenger from Henry VII to the Duke of Milan, and member of Giovanni's 1497–98 crew.

de la Cosa, Juan Alonso de Ojeda's cartographer.

de' Medici, Piero Head of the Government of Florence.

de Ojeda, Alonso Military chief to Queen Isabella of Castile.

de Puebla, Gonsalez Ambassador to England from the Court of Queen Isabella of Castile.

Dedo, Zuane Senator.

del Pozzo Toscanelli, Dottore Paolo Cosmographer, Florence.

Dom Diogo of Portugal Son of Prince Fernando of Portugal.

Dom João of Portugal Son of Prince Fernando of Portugal.

Donato, Thomaso Patriarch of Venice.

Duke of Gandia Son of Pope Alexander VI.

Elizabeth of York Daughter of Edward IV of England and heir to the throne.

Elyot, Hugh Bristol merchant who accompanied Giovanni Caboto on his 1497 voyage.

Emperor Maximilian Emperor of Germany.

Fidelis, Cassandra Intellectual and humanist.

Gherardi, Maffeo Patriarch of Venice, spiritual advisor to Mathye Caboto.

Giorgione (Giorgio Barbarelli) Painter.

Gnupsson, Eirik Papal legate to Norway, Iceland and Greenland, and missionary to the Skraelings in 1121.

Jay, John Mariner, Bristol.

King Ferdinand of Aragon Husband of Queen Isabella of Castile.

King Henry VII First Tudor king of England, reigned from 1485 to 1509.

King Manuel King of Portugal from 1495 to 1521.

Loredan, Antonio Senator and member of the Collegio.

Maimonides Scholar and writer on the Torah, 1135–1204.

Martins, Fernão Canon at the Cathedral of Lisbon, servant to the King of Portugal.

Messer Blemet Hebrew scholar, Florence.

Morton, John Archbishop of Canterbury.

Nicolas of Lynn Fourteenth-century English astronomer, mathematician and navigator.

Paschal II Pope, 1099–1118.

Petrarch Italian poet and scholar, 1304–74.

Picorina, Violante Singer.

Polo, Marco Explorer, 1254–1324, journeyed overland to Mongolia and visited Kublai Khan.

Queen Caterina Cornaro Queen of Cyprus from 1472 to 1489.

Queen Isabella of Castile Wife of King Ferdinand of Aragon. They maintained separate States.

Ramos, Girolama Corsi Poet.

Rull, Gasper Merchant, Valencia.

Sanudo, Marin Writer and historian.

Savonarola, Girolamo Dominican friar and reformer, Ferrara.

Sforza, Ludovico Duke of Milan.

Thorne, Robert Bristol merchant, accompanied Giovanni Caboto on his 1497 voyage.

Vespucci, Amerigo Friend of Mathye and Giovanni, Florence.

Vespucci, Anastasio Monk and scholar, uncle of Amerigo Vespucci, Florence.

Author's Note

The letter was the only means of written communication in the fifteenth century.

Heads of state had their emissaries; merchants and those who could read used one of the many private postal services. An overland 'express post' connected major cities: a relay of riders could deliver mail from Bruges to Venice in as few as fifteen days.

Seals were used, but the art of breaking them was a sub-trade of the letter-carrying business.

Letters were sometimes lost en route or waylaid at an out-of-the-way post. A traveller might carry a private letter, which generally went unsealed and often passed from hand to hand before it reached the person for whom it was destined.

Letters were shared with family, relatives and friends, and were written with that understanding.

Introduction

The last decade of the fifteenth century, Venice was the queen city of Europe.

For two hundred years her nobles controlled the spice and silk trade of the fabulous East and their galleys brought that wealth up the Grand Canal and shipped it along the trade routes of Europe.

Venetian families schooled their sons in the ways of the sea, and trade remained in their capable hands.

From one of those families came the woman Mathye, who married the greatest seaman of them all: Giovanni Caboto. Caboto was a man who dared greatly, but the thrust of his daring was aimed at the heart of Venice.

This is their story.

Chapter One

My darling husband,

Amerigo Vespucci's little servant came swimming up to our door yesterday morning with a note in his teeth. He was followed this afternoon by the man himself. Amerigo has come from Florence where he was visiting his brothers. He intends to leave his position with the de' Medici business at Seville and begin the life of a navigator.

I was unkind enough to ask what experience he had which would allow him to take up such an adventure so late in life. He hinted at an education in cosmography, and offered a pilgrimage to Jerusalem when he was a young man, and his recent voyages from Florence to Seville.

Sebastian was quietly looking at charts at a side-table with Lodovico and Sancio. Sebastian turned incredulous eyes on Amerigo and suggested, innocently, that maybe Messer Amerigo would have to go back to school.

Not at all abashed that a child hit so close to the mark, Amerigo agreed, said he was starting in this very house, and would I lend him my father's copy of *Marco Polo*.

I do know how you feel about lending a manuscript that might give an edge, but poor old Amerigo has so much to learn. I thought it a sin against knowledge not to let him have it.

Amerigo will leave for Seville in a few days, will return it before he leaves. I don't think you need worry about a rival in Amerigo.

Have you convinced King Ferdinand he needs a seaport constructed at Valencia?

What of your chance of a visit home? Our sons have grown inches since you last saw them.

May Our Lord and the Blessed Mother have you in their holy care.

Your own true wife,

Mathye

Fifteenth Sunday after Pentecost, under seal.

DIARII
Venice
September 21, 1492
Amerigo bragging of the leisurely meal he shared with my husband; cheering his plans for exploration. I wanted to tell him to stay out of my husband's life. Don't want Giovanni persuaded in that direction any further than his own determination will take him. Eventually I encouraged Amerigo to the door.

Went back to my desk.

Reworked the music for Psalm 117.

Have sent it off to those discerning nuns at Santa Maria delle Vergini.

I hear my choir arriving for the first practice of the Mass of the Nativity.

Feast of Saint Matthew, Apostle.

DIARII
Venice
October 26, 1492
Gentile Bellini needs two months to finish our portraits. He's been working six.

I'm tired of his plodding up the stairs.

I want them finished before Giovanni comes home.

He assures me – yes.

Thanks be to God.

Feast of Saint Evaristus.

Valencia
November 10, 1492

My darling wife,

The twenty-second Sunday after Pentecost Amerigo passed through Valencia on his way to Cadiz. We spent the morning together. He gave me your letter and I have since received the one you sent under seal.

He is not, my dear Mathye, as unprepared for exploring as

it appears at first glance: he was educated by his uncle, Friar Giorgio Antonio at the Dominican priory at Florence, and by his uncle's friend the learned Doctor Paolo del Pozzo Toscanelli who, though a medical doctor, had a reputation of being a fine cosmographer.

Amerigo is a collector of charts and has many of the best. I have given him one of the northern countries that includes Iceland.

He knows as much about cosmography and geography as anyone who studied with me at Sagres. I am always eager for his company.

Of course, he has no deep-sea experience, and that's a great disadvantage. I suggested, since he was starting late, he should consider attaching himself to me. He didn't respond to my offer. I am beginning to suspect he has plans he doesn't want to share.

I don't worry about Amerigo.

And now to King Ferdinand of Aragon: I have had a second meeting with him. I brought with me Gaspar Rull, who is a merchant of vast means and is interested in investing in the seaport and jetties at Valencia, since he can see how it will redound to his benefit. The King showed considerable interest in what I proposed and was not unimpressed with Rull's wealth. He asked practical questions about my drawings and charts. He was as delighted as a child with my sphere. It was the first he'd seen.

He is sending my documents to the Governor-General of this place for his advice, and will meet with me again before Ash Wednesday.

If the King approves the seaport, this city will be able to capture more of the Mediterranean trade, and money will begin to pour into the King's pockets. I will use my success to get from this King a charter to go in search of a short route to the spices of the East. That, of course, will force me to stay here at least another year. The prospect of a visit home at this time seems bleak. But if there is opportunity, you can be sure I will take it.

May the Holy Trinity bless you and our sons; this is the prayer of your husband who loves you better than life.

Giovanni

Feast of Saint Nympha, martyr, under seal.

DIARII

Venice

December 8, 1492

Seven months since I've seen my husband. How can he stand it! How can I!

I want to knock down walls!

The sight of a woman with her arm linked to her husband's is anathema to me.

The cousins can smell a letter from Giovanni.

Paola was here. I trod gingerly – gave only the banal bits.

Feast of the Immaculate Conception.

DIARII

Venice

December 12, 1492

Gentile has finally packed up his brushes and paints and is out of the door.

He has done a splendid piece of work on Lodovico and Sebastian but Sancio's portrait shows a boy with a certain weakness of character. I now haunt my young son's face to discover what is veiled there.

Gentile has made me look younger. Does he not think I look in the mirror?

Feast of Saint Finnian, monk.

Venice

December 18, 1492

My darling husband,

You won't be home for another year! No! No!

To shroud the disappointment, Isabetta and I went to

Murano. I paid a queen's ransom for those two vases I admired when you and I were last there. I've put them in my music room; they give me pleasure and inspiration each time I raise my head. I spent your money, not mine, so don't put that fierce look on your face!

You'll miss your birthday party. You'll miss mine. I'll be thirty-three, a momentous occasion.

I didn't tell our sons that you will be away another year, since you might manage to surprise us.

When next you see Lodovico you are in for a treat – he is taller, has put on weight.

To catch this phase of his maturity, which is lovely beyond words, I called in Gentile Bellini, had him paint his portrait. I planned to keep them – yes, there are more – as a surprise, but it will be such old news by the time you do get home, I will forget to be enthusiastic.

Lodovico wasn't excited about sitting for long hours, but the painter allowed him to read, and our son put up with it.

In the portrait, he is looking straight at the viewer. His neck, which used to be so thin, is now solid and holds his head erect on a very straight back. Gentile has painted the canon lawyer Lodovico will surely become. I was so pleased with the portrait, I asked him to paint the rest of the family. This was a little more difficult; Sebastian complained his face has too many blemishes: it hasn't.

Gentile has caught the smile that plays around Sebastian's mouth, his Byzantine eyes that are amused rather than grave, the yellow Caboto hair that flies from underneath his cap. This Sebastian has all the answers and all the fun.

I was surprised at Sancio's portrait; he looks older. When I pointed this out, Gentile said he would grow into it. Whereas he painted our other sons in their togas, Sancio is wearing a shirt with a frill at the neck, a chain, his signet ring. His top lip has a very light moustache, not yet visible; next year it will be. Gentile has caught the delicateness of his still frail body.

As for my portrait, it is three-quarter length; I am wearing the green brocade dress, the one with the wine oversleeves – the one I complained was cut too low. I have on the chain you brought from Constantinople and the emerald earrings.

At the last minute, I wrapped a braid of black hair around my head; Gentile liked it and I wore it at each sitting. He has made something attractive of it. I had to sit, or rather stand, for ten hours altogether; close to the portrait you see, just around the outer corners of my eyes, he captured a flick of boredom.

He painted me surrounded by my musical instruments.

Although Gentile is now working on the walls of the albergo of the recently rebuilt Scuola di San Marco, when you return he will paint your portrait to complete the set.

I know you will fall in with my wishes.

Now that the paintings are hung, and a number of our relatives and friends have seen and admired them, even our sons approve.

I am off to meet cousins Piero and Carlo; money is raining into our Fraterna from the Flanders trade. We have to decide what to do with it.

May the great Archangel Gabriel go before you, even when you stay away longer than you should.

Mathye

Friday of the Advent Ember Week.

DIARII
Venice
December 19, 1492
More ready money in our Fraterna than we know what to do with.

Will bid on a galley for the Constantinople trade. Piero is sure the Collegio will approve. We will send only one galley to London.

Put aside three hundred ducats for repairs to the six properties at San Iachomo de Lorio.

Have raised our yearly stipends by one hundred and twenty ducats each.

I don't want to know that Piero spent one penny for a tankard of sack while the galley was unloading at Southampton; he insists on bringing those minute records to the amanuenses.

What is it about money that forces Venetians to put on paper every soldo spent? This constant adding up of sums!

Giovanni gives me two hundred ducats a year. Insists I spend only his. Wants an exact accounting of it.

Every man on both sides of the family spends more time talking about money then he spends in his bed. It's sinful.

Lodovico, thank God, shows no sign of this Venetian fever. But then, all my money is entailed on Piero, Carlo and their children. Gr-rr-rr.

If our laws allowed me to leave what I have to our sons, maybe Giovanni would not feel compelled to follow his unbridled search for wealth.

Saturday of the Advent Ember Week.

DIARII
Venice
December 23, 1492
Tomorrow – Vigil of the Nativity – two straight days of sublime liturgical music.

My choir is ready for it.

Yes.

Wednesday of the fourth Sunday of Advent.

DIARII
Venice
December 24, 1492
Lights flickered among the houses; from the gondola I watched my choir make its way to the Canal – they carried the twelve copper globes.

The wind had fallen. It was cool, crisp.

The one night in the Church year my sons accompany me

to San Zan. San Zan Degolla – the only church in Venice to perform the Procession of the Shepherds.

This is lovely, isn't it, Mother?

Yes, my darling Sancio, nothing lovelier.

My choir suddenly appeared around the last bend – light flickering about them.

On the bank of the Canal we sang the first of the antiphons of the Procession – four-part harmony:

> There were shepherds in the fields
> Keeping watch over their flocks by night.

My choir was in fine voice.

People began to gather around us.

We moved off. As we walked through each calle, more people fell in.

The tramp of our feet on the hard ground told of our passing; windows filled with the old, the young.

On the bridge we sang the second antiphon – three-part harmony:

> Behold, an angel of the Lord stood by them
> The glory of God shone round them, and they were
> sore afraid.

We went on to the entrance of the campo – third antiphon – two-part harmony:

> And the angel said to them,
> Be not afraid.

We entered the campo – the twelve globes gave off stars of light.

The last antiphon – plain chant; the parishioners joining in:

There is born to us this day a saviour, who is Christ the Lord. Glory to God in the highest, and peace on earth to all of good will.

In the dark, the people gave to the words, the music, such a fervour – I wanted to believe they had just come down from the hills, witnessed the event.

We went into the church.

I took my place at the organ.

Brought my fingers down on the first mode of the great Mass of the Nativity.

Vigil of the Nativity of Our Lord.

> *Valencia*
> *February 21, 1493*

My darling wife,

I have heard nothing new from King Ferdinand about harbour installations.

Their Highnesses have now left for Barcelona and will not return until after the Paschal season.

This does not please me.

And there is rumour here that Queen Isabella has sent ships exploring westward. This makes me concerned for my own chances.

When the King returns I will press my case.

I am determined.

My dear wife, I keep you and our sons close in my thoughts.

Giovanni

Quinquagesima Sunday.

DIARII
Venice
March 8, 1493
For a turn around the Piazza with Isabetta.

More Muslim women than usual, in their silent sixes and sevens.

A travelling band of musicians sawing away near the south door of San Marco's.

Along the west façade: harlequins turning somersaults, standing on each other's shoulders, cajoling money from the crowd.

Near the Doge's palace loud and urgent music: we walked that way, stopped, moved in to get a better look – Sebastian in a cockfighting stance. Lute to his shoulder, yellow hair bouncing, challenging Gabriel Soranzo note for note. Loud, funny, cock-of-the-walk Sebastian. We stayed to the end. On the last note he swung his lute over his head, let out a loud whoop, turned, winked at a girl who was holding his cap, noticed me in the crowd, jumped through – kissed my cheek.

Mother, I'm having a lovely time.

Of course you are, my son.

He was off again, challenging another young man. Sebastian is only twelve. I didn't know he came to the Piazza in the evening.

What is a mother to do?

But what is a mother to do?

Monday after the second Sunday in Lent.

Outside Valencia
March 25, 1493

My darling wife,

My brother, who is returning to Venice by a fast galley, will bring this letter to you, under seal. I have not shared the burden of it with him.

I have news.

Christopher Columbus, the Navigator attached to the Court of Queen Isabella of Castile, who last year sailed westward in search of a short route to the spices of the East, has returned with evidence he has reached land.

He passed through Valencia yesterday.

He was dressed in parti-coloured silks, a parrot on each shoulder, followed by two men from that new land and attended by servants and mariners.

He is on his way to Barcelona to present himself to Queen Isabella.

Before he left Valencia I spoke with him. He has found land. I am not convinced he has found the short route to the spice-rich East.

The men he brought back were naked, except for loincloths. Their bodies were burnished a red hue; they had none of the bearing or arrogance I saw in the caravan leaders at Mecca.

He found no spices.

My dear wife, I know this Navigator who calls himself Columbus, I went to school with him.

He is not an Italian from Genoa, as he has let it be known to Queen Isabella and all of Castile. He is PORTUGUESE from BEJA, and a PORTUGUESE of the BLOOD ROYAL.

When I studied at Sagres, in Portugal, there were there two sons of Prince Fernando: Dom João and Dom Diogo. Also studying there was Prince Fernando's natural son, Salvador Zarco. This is the man who now calls himself Christopher Columbus.

To see the two Holy Princes and Zarco/Columbus together, there was no doubt they shared the same parent. They had the same light colouring, the large nose, the chiselled lips, the freckles.

I am sure of what I say.

I spent three years in the company of Zarco/Columbus. He has not changed so much since that time. He is a Prince, with the education and bearing of a Prince. From Mina in Guinea, to Iceland in the north, there is no one who knows more about the open sea and the Portuguese discoveries than he does.

But why has Zarco changed his name to Columbus? More particularly, why has the King of Portugal allowed a nephew of his to serve Queen Isabella of Castile in the area of discovery, an area so sacred to the Portuguese that everyone who studies at Sagres must join the Order of Christ and take an oath of secrecy about Portuguese discoveries?

When I tried to winkle these mysteries from Columbus, he looked at me as if I had broken my sacred oath. You know when a man would prefer you out of his sight, or dead. My dear wife, when he asked, with that certain glint in his eye, where I was living in Valencia, I thought it in my best interest to leave that place that very night, on a swift horse.

As I rode along, I pondered the mystery of the reincarnation of a Portuguese Prince as servant at the Court of Isabella of Castile. The only conclusion I could come to is that he must be a SPY for the King of Portugal.

And why would the King of Portugal want a spy, at the Court of Castile?

A simple answer.

The King of Portugal now controls what Queen Isabella's Navigator will be allowed to discover.

Columbus let it be known that on his way back from his voyage he was shipwrecked off Portugal, and was received by the Portuguese King. I believe this shipwreck was a ploy, and his visit to the King of Portugal was to report what he found, or failed to find, as any good spy must do.

My faithful wife, I know too much about Columbus to stay in Valencia. Even now he must have his men looking for me.

I am safe. My brother, my servant and I are a day's ride outside the town.

Work on the proposed seaport at Valencia on which I spent two years of my life, I have to abandon.

I am disappointed, but a Navigator's life is full of such disappointments.

But there is another story that swirled around Columbus during his time here.

While waiting for Queen Isabella to decide whether she

would back his voyage – so that he would not waste time (or invite suspicion) – Columbus sent his brother to present his proposal to King Henry VII of England. On the way, his brother was seized by pirates and was late returning, but this brother did meet with the English King, did explain the voyage Columbus wanted to make, did show him charts, and the King was interested.

My own true wife, I now have my chance. I will go to this English King. I need the protection of a powerful Monarch.

King Henry VII of England is the one.

He is interested. He will give me the support to do the one thing I have spent my life preparing for – to find a short route to the riches of the East.

I must get to this King before anyone else.

I need your help.

The charts I have been using are worn. Would you make me another mappamundo?

You will understand how crucial this is.

Should you agree to start this work, please buy new leather. Use the cartoon I made for the chart I took to Valencia. You might want to study the Bianco chart.

Would you read Carpini's manuscript on the *Relations of the Mongols or Tartars* which you will find wrapped in silk cloth and stored on the bottom shelf of the cupboard in the chart room?

With the Carpini document is a list of some of the places and people those monks visited. You can leave out the references to Africa, as it has no purpose for this chart, but add the many place names that speak of the land of the Great Khan.

You will see how important this information is: I want to convince the English King that these eastern lands visited by Carpini and his companion – by travelling overland – I will find by sailing westward.

The sphere I have with me is still sound; I will bring it to England.

I do realise the hours I am asking you to work at this season of the Church year. I only hope, for my sake, if not for the Good God's, that you have not undertaken new music for the Resurrection.

I can write you no more. My brother is anxious to return to Valencia to join the galley.

I will come to you before I leave for England.

May God keep you and our sons safe.

Giovanni

Feast of the Annunciation.

Outside Valencia
March 26, 1493

My darling wife,

I am on my way to Cullera where I have a friend who trades to Palermo; from there I will take passage for home. I could be home for the Resurrection.

I will spend a month with you and our sons; we will walk at dusk in the Piazza and admire the Quadriga one more time. I will accompany you to San Zan Degolla and listen to your choir sing the great Mass of the Ascension.

We will go to Montebelluna and be a happy family together. We will give a fine supper for our friends; I am bringing Castilian wine.

I have rarely failed to keep my promises to you, so count on it.

Then I am off to the north where they keep the English King.

Bravest of wives, you must not grieve I am going back to that northern land. I will be as near you, in my heart, as when we watch the firelight flicker on the ceiling-tiles of our bedroom.

Tell Sebastian I hope he is doing well in his studies as I have already written to enrol him in the Royal School of Navigation in Sagres for Autumn 1495. I hope there are a few masters left from my time there; it would make his first days easier.

I am bringing him a chart of Valencia harbour.

I have a Hebrew scroll for Lodovico, and a sketch of a mosque for Sancio.

I will have two presents for you.

The first, I have had with me since June when I thought I would be coming home.

It is a dress.

Yes, a dress!

I remembered we once saw a woman from Valencia on the Piazza. You admired her dress.

Here is how I came by it.

I told Señora Rull I would like to bring you a dress.

She agreed to get it made, but I wasn't so sharp in describing you.

Señora Rull suggested I point out to her a woman at church who had your shape and height.

I did.

She was surprised.

Are you sure your wife is that tall?

Yes, Señora, she is!

She has black hair?

Yes.

That black?

Like the raven.

Her colour, does she have that colour?

Yes.

Than your wife must have Byzantine ancestry.

Indeed, Señora, she has.

She went to the market and selected burgundy cloth with a cream lace and had the dress made.

I think you will like it.

Your second present will be a surprise. It is something I hope to buy for you in Palermo.

Will you think of coming to me in England when I am ready to make the presentation to the King? It is a pretty land in the Spring and Summer.

My darling wife, trust in the Lord I will see you shortly.

Giovanni

Friday after the fourth Sunday in Lent.

Post Scriptum

Tell Sancio the bridge he has drawn is first rate but he needs more rock ballast between the stanchions.

DIARII

Venice

April 5, 1493

If Columbus is a spy, what kind of danger is Giovanni in because of what he knows, or thinks he knows?

Is Columbus powerful enough to harm my husband?

A thought not to be clung to.

This Columbus has found land to the west.

Giovanni will not rest; he will go there.

If my husband finds the spices of the East over the western ocean he will divert that trade from Venice.

I see clearly what will become of us.

How can I live without Venice?

England? England is the outer rim of civilisation, nearer Ultima Thule.

Haec igitur regio, magni paine ultima mundi.

I will not live in a sea of ice. I will not leave the centre of the earth, drag my sons to live among those strange northern tribes.

I will not!

Someone has removed the walls from my home.

No? Then they have blown out my lamps.

Monday in Holy Week.

DIARII
Venice
April 6, 1493
I make a chart for Giovanni, tell myself – never again! Never again arrives – and here I am!

Have put aside the music for the Nativity Credo I am composing for the Convent of Santa Maria dei Miracoli.
Tuesday in Holy Week.

DIARII
Venice
April 8, 1493
Week after week I train my choir, I train my assistant, I train the deacon. Then something happens for which there is no accounting.

Canon Leonardo asked me to prepare new music for the rite of Washing of the Feet for the Holy Thursday service.

I met with Ana and Deacon Garofoli. We worked out a simple programme.

I wrote an antiphon based on Saint John's gospel:

Jesus rose from His supper
Girded Himself with the towel
Washed the feet of His disciples
Saying: Do you know what I have
done to you?

I set it to plain chant.

We selected Chapters Thirteen and Fourteen of *The Passion of Our Lord* for the deacon to read – three verses at a time.

The service started.

The choir sang the antiphon.

Deacon Garofoli began reading the verses from the Passion. As I directed the choir in humming the four-part harmony underneath his reading, my hands seemed to take on a life of their own: became the music; my mind was liquid with music. I wasn't sure I was in the body.

The choir felt it too; their faces gleamed, their voices rose and fell – seamless – sublime.

The deacon, who has an indifferent voice, found one of ringing clarity, and read each verse as if he were watching the scene unfold.

We continued singing, reading and humming until the canon had washed the feet of the twelve old men who were sitting on the bench in the sanctuary.

The feeling of liquidity stayed with me throughout Mass. Only when we went in procession – the priest carrying the Eucharist to the Altar of Repose – did the feeling fade.

After Mass, I asked Ana what happened back there. She said she didn't know, but could we repeat it at the next service?
Holy Thursday evening.

DIARII
Venice
April 19, 1493
Low Sunday – come and gone. My husband has not come home to me.
Feast of Saint Alphege.

DIARII
Venice
April 27, 1493
Giovanni! Home!

There will be fifes and drums until we leave for Montebelluna, which I am determined will happen at the end of the week.

Might as well be living on the Piazza; half Venice has passed through our doors this morning. Giovanni has now moved to the meadow. He tells a shortened version of Columbus's voyage, without the spies and royalty. People go away shaking their heads.

Paola's Uncle Rufin won't go away!

Canon Leonardo, who stayed for an hour, listened to the

tale twice, told me he has read historical documents and believes the voyage is possible.

All the relatives have visited.

Cousin Piero has again hinted Giovanni take over the Flanders galley. Piero wants to leave the sea and allow his name to stand for the office of Provveditore di Comun.

Piero hints. My husband changes the subject.

Giovanni has never divulged even to our sons he is looking for the short route to the wealth of the East. I can't believe those wily cousins still think all his travels are for the purpose of finding backers to support him in search of new land. When I mention this to Giovanni, he says Venetian traders regard him and men like Columbus as dreamers, and he wants it to stay that way.

Now a messenger has come from Doge Barbarigo; Giovanni must present himself to the Collegio tomorrow, at noon, and tell what he knows of Columbus. I am invited. There will be a dinner. When the Collegio lays out a dinner, they want something in return.

Giovanni brought me a double harp.

Has a voice like a new river.

Majestic present!

The dress? For a masque!

Feast of Saint Zita.

DIARII
Venice
April 28, 1493
Gemma spent an hour on my hair.

I selected a strip of blue silk, bound it around my head, anchored it with a chaplet of gold. Put on diamond earrings that reached down my neck. Draped my too-low-cut Venetian red dress with netting, held it in place with a diamond collar. Put on my blue cape.

Giovanni wore the simple black toga and cap of any chancery worker. He carried a mappamundo.

The Cabotos are ready to confront their Doge.

Giovanni returned my grim smile.

I am a reluctant participant in my husband's schemes, but Venice will know he has a wife.

We left our house, stepped into the gondola. Guido poled us to the Piazzetta. The mercers had paused in their selling – moving up the Piazza was a procession of foreign Scuole: Albanians, Armenians, Germans, Dalmatians and four other Scuole behind them. Each group with a hundred or more members, white-robed, carrying banners, candles.

We forced a fast-paced trot across the top of the Piazza. The procession was at our heels as we turned into the Doge's palace.

We climbed the stairs, were met and escorted to the Doge's private dining room.

The Collegio were dazzling in their robes: scarlets, purples, blues. The Doge had on his cap. The meal was already being brought to the table.

Only Doge Barbarigo, who hadn't seen Giovanni since his return, came forward, had a short word with us.

We were placed on either side of His Serenity.

On my left, Zorzi Cornaro – too handsome, too suave.

We talked about the sermon given at San Marco's by the English Bishop, here on his way to Jerusalem. Wondered if he was as rich as he appeared: he had brought twenty-five horses and twenty servants. Neither of us knew why he had come so early – the galley for Jerusalem doesn't leave until June.

The Doge turned to me:

And are you, too, interested in finding new land, Donna Caboto?

I make the charts!

I saw the lines deepen, which formed trenches down each side of his nose and mouth. As quickly, his grey eyes modified their blankness to something resembling a smile. I watched him compose himself and reach for the appropriate response. It didn't come; he fell back on:

I am an old man.

I wanted to say: *You are a nasty old man.*

He turned back to Giovanni where the conversation, since the meal began, was of the arsenal and the assembly-line method of constructing galleys.

The food was plain: a mixed fruit, followed by succulent trout, a salad. The wine was passable.

The Doge crossed his cutlery on his plate. Zorzi rose and gave a pleasant, if short, speech of welcome.

My husband unrolled his mappamundi. Two servants appeared, as if part of a stage play; each took an edge.

Giovanni gave the facts of Columbus' voyage: the latitude he followed, the number of days it took, the leagues covered. He pointed out the empty spaces on the chart where Columbus would have landed.

Here and there I saw an eyebrow raise, an eyelash flicker. Each of these men, at one time or another, had taken galleys north to London, east to Beirut and through the Sea of Marmara to Tana, hugging the coast all the way.

The open sea was a mystery to them.

Giovanni's story was simple. When he finished, the Doge asked the one question my husband was waiting for:

Will you go in search of new lands too, Messer Caboto?

I have not been as fortunate as Messer Columbus, Serenity. He has found a Queen who believes in him.

The meeting was over. Everyone had what they had come to hear.

Thursday after the second Sunday after Easter.

DIARII
Venice
April 29, 1493
Taking Gemma and Justina to Montebelluna.

Justina does the drudge work – rarely gets a break.

Gemma pouts when I take along Justina.

Feast of Saint Robert.

DIARII

Montebelluna
May 4, 1493

My heart never fails to gladden when we take the road to Montebelluna. Our sons galloped their horses – were in the pasture when we arrived.

Our horses were as eager to be free as we. They bolted their reins, snorted, kicked up their heels, bit at each other's flanks.

The first evening Giovanni said:

I feel in a state of supernatural grace when I am with my family.

You should, you are so seldom here died on my lips.

Each day we walk in the fields, sometimes startle the servants by helping broadcast the grain.

We go riding over the countryside; take our dinner in a basket, eat among the insects.

We sit for hours in the lowering night telling family stories.

Last evening, Sancio asked:

Why are there no stories about me?

Our four heads swivelled in his direction. Our silent Sancio had asked a question.

Yes, Sancio, I have a story about you:

You were three. Someone had given you one picolli. You could buy a sugar-mouse with one soldo. You went down to the kitchen, found Gemma. She and Guido had married that month and were looking for a house. You gave her the picolli and asked her to go to Codussi's and buy you a sugar-mouse.

You told her:

Keep the change and buy yourself a house.

Sancio laughed. We all laughed, but Sebastian almost fell off his chair. I wondered if he remembered it was his story I was telling.

Feast of Saint Joseph, spouse of the Virgin Mary.

DIARII
Montebelluna
May 8, 1493
Rain all day.

Played six games of draughts with Sancio. Passed him off to Sebastian. Poor lad, that was the end of his winnings.

Beat Giovanni twice at chess!
Saturday after the third Sunday after Easter.

DIARII
Montebelluna
May 9, 1493
Lodovico is too polite with his father. A studied politeness. When Giovanni speaks to him he sits bolt upright. His 'Sir' is clipped.

Giovanni doesn't help. I've asked him to be more relaxed with the boy. He doesn't seem to understand what I am talking about.

Lodovico never quite got used to Giovanni coming and going in our lives. As a child, each time his father returned from the sea he stayed surprised for a week; surprised to find him still here in the morning. Some residue of the unforeseen has stayed with our son.
Fourth Sunday after Easter.

DIARII
Montebelluna
May 11, 1493
It's not possible to have a conversation with Giovanni about giving up his quest. I raise the subject, he talks charts, spheres, mappamundi, Mecca, Marco Polo, Carpini, Contarini, Avicenna, Ptolemy, and on and on.

His face glows, his voice strengthens.

I want to say: *but the Doge will hang us all between the columns if you divert the spice trade from Venice to another country.*

I do not say it.
Feast of Saint James the Less.

DIARII
Montebelluna
May 12, 1493

Ordered a very fine English jerkin and hose for Giovanni's birthday; gave it to him this afternoon with the thought, if it doesn't fit, there will be time to have it adjusted. He will be in full fig at his supper-party.

It fitted splendidly. The deep blue silk of the jerkin sharpened his blue eyes, set off his high colour, his yellow hair. He was admiring himself in the mirror.

I was charmed by his pleasure, about to say:

Shall we dance?

I saw that look appear on his face.

Whose money did you use?

Mine, of course. Should I give my husband a gift using his money?

But you know I want you to use my money.

I lost control:

I won't account to you for every soldo I put in the collection box! You spoil everything with your infernal need for me to spend your money! I wish you never had a picolli to put in your pocket! I will spend my money how I want – on whom I want.

Giovanni just stood there. If I were a child I would have spit; it was a great temptation. I turned and marched into the meadow. Banged the door.

I thought: *if you follow, I shall go back to Venice.*

I sat in the garden for an hour, wondering why I still allow Giovanni to put me in this state about money.

When I accuse him of pride, he says a man has to care for his family.

I've had enough of it.

Feast of Saint Pancratius.

Giovanni: But of course, every Priuli son is sent out 'hunting birds.'

Me: Pardon?

Giovanni: Every Priuli son is sent out 'hunting birds'!

Me: Explain.

Giovanni: You have never heard that expression?

Me: Never.

Giovanni: Noble families who have fallen to the ranks of the shamefaced poor, will try to add to their coffers by marrying off their sons to daughters of rich nobles, or rich cittadini, or to members of the popolari, as long as the family has money.

Me: Did your uncle send you 'hunting birds'?

Giovanni: After my cousin took over the business, my uncle lost interest in my future. But he would not have been above sending his son to see what he could snare. And besides, you snared me.

I pull his woolly hair.

Me: I'm ashamed to be a member of this grasping nobility. We won't send our sons 'hunting birds'!

Giovanni: That's why I am going to see the English King.

Me: If you don't see the English King?

We change the subject. But what a tattered system of money grubbing.

We have finally agreed – or rather Giovanni has said: In the name of the Good God, *which is usually my line*, I will never again ask who owns the money you are spending, but I will look at the books.

We have another truce.

Feast of Saint Boniface.

DIARII
Venice
May 17, 1493

Whenever I dance till dawn, I sleep two hours, am ready to plough a field, write a Jubilation Mass.

Giovanni has turned over – is dead to the world.

I hear the distant rattle of a cart in the Piazza. The day has begun – just.

We were halfway through Giovanni's birthday supper before he realised our thirty-seven guests numbered his age. His uncle never celebrated his birthday. I put in all the childish tricks. It never fails to please.

After supper, four of our Guild of Singers gave us the Petrarch madrigal I put to music. They out-sang themselves.

We had a contest among the tables to see who would sing the funniest songs; the servants were the judges. As usual, they awarded all the prizes to the children's tables.

We accused them of taking bribes.

The dancing master arrived with his drummers and fife players, prepared to teach us the newest dance from Greece. He wore his local costume: white dress, leggings. His body thin, wiry; his face like an arrow. He put us in two rows and walked us through the steps.

The fifes screamed, the drums loud and insistent. We hopped on the right foot, on the left, slapped our thighs, swung in circles, bolted up the middle of the line; it went on for an hour. When it was over, we crowded onto the balcony. The dozen or so gondolas lined up outside the window watching our frolic moved off into the dark.

More fruit juice and wine were brought.

Lodovico, Sebastian, Sancio, Marco and Giacomo performed a moresche: masques – grotesque, funny. Sancio smiling his shy smile. Giacomo – his long lean body, looking more like Piero every day.

Lisa and Maria danced a gelosia with extraordinary grace and agility.

Paola and Adriana beamed.

Paola told me that Ser Donà has hinted he would like his son to marry Lisa. Paola is not averse to it; Piero is – a large dowry is expected.

About the third hour of the evening the younger children were sent to bed or taken home. Isabetta had a little tiff with Marco, who neither wanted to sleep here nor go home. Lorenzo put his hand on the back of his neck – marched him out of the door.

Adriana used the general stir to take Alvise home. His legs had long since stopped taking direction from his head.

Alvise Querini drinks no more wine than any of us; but what makes us happy puts him under.

They let Maria stay.

We did the new dance at least three times, dragged out all the old ones we knew, and some we didn't.

Giovanni and Isabetta danced the wild chacota they both learned in Portugal in their youth. It amuses me to watch Lorenzo during this performance. His eyes narrow, he makes his way to me for assurance.

When we finally closed the door behind Piero and Paola (who always stay for the last glass and tell, or listen to, the last story, which no one remembers the next day), we heard the crier in the Piazza:

It's a fine cool morning. The galley has returned from Tana.

Giovanni assured me this was the best of birthdays. We rolled up to bed.

I'm off to add verve to the Credo for the nuns at the Convent of Santa Maria dei Miracoli.

Feast of Saint Innocent.

DIARII
Venice
May 18, 1493
Giovanni has taken our three sons to hear Friar Girolamo

Savonarola preach a sermon on Grace. This Dominican, from Florence – the second time he has been here – has gained a reputation for Hell's fire-and-damnation sermons. Tonight is supposed to be a mild one.

Sancio, delighted to be taken out with Lodovico and Sebastian, and at night, was shivering in anticipation.

Have at least an hour to work on the Credo. With all the interruptions it is still coming along nicely – maybe because of them.

Tuesday after the fifth Sunday after Easter.

DIARII
Venice
May 19, 1493
I wish Paola were less interested in what Giovanni intends to do in England.

Giovanni is vague. She won't take the hint.

Feast of Saint Dunstan.

DIARII
Venice
May 20, 1493
I hear Sebastian shouting the news over the back fence to Ser Barozzi that his father has arranged a working sea-voyage for him for the coming August – as far as Modon – with Nicolo Pisani.

Sebastian is laughing and stumbling over his words.

It grieves me to give up my son, even for a month.

Vigil of the Ascension.

DIARII
Venice
May 21, 1493
My husband's mind is already on the road to England.

He is back at his chart-making.

I refuse to recognise his spiralling away from us.

Ascension Day.

DIARII
Venice
May 22, 1493
Will the English King protect Giovanni from Venetian wrath if he finds a short route to the wealth of the East, and that wealth flows away from Venice and into the coffers of the English?

My husband will not understand that if a hint of his plans reaches the Doge's spies they will lure him under a dark bridge on a wet night and garrotte him.

My husband will not see this.

Feast of Saint Julia, patron of Corsica.

DIARII
Venice
May 23, 1493
Giovanni and I sit in the shade on the altana sipping the yellow Castilian wine.

The Canal is flat and luminous. The traffic scarcely moving in the first fiery day of summer.

Three galleys leave the Rialto, pass our door. All going to Constantinople. Ours among them. The oars are out. The oarsmen on their feet and straining.

Come with me to England?

Our sons . . .

My husband turns his head, looks over the burning Canal.

We finish the sharp yellow wine.

Feast of Saint Augustine.

DIARII
Venice
May 26, 1493
Giovanni has changed his plans.

Canon Leonardo has convinced him he may find documents in monasteries or university libraries that tell of westward voyages taken by Franciscan monks – as early as the eighth century.

Canon Leonardo has given him names in Florence, France and England. Giovanni has written to a number of these institutions and offered to give a lecture on what he plans to do – on what Columbus has already done.

He'll be travelling off the beaten track. I've insisted he take Luigi who likes the rough and tumble of overland travel.

I may not hear from my husband for months!

God help me.

Feast of Saint Augustine of Canterbury.

DIARII
Venice
May 29, 1493
Giovanni has returned from a meeting with the Collegio.

He is elated.

He has again persuaded them – as a navigator, he deals with Kings and needs to keep the title of ambassador!

He has his documents.

How does he manage this?

Vigil of Pentecost.

DIARII
Venice
May 30, 1493
At Mass today, Giovanni whispered:

I swear before the Living God I will leave the sea by 1500.

No, no. Don't swear it.

After Mass he said he swore it as much for himself.

He prays for a wealth we don't need; if he gets it, we lose Venice.

Why won't he see this?

Pentecost Sunday.

DIARII
Venice
June 1, 1493
For twenty-four hours after Giovanni leaves I am troubled –
keep to my bed.

The twenty-four hours are up.

To work!
Feast of Saint Pamphilus, scholar.

Chapter Two

DIARII
Venice
June 3, 1493

Amerigo Vespucci ducking into the Doge's palace.

Waited for a note to tell of a visit.

Nothing.

Sent Guido around to White Sails Inn. No one has seen Amerigo, nor is he expected.

Isabetta, who knows more about what goes on in Venice than anyone, has heard nothing. Lorenzo said Amerigo would not come to Venice without visiting them.

Amerigo is in Venice.

Feast of Saint Kevin.

Pisa
June 19, 1493

My darling wife,

Messer Trevisan is leaving for home in the morning; he will bring this letter.

I visited the universities at Padua, Ferrara and Pisa. I was received courteously but sceptically.

Only in Ferrara were the scholars open to my ideas; they had heard a talk by young Ludovico Toscanelli, the nephew of the cosmographer Dr Paolo del Posso Toscanelli.

When I arrived at Florence I went in search of young Toscanelli.

He invited me to view the vast library inherited from his uncle. We spent an evening looking through books on cosmography and mathematics.

As well, he showed me his uncle's letter-book and allowed me to copy a letter Dr Toscanelli had written to Fernão Martins, Canon of the Cathedral of Lisbon, an employee of the Portuguese King. In this letter Toscanelli said the lands of spices are to be reached by sailing west; let me quote you the exact words:

> And do not wonder that I speak of the West referring to the lands where the spices grow, which are commonly said to lie to the east: for those who sail steadily westward will find those regions to the west and those who travel eastward overland will find them in the east.

There was also in the book a letter from Columbus referring to the Toscanelli letter to Martins.

How would Columbus have heard of correspondence between Toscanelli and an employee of the King of Portugal, if he were not close to the Portuguese Court? How nicely this ties in with my suspicion of Columbus as Portuguese spy.

As well, I saw a chart of Toscanelli's that concluded the city of Quinsy in Cathay will be found in the latitude of Lisbon, at a westward distance of 5,000 sea miles. I believe it will be found further north and, because of the curve of the earth, within many fewer sea miles.

Maybe as few as 1,500.

Toscanelli let me copy the chart. I promised I would send him a copy of my mappamundo. Ludovico is not, I think, the scholar his uncle was, but he is a generous young man and shared freely his uncle's work. I felt constrained to offer something of mine. If you are not burdened with music, would you make a start on a mappamundo for him? I told him he could expect it sometime after the Nativity. Can you manage that?

Meeting young Toscanelli and getting access to his uncle's work was a great moment. We talked late into the night. He was a gracious host and offered a bed but Luigi and I walked to our lodgings through the empty streets.

When I visit the English King I will be better prepared than when in Lisbon and Valencia. I will have Toscanelli's letter and chart to add to the knowledge of the ancients, and my own charts and sphere.

Since I will be going to monasteries off the post route, you will get few letters from me. If I meet trustworthy travellers bound for Venice, I will send knowledge of my whereabouts. From Paris I will send a letter to you by a fast express via Milan which should reach you in good time. I shall write again from Bruges.

You know how my heart aches for you.

God be with you and our sons.

Giovanni

Feast of Saint Gervase, under seal.

DIARII
Venice
June 20, 1493
Astounding happenings!

Lorenzo has to move to Florence to prop up the family banking business.

Isabetta, Martino, Marco will follow in July – stay for two years or more!

Lodovico wants to go with them!

For a year!

He wants to work with that Friar Savonarola, who came here last year – preached sermons calling for Church reform.

With Isabetta going, he is sure I will approve.

No! I will not approve!

I will not give up Lodovico and Isabetta at the same time.

No!

I will not!

Second Sunday after Pentecost.

My darling husband,

Isabetta is moving to Florence.

Lodovico wants to go too!

I'm daunted.

Lorenzo will leave in a week.

His father is ill. His younger brother was supposed to take over the Bank but is incapable. His mother is trying to keep the business going; she asked Lorenzo to return home.

Apparently his father did all the work, not training his younger son.

Lorenzo said it will take two years or more to put new managers in place.

You are somewhere in the frozen north; my friend from childhood will go to Florence; our son wants to follow!

My dear husband, I am daunted.

I was prepared for Lodovico to go to the University of Padua in October, not to a foreign state on the other side of the Peninsula.

Remember, you took our sons to a sermon by Friar Savonarola at San Marco's. That Friar also preached a series of sermons on corruption of Church leaders, hinting at the life of our new Pope, Alexander VI. Lodovico attended them all, spoke to the Friar. Do you remember this?

Now, this son of ours – who in his lifetime has rarely asked for a second piece of bread – wants to spend a year at Florence under the influence of this friar before he begins his studies at the University of Padua.

He says, as a future canon lawyer, he can do no less.

I am aghast at this request. I don't want our son in Florence. Florence has the reputation of being the Sodom of the known world – clergy leading the way.

I went to see this friar – he is again visiting Venice. I was astonished at his appearance: keen black eyes, prominent beaked nose, lips so full he can hardly keep his mouth closed, a most unpleasant speaking voice.

But I liked his scrubbed look; the patch on his habit I found endearing.

He remembered Lodovico, and his questions. He suggested our son could do worse than spend a year listening to his preaching, which, he said, is more to scourge the clergy and the venal people of Florence than to propound deep theological thought.

Lodovico is just realising the extent of the corruption among clergy; he believes this friar is the one to start the reform. He wants to be in Florence to witness and be a part of this.

Isabetta, whom Lodovico has engaged in his crusade, says she is delighted to have him stay at their home. I was hoping she would say it was inconvenient.

I told Lodovico I would give him an answer before he is finished his studies in October.

Yes, my darling husband, I am daunted. But you would never understand that, as you have never been daunted.

Nevertheless, your wife prays each night that the Light of the Spirit of God surrounds you.

Mathye

Second Sunday after Pentecost, under seal.

DIARII
Venice
June 25, 1493
Isabetta's farewell dinner.

A choice table: Isabetta and Lorenzo, Adriana and Alvise, Piero and Paola, me, Isabetta's mother and father – Ser Barozzi wearing a splint on his arm from a fall over his back steps – all our children.

The fire was lit. The candles gave off a pink glow. The children, catching the tone, were subdued. The servants bent over us in a more solicitous manner than usual. Our stories were kind and raised only chuckles.

Isabetta's new cook, whom I shall steal while she is away, served wild boar, dressed, and brought in on a trestle. There were roasted doves, poultry and sturgeon. The confectioneries, moulded in sugar, represented the arms of each family. The wine, from their own vineyards, was nutty and full-bodied; I have not tasted better.

Alvise was only mildly drunk.

Adriana made sallies down the table, none of any weight:

I don't trust sailors. Haven't looked at Jacopo since he became my gondolier.

After the confectionery, Lorenzo stood, raised his glass:

To my dear friends, my dear family, whom I am leaving – if only for a while. I shall miss you. Think how delightful the banquet for our return.

His voice faltered. He went to the fireplace, smashed a murano glass. The tables came to attention. Murano glass, even in Venice, is precious.

Ser Barozzi rose. It had been a long time since I heard him give a toast.

To my beloved son-in-law, who brought the joy of a good man to this old man's family. To my only daughter whom I love beyond measure. And my precious grandchildren. Godspeed.

Another murano glass hit the fireplace.

Alvise ordered them under the pain of mortal sin to come back in two years.

Another crash.

The servants started to crowd the door. The children, who had not before witnessed this ceremony, were round-eyed with amazement.

Piero was on his feet; cautioned Lorenzo to be sure to earn a million ducats down there in Florence, make the move worthwhile. He invited Isabetta to return to Venice to spend it and make us all eternally rich.

Crash!

Donna Barozzi, whom I had never seen on her feet, gave them her blessing, said she was not in the habit of breaking glass intentionally but was always inclined to follow the host in the matter of table manners.

Crash!

Adriana, who has more money than any ten families need, started laughing before she stood, set the table laughing with her:

> In the morning I think I'll buy the glassworks.

Crash!

Paola, whose family owns the glassworks:

> They're not for sale.

Crash!

It was my turn. I wanted to bring the table back to the moment but not lose the jollity:

> When Isabetta told me she and her family would be gone for two years, this is how my world felt.

I picked up the murano glass and another at my place and swung. Crash! Crash!

Isabetta:

> You can be sure this is the last time we will leave home.
> Imagine the cost if my husband had decided to drink from a murano vase and toss it.

Crash!

Flushed and in high glee she pushed back her chair. We followed her to the altana, had a last glass of mellow wine, started to drift toward home.

Feast of Saint William.

DIARII
Venice
July 2, 1493
Isabetta and I spent our last evening together.

We sat on the altana, gossiped: people passing in gondolas, the lack of talent in the newly elected Savi di Terraferma, fashion – as if we had all the tomorrows.

Drank two jars of sweet Cyprus wine – at least Isabetta did – was almost blind when she stood. Gemma and I had to walk her home, the back way. At the door she ducked inside, never looked back.

They were off before I was out of bed. This morning feels like any other morning.

It isn't.

Feast of the Visitation.

DIARII
Venice
July 4, 1493
Lodovico has joined the Companion of the Hose; he presented me with the accomplished fact.

Another surprise.

Their Statutes of Incorporation have all the right words:
... nothing is more pleasant, or binds us more closely together, than sharing good morals ...
In reality it is an eating and drinking club.

I suggested he join the Scuola di Sant' Orsola to balance this frivolity, although I can't imagine Lodovico frivolous. He readily agreed and has gone off to have his clothes made for both societies.

I see a change in Lodovico. He goes out more often, joined the dancing at cousin Piero's last week without having to be dragged. Sebastian, who loves to dance, has noticed it too.

Mother, the son and heir has found the use of his legs.

Be generous to your brother.

I'll give him a lesson or two, sharpen him up.

He'll give you a lesson or two – in Greek, sharpen you up.

Fair exchange, no robbery.

Fourth Sunday after Pentecost.

DIARII
Venice
July 19, 1493

Messer Giannotti arrived at my door straight from Paris, a note from Giovanni – on a half page, from his log – and a letter for Sebastian.

They met on the road to Besançon.

Giovanni had been to Saint Ruf, Vienne, Cluny, and Tournus. Monks warm-hearted, food good, beds clean. Some understood what he was talking about, but none wanted to part with their silver in support of his efforts.

He is light-hearted.

Luigi fell from his horse – injured his ribs.

Not received my husband's letters from Marseille!

Feast of Saint Rufina, potter.

Marseille

My dear son Sebastian,

In a month or so you will take your first working voyage to sea without your mother, me, or a servant to watch over you.

You will, however, be under the guidance of Messer Pisani. He will treat you as he treats his own son, Francesco. I am sure of it.

Messer Pisani's eldest son was your age when I took him on his first short voyage to Modon.

I am confident of your wellbeing on his ship.

You and Francesco will be given the task of caring for the ropes, keeping them whipped and clean.

There will be other tasks you will perform on your thirty-day trip, but this is the one task the Master is counting on you to do; make that the object of your day: the first thing in the morning, the last at night.

You will be expected to be a part of the detail that keeps the decks clean: coiling ropes, scraping and sweeping.

You will stand watch during the daylight hours. Keep a sharp eye to the horizon and report immediately to the helmsman anything out of the ordinary.

Do not touch the sails unless particularly invited. This is heavy work for which you are not yet strong enough.

When in the port of Modon, get permission before you leave ship. Never leave alone. I am sure Messer Pisani will assign one of his mariners to you and Francesco when you go ashore. Be back before sundown.

Follow these simple rules, my son, and you will have a memorable first voyage.

I bless you,
Your Father

DIARII
Venice
August 8, 1493
Lodovico – for approval.

His second Companion of the Hose dinner.

My, but the young are handsome.

I had to look twice at this son, newly minted into manhood. Variegated hose; pink silk jerkin – just manages to make him appear decent; cape of deep blue – gave him a distance I could not cross.

He has refused to dye his hair yellow to meet the fashion of the Companions.

My son swirled his cloak for my admiration.

Mother, will I do?

Like a new-minted gold ducat.

He gave me a formal bow, was out the door.

Guido was waiting, in his new livery.

I watched the two of them strut toward the Canal – two peacocks.

Ninth Sunday after Pentecost.

DIARII

Venice

August 9, 1493

Can I stop Lodovico from going to Florence? There are good reasons: he's too young to be on his own, so far away. The plague may strike – I will not be able to get to him for ten days.

The young men of Florence are debauched – everyone says so.

But can I keep him wrapped in tow?

Do I want to?

Yes!

What am I saying?

Feast of Saint Oswald.

DIARII

Venice

August 10, 1493

What if Friar Savonarola is a true reformer?

What if renewal has already begun in the Church at Florence?

Will my son forgive me?

Ever?

Feast of Saint Lawrence.

DIARII

Venice

August 11, 1493

Queen Caterina Cornaro's liveried servant – Saracen no less – arrived at my door an hour ago, embossed invitation in hand.

The Queen is giving a supper party at Asolo, the fief awarded her for surrendering the throne of Cyprus to Venice.

I'll go.

All the intrigues, and half the rumours of intrigue, will be passed down the table with the latest news of the latest madrigal.

Twenty years ago Caterina was a beautiful young woman betrothed to the King of Cyprus.

Neither her King nor their son survived the first year.

Like any corrupt stepfather, the Doge, in the name of Venice and God – poor God – sent Councillors to Caterina in her bereavement; they never left.

In quick succession, any claimant to the throne of Cyprus disappeared or was shut up in a convent.

Four years ago – was it just four years? – the Collegio stopped pretending, sent her brother Zorzi to bring her home.

Cyprus, the prized outpost on the Beirut trade-route, was snuggled into the heart of the Republic without a shot being fired.

The Collegio tore Caterina from her throne. How much more quickly will they sacrifice Giovanni if he is the cause of diverting our spice and silk trade to England?

My husband will not understand this; will not see that every man, woman and child exists or is destroyed to keep the spice and silk trade moving in and out of Venice.

No wonder I have nightmares.

Feast of Saint Clare of Assisi.

Venice
August 15, 1493

Dear Isabetta,

Of course, I will write to you often.

How can I leave you on the Tuscany Plain without news of La Serenissima Repubblica?

Truth is, I miss you more than I can say. Why wouldn't I; from the time we could walk – before – as babes in arms – we were in and out of each other's homes. Your mother says so. Thirty-three years is a long time.

Let me start with the choicest bit:

Our ex-Queen of Cyprus has moved to her new palace at Asolo.

The Collegio have shined up that little hill town – put in a bricked main road, built her a palace.

I've been there.

You can imagine I was amazed when her high-hatted Saracen delivered the embossed invitation.

I got out the family jewels, all the biggest and gaudiest bits, boxed them up and took them with me. I wore only my mother's amber.

Caterina met me at the door of her castle wearing the Cornaro pearls, a ring on each finger.

She is still vivacious: son dead or murdered, husband most certainly murdered, crown and country the pawn of Venice, and Caterina is still vivacious. What a magnificent Queen she must have been! At thirty-eight she is comely. I remembered her as delicate; I often saw her, at Sunday Mass at San Marco's, swoon against the wall.

She showed me around her castle and grounds, which are luxurious, suitable for a Queen – a Cornaro.

Her public rooms are covered in damask, mostly gold and blue.

She has had Carpaccio paint the story of her life in Cyprus on her study walls: the Queen is eighteen, the King is handsome, the child beautiful, the courtiers serious, the walls of the fortress strong, the soldiers armed, ready. The worm is not in evidence.

She rarely opens the door to this room, so the rumour goes.

The Collegio gives her a stipend of eight thousand ducats a year.

I was the only guest that first evening. They say she keeps a hundred servants – if so, they are well hidden.

There was a reason I was there alone; this is Venice after all: I was selected to hear the first version of a plan to support artists. Maybe the only work she can do that will not bring her to the attention of the Collegio – a minor stroke of minor diplomacy.

Her vision is grand.

She intends to use the guest houses on her estate for artists who need a period of quiet to polish their art. As well, she wants to open her palace to performances and lectures.

We spent a whole evening brooding over how she might approach this, who might be her first candidates: I suggested Violante Picorina, the singer. She needs it; singers make less money than musicians. As well I gave her the name of the painter Giorgione. All the good jobs are tied up by the Bellini brothers, and he's just starting his trade.

Caterina hinted the proposed supper-party the next evening would be small. In fact there were only ten of us.

The dinner was pleasant.

Caterina wore a small gold brocaded cap, over it a chaplet of gold, studded with pearls and precious jewels. Her dress was dark wine silk – to deepen those amber eyes – with a stomacher studded with pearls and rubies; she wore a gold chain with a carbuncle and pearl drop, only one ring; it was a magnificent ruby.

I was modest – wore all the family emeralds: necklace, earrings, bracelet, brooch. Ha! Ha! No rings.

Caterina presented her proposal to the group in a clear-headed way. It was a pity she was pulled from her throne; I suppose the alternative is too grim to contemplate.

Others at the table suggested any number of people whose work might benefit from a year in the country – including Marin Sanudo, who is writing a history of Venice.

By the way, the Dolfins were there; they are going on a pilgrimage to Jerusalem. Dorotea's child was still-born. They are quite grief-stricken. If they don't have a child soon it will be too late. She must be thirty-five.

After supper – the wine was excellent – we sang a number of madrigals; both Caterina and I accompanied on two exquisite lutes she brought back from Cyprus, and the evening was over.

Tomorrow we put Sebastian on Nicolo Pisani's carrack to Modon – his first working voyage. Then I am off to Montebelluna with the rest of the family until the feast of Saint Gregory.

Carefree.

Blessings on all your family, blessings on you.

Mathye

Feast of the Assumption of Our Lady into Heaven, under seal.

DIARII
Venice
August 16, 1493

Sebastian, Lodovico, Sancio, me, all the servants squeezed into two gondolas, made a procession to Nicolo's carrack.

Ser and Donna Barozzi on their balcony waving handkerchiefs.

Sebastian putting his strength into hugging us.

Not letting the servants touch his clothes' bag; hefting it on his shoulder, climbing the rope ladder with one hand.

When his feet touched the deck, doing a little gigue.

Immediately the carrack moved out into the Canal.

Sancio took his pipe from inside his toga – shyly began playing.

Sebastian continued the gigue for a few seconds, raised his fist in the air, shouted:

Hold the party! I'll be back in a month!

Grinning his glittering grin, disappeared into the bowels of the ship.

I have no doubt that Sebastian is the happiest boy in the universe.

I'm glum.

Feast of Saint Joachim, Father of the Virgin Mary.

Most dear wife,

Your letter was waiting for me at Bruges.

I needed it.

I am now more than two months on the road.

I will go on to the universities of Oxford and Cambridge, then back to Bristol where I have every hope my future will begin.

I wish I had been home when Isabetta told you they were moving to Florence. It must have been distressing for you.

Yes, Lodovico is a surprise. But a year with Isabetta and Lorenzo, at Florence, will ease him into the broader world. If he were a less serious student I might feel anxious. I am sure he will return at the end of the year and go to the University of Padua. However, I know how grievously you will miss our son.

Isabetta is a great loss to you, but she will be back in a couple of years. She loves Venice more than you, if that's possible.

I have written to Lodovico.

You had every reason to be daunted by these events but I had hours of disquiet after reading your letter. You suggested I had 'never' been daunted.

It is true, in my work, never.

But during the three months before we married, I was constantly daunted; that uncle of mine educated me to be the master general of his galleys. Then his only son changed his mind and decided he wanted to go to sea, instead of becoming a priest.

I was expected to give way to him.

I did.

I was not disappointed by this turn of events; on the contrary, my education at Sagres had prepared me for a more exciting life. I had studied cosmography with the best minds in the world; I had read all the available Arabic and Latin manuscripts on the subject. I had taken Portuguese caravels as far west as man had gone.

I had been to Iceland.

I made charts that can guide a ship safely from Iceland to Guinea to Cape Verde.

I was already convinced it was possible to sail west and reach the East. I knew whoever found that route had the wealth of that fabulous land in his pocket.

I left my uncle's house satisfied that I had escaped.

I was twenty years old.

The Republic gave me a galley to ply the trade to Constantinople.

I had long talks with caravan leaders who brought the spices from the golden East.

I took the Red Sea to Mecca, bribed my way into that Holy City.

Later that same year I returned to Venice and we met. Remember? My cousin had invited a dancing master to teach us a German saltarello. The room was full of the golden youth of 1476.

We danced.

I was captivated by your Byzantine eyes, your black hair with its green sheen.

You enticed me, and I was enticed.

I have no memory of the next twenty-four hours. I assume I remembered to eat; to put on my clothes the right way round; to greet people in the rough Venetian tongue.

You were so sure we would have what we wanted, I conveniently forgot your wealth, your ancient name.

I announced my happiness to anyone who would listen.

Within a week I had a visit from your legal guardian; he told me he would never permit our marriage, that I should leave Venice and not return. I threw him out of the house. The next day your uncle summoned me to his home and repeated what your legal guardian had said.

That same evening we went dancing at the Dandolo home – did we do anything but dance that summer? You told me your uncle wanted you to marry into the Polani family. You laughed! I went outside and was very sick.

I lost all hope when my uncle suggested I captain a ship that didn't call at Venice. He reminded me I had neither wealth, name, nor citizenship.

There was an old cob from the Levant at the quay. Sometime before dawn the next day I packed my bag, climbed out of the window of my uncle's home.

I was sitting on the sea wall waiting for a sign from inside the cob when my life at Sagres flashed before my eyes: my education there, and all that it had promised. I saw my future could be brighter than that of any man you might marry. I let out a howl of joy, threw my fist in the air and turned towards home. I crawled back through the window, went to bed and slept.

When I woke I felt again I was carrying the weight of the house on my chest. The confidence I had on the quay had left me. I realised all the barriers ranged against our marriage. And, as my uncle reminded me, I wasn't even Venetian.

Why didn't we talk of all those difficulties?

Every time we met we spoke only of our coming marriage. Not once did you indicate by half a frown that what we wanted wouldn't be accomplished. I would leave you joyous beyond believing; then halfway home the weight of the game we seemed to be playing would fall on my head.

Do you remember introducing me to Patriarch Gherardi? My dear Mathye, that Feast Day is burned into my soul; it was after Mass on Pentecost Sunday, June 13, 1476 at San Marco's. I didn't know until that morning he was your spiritual director.

You told him we would marry. He seemed genuinely happy for us.

I followed him back to his palace. He received me graciously;

listened to my story; looked grave all the while. I felt I had failed, that the visit had been useless.

At the door, he placed his hand on my shoulder and said, 'My son, canon law stipulates it is the man and the woman who make a marriage, not kinsmen or guardian.'

The rest is our life together.

As I write this, it now seems incredible that I never once discussed those problems with you.

What kind of young man was I?

So you mustn't say I have never been daunted – my dear Mathye, you are still the only person in the world that, even now, can leave me daunted. You unhappy, I would turn over Venice to make you smile.

These memories have made my head spin.

I am sending this letter by a special messenger whom I met at this Inn. He has come from the King of England and is on his way to the Doge. He told me he has already ridden two horses to their deaths. He is to be in Venice in ten days. You will verify his boast.

Tomorrow at dawn I leave for the isle of the English King.

Luigi will come on to London. He will take your family galley home if it is still there. He's been a good servant to me.

I keep you close in my heart with my prayers.

Giovanni

Feast of Saint Joachim, under seal.

Montebelluna
September 8, 1493

My darling husband,

The road to Hell is paved with those who said they didn't know, but I didn't know you were suffering in that way. You concealed it from me. You did.

I didn't know.

Once I had decided it was you I would marry, my mind was at peace. My legal guardian and my uncle behaved as if life were proceeding as it should. It's the Venetian way – to pretend all is well, while behind the scenes they are trying to undo what they say they have approved.

Poor Giovanni. I didn't know.

I have since asked cousin Piero what was the atmosphere in the family at that time. He said, 'hornets' nests.'

Patriarch Gherardi did come to my house that Pentecost Sunday. I remember thinking it strange, as he had already gone back to his palace; he rarely made the trip twice a day. He wanted to know if I was sure you were the one.

I suppose he must have gone to see my legal guardian, and maybe your uncle. Soon after you were made a citizen of Venice. I remember being surprised to discover you weren't born here.

I wanted to marry after the Feast of the Nativity. Why did we marry in July? I was enjoying showing you off.

I liked your blue eyes that made me fall back the first time I looked into them.

I liked the way our bodies matched when first we danced – many of my friends were shorter.

I liked the look of you in your black Portuguese clothes.

I also thought we might have the Biblical year of grace – but in three months you were off to Constantinople.

A few days after you left home, I was overwhelmed with the thought that for the rest of our lives it would be like this: you would be home for three months, away for three months – we haven't been that lucky!

Nurse sat by my bed for a week.

After I recovered I told myself I would not, like the ancient Penelope, unravel each night what I knit up each day.

I went to Patriarch Gherardi and asked him to find me a church that needed a choir director. He gave me San Zan Degolla.

After you and our children, it is the best that has happened to me.

But you rarely return to me after three months, my husband.

My love and the Holy Mother's surround you.

Mathye

Feast of the Nativity of the Blessed Virgin, under seal.

DIARII
Montebelluna
September 8, 1493

San Zan Degolla! First went there seventeen years to the day!

Nurse with me.

As I walked up Calle dei Tentor it washed over me – I had never met Canon Leonardo – that Patriarch Gherardi, concerned for my welfare, might have insisted he take me on.

I still can hear the soft fall of our shoes on the bricks as we made our way to the campo.

I stopped for a drink at the well.

We found the canon's house tucked behind San Zan.

By the time the servant invited us into one of the public rooms I wasn't hearing a word Nurse was saying.

The door burst open, the Canon rushed in. I thought he was old. He must have been thirty. Younger than I am now.

You are an answer to my prayers! The last two years, my deacon, who doesn't know music, has sung my Masses!

I giggled.

I saw Nurse turn her eyes on me.

Follow me.

We were off in a line: Canon Leonardo ahead, cassock flapping about his legs, me at his back, Nurse behind.

We made the rounds of the parish, meeting a man here, a woman there. All introduced as:

Your choir.

When we returned to the church I posted on the door my first notice for choir practice.

Who would I have been without it?

Nativity of the Blessed Virgin.

DIARII

Venice

September 11, 1493

Piero and Paola were here. We sat on the altana, had a glass –
as we've done so many times.

Piero left for the Rialto.

Paola stayed.

Mathye, you had Piero. I never had a cousin or a
brother.

Yes, we shared the same nursery until he was ten.
Where he went, I went – until he went to sea.

I envied you that. You and Piero have something
between you I will never have.

But you had a mother and father, Paola. We had only
ourselves – and Nurse.

I saw her bruised eyes clear.

Paola – so possessive, after she married Piero.

So jealous.

So questioning.

It doesn't pass.

Feast of Saint Theodora.

DIARII

Venice

September 14, 1493

Sebastian is back. Smelling of salt and sea weeds.

At least an inch taller.

The house is rocking with his scratchy, high-pitched voice.

How I love this noisy, happy son!

Feast of the Exaltation of the Holy Cross.

DIARII

Venice

September 15, 1493

Unexpected!

A note from the new Patriarch, Thomaso Donato.

First thought: he wants my choir for one of his deacons.

No!

He wants me to write a morality play to commemorate his being raised to the Patriarchy.

Will I come to his palace to discuss it?

I will.

I will.

Feast of Saint Nicomedes.

Venice
September 16, 1493

My dear Isabetta,

Remember how, with half Venice, we were at the Piazzetta to see Patriarch Gherardi off to Rome?

Remember how, as he was about to board the galley, he turned to me and said:

When I return, I will give you a commission to write a Te Deum to celebrate the election of the new Pope.

Do you remember that?

When the Patriarch died on the way home I assumed it was the end of the Te Deum.

It's not.

The new Patriarch invited me to his palace to talk about it.

He doesn't want a Te Deum for the Pope, who has the reputation of being dissolute; he wants a morality play, to celebrate his own elevation to the Patriarchy.

He suggested I base it on the twelve fruits of the Holy Spirit.

It's to be presented at San Marco's on Saint Stephen's night.

I have just three months!

Patriarch Gherardi had added a codicil to his Will. I'm to get 175 ducats. That's as much as the Admiral of the Arsenal makes in a year.

The new Patriarch said I can have whomever and whatever I want within his jurisdiction. I am to use his name.

I asked for the nuns of Santa Maria delle Vergini who, of course, are under the jurisdiction of the Doge; the Patriarch thought he could arrange it. These nuns are the best-trained singers in Venice.

When I arrived home and closed the door, I did a little dance, to the astonishment of Gemma. Within minutes she was shouting the news over the back fence to Bianca. Within ten minutes your mother had come by and we were celebrating with a glass of Pellestrina wine.

My dear Isabetta, I miss you, but this day I am rapturously joyous.

Mathye
Feast of Saint Ludmila, under seal.

Venice
September 18, 1493

My darling husband,

If the post has caught up with you at Bruges you have my letter – know the story of my commission. I sent a copy of that letter on to Bristol where there will be a sack-load awaiting you.

I was at the new Patriarch's palace this morning and signed the contract. It was the first time I had been there since Patriarch Gherardi died. It took me some time to adjust to the place without him.

I took our three sons and Nurse.

The Patriarch's secretary showed us into one of the formal rooms where the contract, with seals and ribbons, was laid out; and on a smaller table were wine, cheese, bread.

His Beatitude, who is a Dominican, and quite young for such an exalted post, apologised for not telling me sooner. He said he didn't want to sign documents until the Pope had confirmed his appointment.

He is a man of some charm. He poured wine, we sipped and talked about how I might present this work. I let him do most of the talking; I didn't want to divulge my best ideas.

Out of the corner of my eye, I saw Sebastian wink at Lodovico, pretend to add water to his wine; Lodovico took the water cruet, poured his glass half full. Sebastian gave that mocking little bow of his that allows him to get away with so much.

Finally the Patriarch got round to signing the contract.

The young secretary made flourishes affixing the ribbons and seal; sweat formed on his top lip. The Patriarch's eyes twinkled.

His Beatitude took up the newly minted contract and read it with that melodious voice of his, which judicious use of, I suspect, helped him get where he is.

Here is what the contract says:

I, Thomaso Donato, Patriarch of Venice, grant power and full authority to Mathye Caboto, Maestra di Cappella dei San Zan de Degolla, in order that she may more quickly and more easily write a morality play to the greater Glory of God. To be performed on Saint Stephen's night, at the church of San Marco in the year of Our Lord fourteen hundred and ninety-three.

I grant her the authority to make use of whatever singers she may need, with whatever materials that may be necessary of whatever kind it may be.

I grant her the authority to make use of the Cathedral Church of Aquileia and, with the cooperation of the Doge, the Church of San Marco, for whatever times, outside the ordinary liturgical hours of the Church year, as are suitable for the preparation of this work.

The said Mathye Caboto will receive one hundred ducats on the date of the signing of this document, and a further seventy-five ducats on the day the morality play is completed and presented to the said Patriarch at his Palace.

Given at our Palace, Thursday, of the Twelfth Sunday after Pentecost, in the year of our Lord's Incarnation, fourteen hundred and ninety-three.

That is a handsome sum of money. I am working like a Trojan. It will take another two months to complete, and a month's practice.

I am already spending most of my days thinking about it.

I will send this letter to Oxford with a copy to Bristol.

I hope, my beloved husband, you are wearing warm clothes in that frozen land.

The Holy Trinity be with you and guide you.

Your own true wife,

Mathye

Saturday after the fourteenth Sunday after Pentecost, under seal.

DIARII
Venice
September 19, 1493
Ana is delighted she will prepare the choir for the Nativity services. I am protective of my choir – only a commission of this magnitude would permit me to give it up.

Deacon Garofoli hinted he would like to direct the choir in my absence.

I didn't respond.

His musical education is weak; he is an indifferent student.

Both were at the Guild of Singers last night: Ana, smug – the deacon, glowering.

Fifteenth Sunday after Pentecost.

DIARII
Venice
September 20, 1493
Walking back from a Low Mass at San Marco's – I attend daily for Giovanni when he is at sea – met Natalin di San Giorgio on his way to Chancery. He started a rambling story about himself and my father as lads stealing figs from stalls on the Piazzetta. Had heard it so many times:

We made a hook on the end of a long piece of wire.

Your father distracted the mercer. I hooked off the figs.

All the while a sweet phrase of music was tumbling in my head; tried to edge away; he held me with that eye – wide, black:

Arch lads, we were. Yes, we were.

Home, I raced to my music room, snatched parchment, couldn't get a note right, kicked my footstool across the room; it hit under the window – at that precise angle – shattered the glass. I sit in my study twiddling my thumbs while Guido repairs it and mutters about how it could have happened.

I do not confess my sins to my servants.

I do not pray for Natalin di San Giorgio.

After much thought I invited Girolama Corsi Ramos to write the text for the morality play.

She's a better poet and works faster.

She came with two pieces today – almost perfect.

I will give her fifty ducats.

Feast of Saint Eustace of Egypt.

DIARII
Venice
September 21, 1493
I have moved the organ to the top of the house with my lute, zither, timbrels, bagpipe, harp, flute, recorders. The servants were astonished; I encouraged them along with a few soldi.

No one has lived in this room in memory. Justina spent days cleaning.

There is a good fireplace and a western light – it soothes me.

When I am here I am so concentrated – after a few hours I go down to bed and fall into a deep sleep, deeper than at any time since childhood; I don't wake until supper time.

I have the Te Deum sketched out. That is not difficult. It is the representation of the Fruits of the Holy Spirit that will crack my head.

I'm glad I wasn't offered this when I was young.

Feast of Saint Matthew, Apostle.

My darling wife,

Six letters at Bristol! I was hungry for them.

My journey through a dozen universities and monasteries of Europe has sharpened my Latin, opened a few minds, and brought me bits of new information.

The Toscanelli letter is important.

At Oxford University, I saw a manuscript: *Invento Fortunata*, by Nicolas of Lynn, a Minorite monk, who was a mathematician and an astronomer, and taught there.

Nicolas wrote of a number of voyages he made to the Norse Settlements at Greenland and 'beyond', beginning in 1355. There were charts that show where these settlements were located.

Believe me, my dear Mathye, if these charts are in any way accurate, I will be following the paths that men have already taken.

I am anxious to begin my work here, to meet the men who will be my partners in this adventure.

Luigi left for home on the Feast of Saint John Chrysostom.

God bless you, my darling.

Giovanni

Feast of Saint Matthew, under seal.

My darling Mathye,

I have moved out of the Inn and found very good lodgings in Broad Street. I have a bedroom and a chart room. My breakfast and supper are provided; I take my dinner at one of the many good inns.

This city has improved since I was here in the 1480s.

There is a very strong Common Council; they are trying to

get rid of houses that overhang the streets. Anyone who wishes to build one that juts must now pay a yearly tax.

There are almost as many church spires piercing the sky as at Venice, and their bells are as cacophonous.

The port is a beehive with local and foreign ships arriving and leaving almost every hour of the day.

The main streets have been paved.

Bristol is a small town but not an unpleasant one to live in.

I am rested from my travels and am waiting to meet with Richard Americ – a name which always reminds me of friend Amerigo Vespucci.

Richard has rufous hair. He looks like a Norseman. He has been in London since I arrived. He will be back in Bristol around the Feast of Saint Pelagia, when I hope to begin my work.

Last night I dreamed you were with me. We had a home; we were walking around arm in arm admiring the ceilings.

My dear good wife. I bless you.

Giovanni

Feast of Saint Jerome, doctor of the Church, under seal.

Bristol
October 2, 1493

My darling wife,

I have met with Richard Americ, who is now a customs official and a man of some importance, also with Thomas Canynges; both men have fleets of ships.

These are the ones I need by my side when I am ready to approach the English King.

I have shown them my sphere and charts, let them read Toscanelli's letter.

They were not uninfluenced by my status as an ambassador of the Republic of Venice.

They say they are prepared to consider a voyage to the West sometime in the future.

My dear Mathye, this life is continuously exciting.

I hope your morality play is going well. I am sad that I won't see it. But then I miss so much.

I have received four more of your letters written when I was in France.

Whenever possible I will have my letters conveyed privately to London and put aboard a galley for home.

May you and our sons be in the care of the Holy Spirit.

Giovanni

Feast of the Holy Guardian Angels, under seal.

DIARII
Venice
October 3, 1493
Spent an hour in the choir of San Marco looking into the Dome of the Pentecost.

Wanted to select a costume for the nuns from the multitudes the Apostles preached to on the first Pentecost.

Have never looked at that mosaic with such intensity; my eyes hurt when I came into the Piazza.

Selected the dress of the people of Pontus: a green tunic with a cream-coloured cloak, padded at the shoulders; just above the deep fringe, stripes of red and green. It falls in a most dramatic way.

To represent the virtues the twelve cloaks will be:

White – Modesty
Yellow – Joy
Green – Peace
Blue – Patience
Orange – Goodness
Red – Kindness
Gold – Charity
Silver – Chastity
Purple – Generosity
Wine – Faithfulness
Pink – Gentleness

Umber – Continency

The nuns will look splendid.

Have sent young Giorgione to make a sketch for the seamstress.

Seventeenth Sunday after Pentecost.

Venice
October 5, 1493

My dear Isabetta,

The morality play is going slowly; looking for inspiration, I went to San Marco's. A mist was falling outside. In the narthex, two men from the market, each with a bullock, were arguing over the price of mullet.

As I entered the nave, I had to skirt around a half-dozen boys who were shouting and kicking a ball.

A couple of women, wearing more jewels than are in the church treasury, were parading up and down discussing the new property tax.

On the high altar, a number of young Dominican nuns, with blue aprons over their white habits, were wrestling candleholders to the sanctuary floor, where another group was scraping off wax. Occasionally they would break out in a frottola; they had pure, sweet voices.

I was looking closely at the high altar, as if I had not seen it before, when I heard a shout: 'Out of the way!'

Up the nave trotted a man with a braying donkey, hauling a rattling cart loaded with altar wine. A canon appeared from behind the high altar, took charge of the wine, and from somewhere inside his cassock drew a purse from which he counted a number of scudi, which he gave the tradesman.

The young boys, hoping for a soldo, rushed the altar with shouts of 'Let me carry, let me carry!' They made short work of bringing the load to the sacristy.

I left the racket and went to the choir and fell into the Dome of the Pentecost.

I spent an hour studying the clothes of the people in that mosaic. The colours are exhilarating, the details quite grand.

Now I must turn it all into music!

Bless you and all your family.

Mathye

Wednesday of September Ember Week, under seal.

My darling husband,

I told Lodovico he can go to Florence.

I thought I would weep buckets.

I didn't.

Lodovico was at his desk. He stood. Bowed. Kissed my cheek. Smiled his sweet smile.

And I didn't weep.

I will send Guido with him. He will remain until Isabetta hires a new servant for him.

That's done!

May choirs of Seraphim be with you, my darling.

Mathye

Feast of Saint Justina, potter, under seal.

DIARII
Venice
October 7, 1493
Not nearly as joyful about Lodovico leaving as I pretend to Giovanni.
Feast of Saint Justina.

DIARII
Venice
October 8, 1493
Problems to solve in the morality play – how to make the music represent:

the soul's battle for salvation
the harvest from the Holy Spirit
the soul in praise and wonderment

The music pounds in my head, generally at the most awkward moments – in the gondola, on the way to church – when I don't have anything at hand to write it down.

Friday of the September Ember Week.

DIARII
Venice
October 16, 1493
This music is taking me away.

I hear Lodovico and Guido plot their move to Florence; they seem to be doing well without me.

Lodovico wants to go there when he finishes his studies in October.

I will keep him here for Saint Stephen's night!

Feast of Saint Gall, hermit.

DIARII
Venice
October 21, 1493
If I can get a stretch of two weeks without interruptions, I will finish the morality play.

I will.

First time I've not walked in procession on the Feast of Sant' Orsola – first time Lodovico has.

Feast of Sant' Orsola.

DIARII
Venice
November 7, 1493
Luigi arrived today with six letters from Giovanni – my husband is as optimistic of the future as our sons.

Twenty-second Sunday after Pentecost.

DIARII

Venice

November 10, 1493

Tomorrow, first practice with the nuns at Santa Maria delle Vergini.

That will be the test.

Wednesday of the twenty-second Sunday after Pentecost.

DIARII

Venice

November 11, 1493

Those nuns' voices are stolen from the spheres.

Have made only slight changes in pitch to better suit one or two who can soar to the heavens.

The work will be ready, yes!

Feast of Saint Martin, Bishop.

DIARII

Venice

December 6, 1493

Ana asked Fedrico Vettori not to sing the Nativity Mass.

Fedrico – the oldest member of the choir, there since he was a boy.

His voice has become too thin.

He wouldn't leave.

I invited him to my home. Opened a bottle of our best wine – told him as kindly as I could.

But Donna Caboto, who will sing countertenor?

I didn't respond.

He complained to Canon Leonardo – as he said he would.

The good Canon didn't ask Ana to take Fedrico back – his ear is as good as mine.

Grief I didn't need.

Feast of Saint Nicholas.

DIARII
Venice
December 26, 1493

With all servants trailing, we left home an hour before the first hour of the night. The nuns and I had planned to be in the choir before anyone arrived.

The Canal was full of gondolas, there was a low hum of voices, people were singing Nativity hymns – not extraordinary on Saint Stephen's night. We stepped out at the Piazzetta, walked through a slight covering of snow to the Piazza; it was bathed in a 'full moon social'. Guido put out the lantern.

People coming from all directions.

The church was half full when we arrived. The nuns, a few minutes later, had to push their way to the choir.

Our Scuola, who came in procession, stood on either side of the nave to make space for the nuns when they were ready to pass into the sanctuary. I looked down upon the throng and tried desperately to control my excitement:

These people expect something new.

The nuns left the choir, in a line of twos. I heard the swoosh of their cloaks as they walked down the stairs. I made the sign of the cross – waited.

Feast of Saint Stephen, first martyr.

Venice
December 27, 1493

My darling husband,

The morality play was sung last evening. San Marco's was full.

Our sons, Girolama Corsi Ramos and I went to the choir-loft and looked down upon the scene. Patriarch Donato, as a surprise, had the church lit with five hundred tapers.

The Doge, his chief priest, all his canons, acolytes, the Patriarch, the Bishops, and at least a hundred priests came in procession from the Doge's palace.

Only the Doge, the Patriarch, and the chief priest sat in the sanctuary, which left the space needed for the morality play.

The twelve nuns entered the nave singing the new Te Deum; some unusual fall of light from the large number of candles playing over the silk of their multi-coloured robes made them look taller, thinner – it was an effect I hadn't imagined; it added a sinister look that suited the battle for the soul.

As each virtue sang her part, the group formed a different zodiacal sign so that the singers, throughout, were doing what appeared to be a measured dance; stops occurred only when the soul was in danger of losing its way.

Each time a voice cadenced from the mixolydian mode to the aeolian and reverberated among the domes, I shivered.

When it was over the people applauded. I was shocked; I had never before heard clapping at San Marco's.

Outside, the night was a riot of good will. Even the nuns were embraced.

Most of the other Maestri di Cappella of Venice were there. I spent a half hour taking accolades.

Our servants came, and every member of the Guild of Singers. All the way back to the house the Guild serenaded us. People in other gondolas joined in.

We had supper and danced late into the night. Without you and Isabetta no one dared the chacota.

I feel as light as a bird.

My darling husband, you missed one of the great nights of my life.

I missed you.

Bless you in everything you do.

Mathye

Feast of Saint John, Evangelist, under seal.

DIARII
Venice
December 27, 1493
A note from the Patriarch. One line:

Be proud, Mathye; be proud.

Now I will sleep.
Feast of Saint Fabiola.

Chapter Three

DIARII
Venice
January 6, 1494
Head bent against a black rain, almost ran into Amerigo
Vespucci in the Piazza.

Placed my hand on his arm. He shook it off as if scalded.
Took me a minute to recover.

Sent Guido after him.

He had disappeared in the warren of roads behind San
Marco.

Have searched my conscience for any slight given when
last we met, remember nothing.

I hate mysteries.
Feast of the Epiphany.

Venice
January 9, 1494

My dear Isabetta,

Lodovico will bring this letter.

He has become quite sociable. After you left he joined the
Companion of the Hose.

He is beginning to use the knowledge he's been storing;
you will see it flower. You must write to me.

Thank you and Lorenzo for taking him on.

I'm glad you are able to accommodate Gemma, as well as
Guido. They've not been separated since they came to work
for us. I thought it a pity to leave her behind.

I don't look forward to giving up my first-born.

Well, I must get used to that too.

The Divinity of Christ bless you and your family.

Mathye
First Sunday after the Epiphany, under seal.

DIARII
Venice
January 9, 1494
Sebastian and Sancio came to my room when the fire was lit.
It's been a long time.

They brought a large new chart of the Peninsula Sebastian
had drawn. That son of mine is becoming a fine chart maker.

They are plotting the journey to Florence – the distance
travelled each day, the towns stayed in.

I'm not the only one who is lonely.

I took out the card table, put a hundred soldi in the pot. We
had a rollicking game of scartino. Sebastian and I were taking
all the winnings. Sancio was looking grim. I gave the wink to
Sebastian. That combative son – for once – fell back and let
Sancio take a few hands.

I had fruit juice and ring biscuits brought up.

Mother, do you think they took enough food for the
road?

Sancio, they took enough food to get them to
Jerusalem.

My sons are gone to their rooms; the house is a sepulchre.

Not even my double harp comforts me.
First Sunday after the Epiphany.

DIARII
Venice
January 13, 1494
I want to sit on the altana all day – drink sweet wine.

Why do all fifteen-year-old men, at a distance, look like
Lodovico? My heart leapt as I saw one stride across the Piazza,
disappear behind the Campanile, reappear and enter the
Piazzetta.

Until he left, I didn't realise how Lodovico cared for his
brothers: small things – cap on just right, shoes clean, studies
done, keeping an eye on Sebastian in public.

Yes, it was time for Lodovico to leave.

To be on his own.

To be carefree.

Not to play the father.

Feast of Saint Hilary, doctor of the Church.

Florence
January 27, 1494

My dear Mother,

Donna Isabetta and Messer Lorenzo met us at The Hawk.

I have had a fine week.

Martino has three chestnut maremmana horses, each sixteen hands; we have to use a wine keg to mount them. We ride every day. In May he will go to the University of Paris to study medicine.

He says I can use his horses while he is away.

I have given Donna Isabetta the murano bowl; she was pleased.

I have met with Friar Savonarola.

I am attending his sermons at Saint Mark's; he is preaching on Genesis, but in every sermon he works in a condemnation of wicked priests and the Court of Rome.

The Friar is totally fearless.

His church is full every morning and many young men, influenced by his call to lead a pure life, are entering his priory.

He has rooted out all the worldly friars.

Your son, with deep respect,

Lodovico

Feast of Saint John of the golden mouth.

Post Scriptum

Just outside Siena we dipped over a hill and ran into a band of robbers; they looked at our large train, whipped their horses and disappeared into the countryside. My heart was pounding.

DIARII
Venice
February 1, 1494
Working on chart for Toscanelli, and the Te Deum to welcome the Bishop of Cyprus – keeps me from wandering to my sons' wing of the house.
Feast of Saint Bridget, patron of poets.

DIARII
Venice
February 5, 1494
Two letters from Giovanni, full of suppressed spleen.
   These English are not doing his bidding.
Feast of Saint Agatha.

                                              Venice
                                      February 7, 1494

My dear Lodovico,

   How I do miss you, my beloved son.

   I wait for your tap on my door.

   I never hear your brothers pillow fight any more. I fear they miss you as much as I.

   Sebastian and Sancio have again taken up the habit of coming to my room in the evenings. We cosy around the fire, sometimes talk, sometimes play scartino. Always we sing a madrigal or two.

   Sancio has started to wobble between soprano and scratchiness.

   We miss your rich voice.

   You seem to have started your year well. We wait for your letters.

   May Jesus and the Holy Mother be with you always.

   Your Mother

Feast of Saint Romuald, abbot, under seal.

My dear Mother,

Friar Savonarola has a weekly meeting based on the books of the Hebrew Bible. It is held in the library of his church. I found there some of the great scholars of the City, including the very wise Messer Blemet and Messer Giovanni Pico della Mirandola. There is a set topic for each evening's discussion; you can imagine I prepare well.

There is a general feeling of respect and admiration in Florence for the Friar.

There used to be bands of young boys roaming the street, pestering people for money and pelting them with rocks when they didn't give it. These same young boys were gathered up at night by rich young men and used for their own purposes.

Friar Savonarola has collected all those youngsters and formed them into holy societies. Banks of seats have been built in Saint Mark's and they are now seen at all the Masses with wreaths on their heads.

Mother, I am in the right place.

The air seems to crackle with the excitement of reform.

I have a letter started to Sebastian and Sancio. It will be in the post by the Feast of Saint Andrew.

Your loving son, with deep respect,

Lodovico

Feast of Saint Flavian.

My darling son,

I am reluctant to urge you to further study.

But Messer Blemet has a reputation that has reached Venice – it is a pity to be in Florence and not study with him. He is one of the living scholars of Maimonides – the great twelfth-century writer on the *Mishneh Torah*. An hour a week would broaden your knowledge immeasurably .

I have studied Maimonides with Patriarch Gherardi all my life. His Beatitude's idea of spiritual formation was to assign me a chapter from *The Guide of the Perplexed* which, until I married your father, I was expected to recite at his weekly visits to our home.

Even after your father and I married, the Patriarch – reading whatever manuscript by Maimonides for the forty-first time – would give me his latest insights, invite mine.

I didn't always appreciate it.

Now, I take great comfort in reading Maimonides. I marvel at his skill in fusing revealed religion with the natural religion of the Greeks. I hope you can share some of those pleasures.

My dear son, whatever you decide, I want you to know this is a year apart, when anything is possible.

Bless you, my son, during this holy season.

Mother.

Second Sunday in Lent, under seal.

Florence
March 12, 1494

My dear Mother,

Messer Lorenzo has found me an excellent tutor. His name is Domenico Niccolini. He is retired from the Chancery and is writing a book on the history of law in Florence. He keeps my head down for two hours every morning.

And I have joined Messer Blemet's group. We meet once a month in his study which is overflowing with books, manuscripts and copies of his own works.

He has a little white dog that barks and frisks around each of us as we enter. The great man shouts at it, which makes it bark even louder. Finally it jumps upon his lap where it sleeps and snores throughout the lesson.

There are six of us. We discuss a chapter of whatever

Maimonides manuscript we are assigned. This month we study *Treatise on Resurrection*, which is only available in Arabic. Messer Blemet translates as he reads. We take notes.

Our good teacher said that Saint Thomas Aquinas learned everything he knew from the writings of Maimonides.

Is that true, Mother?

I have a new servant; he has been with Messer Lorenzo's family for five years.

Guido and Gemma will be leaving for home in a week. They will tell you the bits of news I have left out.

Venice, my dear Mother, is more beautiful, but Florence must be the most exciting city on earth.

And you allowed me to come here!

Your son, Lodovico, with loving respect.

Feast of Saint Maximilian.

Post Scriptum

This morning I was studying in my room and heard organ music; for a moment, before I lifted my head, I thought it was you, Mother. There is no organ in this house. I didn't hear the music again but all day I kept listening for it.

Florence
March 19, 1494

My dear Mother,

Of late I have been going to the Loggia of the Tornaquinci with Messer Niccolini. He meets a number of like-minded men who spend a pleasant hour discussing a work of Aristotle, Plato, sometimes a Roman poet.

With other young men, I usually stand on the fringes and listen. The discussions are wide-ranging and have encouraged me to consider taking an arts degree before I begin canon law. It will force me to spend more years at university than I planned, but you know my thirst for knowledge. I will not find it a burden.

Many of the friends of Messer Niccolini know their Latin

poets as if they were personal friends. But they studied Greek and Hebrew literature in translation. I am ahead of them there, but am not a seasoned scholar, and four years in an arts programme will do that for me.

I hope, Mother, you will agree with my change of plans.

Friar Savonarola's sermons are sometimes discussed at these sessions. Messer Niccolini supports the Friar's position on reform but there are a number who consider his constant attacks on the worldly too strident and unnecessary.

Your loving son, with due devotion,

Lodovico

Feast of Saint Joseph.

Florence
March 20, 1494

My dear Mother,

I am having a lovely time.

Martino gave a supper to celebrate receiving his Licentia Ubique Docendi and to mark his departure for the University of Paris. There were many of Messer Lorenzo's relatives and a large number of young people.

Mother, I met a young woman; she is from a family of painters and is already selling her work.

We sat next each other at supper and talked all evening; I have taken a good deal of hazing from Martino and young Marco. Her parents were at the supper; her father is a distant cousin of Messer Lorenzo.

I have seen her almost every day since. Her name is Alessandra Cavalcanti. She lives only four doors away. Martino visits the family; I trail along. She attends all Friar Savonarola's sermons with her parents. I manage to stand next to them in church.

Mother, I am untying all the knots.

Your devoted son,

Lodovico

Feast of Gabriel the Archangel.

My dear son,

I am delighted you are having such a wide variety of experiences at Florence.

An arts degree will be helpful and deepen your learning in Greek and Latin.

You might consider reading, for pleasure, any of the books by Ovid you have not studied. Read all the books of Homer's *Odyssey*. Think as well of reading again Sophocles' plays and Xenophon's *Persian Expedition*.

Since you are in Florence, be sure you read Dante's *Divine Comedy* again.

Six years at university will be a triumph for you.

May the Three Persons of the Blessed Trinity keep you in their holy care.

Your Mother
Tuesday in Holy Week, under seal.

DIARII
Venice
April 2, 1494
Gemma and Guido back from Florence.

Martino and Lodovico have a large circle of friends.

There is much feasting and dancing.

Is this really my Lodovico?
Easter Saturday.

DIARII
Venice
April 4, 1494
Guido poled me back from San Zan Degolla.

I had sung the dawn Mass – fasting since the first hour of the night.

Feeling faint, I asked him to remove the canopy.

Donna Caboto, you are pale.

I am hungry, Guido.

He stopped, uncovered a basket, removed two oat cakes wrapped in a cloth. Passed me a jar of water, a goblet.

You are the best of servants.

It's Nurse, Donna Caboto; she says you are not at your best in the morning.

Thank Nurse, and Cook. Thank you. You take good care of me.

Guido smiled, went back to his poling.

I lay back in the gondola.

Munched.

Sipped.

The salt-laden air, the smell of the rushes along the Canal, the ever-present scent of the wooden pilings laden with water – filled my nostrils, permeated my lungs, seemed to return to the air through my pores.

I was soothed.

The white caps glistened, sparkled.

The palaces crowding the Canal caught the light – every month, seemingly, a new one, crested with Istrian marble, red porphyry.

Along the curve of the waterway, servants began to appear on balconies, spread carpets – the wealth of Constantinople and beyond.

The bells of convents, monasteries, churches began tolling the hour. Venice awakening to another glorious Easter Monday morn.

DIARII
Venice
April 6, 1494
At the dawn Mass at San Zan Degolla, I see, lined up against the north wall, the twenty-five nuns of the Sisters of the Atonement.

Canon Leonardo has thrown me into their midst.

This Order accommodates the natural daughters of Venetian

noblemen. Their fathers have clapped them in the convent – they are either too poor, or too mean, to provide them with suitable marriage dowries.

Certain nuns have brought as little as ten ducats. The establishment, in consequence, is almost always in need. After ten years they are just getting a chapel.

I have been asked to advise on liturgical music. The abbess tells me only three of her nuns can read music – not well.

Canon Leonardo wants me to take on the job of teaching those nuns music.

I won't do that.

Where to turn?

The people who ought to help are those aristocratic nuns of Santa Maria delle Vergini. Every nun a choir nun. Every nun with the education of a princess, and enough personal servants to put any princess to shame. They could easily spare a half-dozen teachers. They won't. They'll make a thousand excuses.

Ah, well!

My choir sang like angels this morning.

Wednesday in Easter Week.

DIARII
Venice
April 7, 1494
Sometimes things come to you.

I was at the Scuola di Sant' Orsola giving out food.

My companion was Donna Marcello.

She hinted she might be looking for food herself next year. Her late husband's money is entailed on the men in his family; she has been told to live on her dowry, her three daughters not provided for. This is a great sin – that family is not without means.

I told her of the Sisters of the Atonement and their need to learn music.

She's a good musician. Her eyes gleamed.

We put together a programme on the spot.

I went back to the abbess with the proposal that a teacher of music be hired for five years:

The first year the teacher will take five nuns as students. The nuns who complete the programme will move on to the next level. As well, each student-nun will teach the programme of the first year to another nun. The teacher will stay with the original group of five and take them to the second year, the third and on. In five years five nuns will be at the level to become teachers; in ten years all of them: a way of earning a living.

The abbess is grateful.

But where to find a salary for Donna Marcello?

Thursday in Easter Week.

DIARII

Venice

April 9, 1494

I can always count on Adriana.

She suggested I ask the Scuola Grandi di San Marco for the salary. Alvise is a patron – says the Scuola has money.

She pointed out – as she would – some members of that confraternity most certainly have fathered one or more of those nuns.

That the convent of the Sisters of the Atonement could become self-sufficient will prick their interest.

Saturday in Easter Week.

DIARII

Venice

April 11, 1494

I was met at the door of the Scuola Grandi di San Marco by Alvise. His greeting was polite.

He led me into the albergo.

The sixteen men of the Banca were ranged along the wall, each with his cowl over his head. I was seated near the end of the bench. I could see only sharp noses, an occasional blue cheek.

The man on my right, whose face I had never seen before, turned. The eyes that greeted me were blank, then affronted.

I wasn't comfortable.

Alvise nodded. I stood, started my story.

No man raised his head or again looked at me until I came to the end. Alvise bent and spoke something to whoever was sitting at the end of the bench. I didn't catch it. It might have been in code.

There was a ruffle of sleeves. One or two faces turned in my direction.

Alvise stood in his place:

Donna Caboto, the Scuola will put your request to the vote at the next meeting of the Banca.

I nodded. Murmured my thanks.

The bodies on the bench dropped their heads, their cowls leaving no feature exposed.

Alvise escorted me to the door.

Winked.

Feast of Saint Stanislaus.

DIARII
Venice
April 14, 1494
A note from the Scuola di San Marco: they will pay half salary for five years for Donna Marcello if I can get another Scuola or another person to pay the other half.

That's easy. I'll bribe Adriana to pay one quarter, by agreeing to pay the other.

Yes!

I do this work for my sins.

Feast of Saint Bénezet, bridge builder.

My dear Mother,

I have good news.

I have met Friar Brugnuli, a Dominican and one of the canon lawyers to the Bishop of the See of Ravenna, who lives in this city; he is a good friend of Friar Savonarola.

He is quite old, maybe sixty-five.

When I told him I intended to take a degree in canon law at the University of Padua, which is where he studied, he asked me if I would like to work with him for a couple of hours a week.

We have met three times. Each time he has a piece of work I can usually finish in the allotted time.

I have not been offered money but I consider I am well paid by watching a canon lawyer at work.

Friar Brugnuli has the reputation of being one of the best Latin scholars in Florence. Already I believe my style is improving.

I am, my dear Mother, your devoted son,

Lodovico

Third Sunday after Easter.

Florence
April 22, 1494

My dear Mother,

The more time I spend with Alessandra the more I am intrigued with the business of her work.

I had the impression she painted all day, but that's not the way it is at all. She paints only in the morning. In the afternoon she does the business of painting: she writes letters to patrons and invites them to view her work.

I hinted that she show me her studio; she reminded me I don't purchase. I offered to purchase a painting on the spot. Her reply was:

I don't coerce my friends.

Mother, I commissioned a painting for your birthday. She showed me her studio. You will see how luminous her work is. I overheard her father say she was the best apprentice he ever had.

Did you know the colour blue is used only at the request of the buyer? Alessandra says the price of a pot of ground lapis lazuli is more expensive than the Doge's cap.

When Alessandra is commissioned to do a painting, she figures out all the costs and presents the person with a bill for the full amount. Before she starts painting she asks and gets half the price.

When it is two-thirds finished she presents the buyer with another bill.

Only one-tenth of the price is left to collect when the painting is delivered.

I stupidly asked her why she worked this way; she reminded me that members of her family have been painters for two hundred years and they like to eat well.

I am endlessly surprised.

After Martino left for Paris, Alessandra asked me to continue to visit her home. Now I am accepted as naturally as if I were one of the family.

Instead of my new servant accompanying me to Saint Mark's to hear the Friar, I go with the Cavalcanti family.

Donna Isabetta gave permission.

Mother, I am having a lovely life.

Your devoted and loving son,

Lodovico

Feast of Saint Theodore.

My dear Mother,

I am in Alessandra's garden. She is painting and won't let me look over her shoulder.

She says, 'Tell your mother I have a sharp tongue.'

What she calls sharp, I call candid. Let me tell you: a few days ago we were in her garden and her mother joined us. I suppose I must have pulled a face, since I get so little time alone with her. Alessandra caught the look and without a break in her conversation with her mother, she said, 'Stop that, Lodovico.' She gave me a little push.

I laughed; I was caught red-handed in an act of selfishness.

Mother, Alessandra is beautiful! She is about to my shoulder. Her hair is the colour of chestnuts. Her skin is a light shade of olive; if she goes into the sun, she burnishes a copper tint which is very attractive and comes from her mother's side, as that family has red hair. She is a distant relative of the Sforza, whom Alessandra always refers to as 'the condottieri'.

Her mother, as you might say, has a voice stolen from the spheres, but Alessandra's is not of that quality, although we sing together often.

She has a funny turn of phrase rather than a sense of humour – she knows how to bring levity to an awkward moment. I am impressed with this, as I approach an awkward moment with a bank of arguments and often end in confusion, as you know.

Last Sunday, I was a guest at a meal in her parents' home. A friend of the family, Michelangelo Buonarroti, who has a reputation of being a fine sculptor, was there too. We were eating in the garden. With a swipe of my arm, I stupidly knocked the bread basket off the table. I picked it up and to cover my embarrassment I asked Alessandra if she wanted bread.

I've had so much bread I'm rising.

After that sally no one remembered the bread had been picked from the ground.

Sometimes I think I'm the younger one, although I am three months older than she is.

She has no sisters or brothers.

She makes decisions quickly and definitely, and they seem to be the right ones; I see her do that when she talks about her painting. I think you will like each other.

There is great harmony between us. I am happy.

Your loving and devoted son,

Lodovico

Fourth Sunday after Easter.

Post Scriptum

Mother, I am sending by this post some jars of Trebbiano wine from San Giovanni in the upper Arno valley. Donna Isabetta says it would waken the dead to its praise.

Montebelluna
April 30, 1494

My dear Isabetta,

My beloved son is doing what sons are wont to do – he is giving his attention to a young woman.

After he met Friar Savonarola, I thought he might follow him into the priory.

Now he seems to have become enthralled by the first young woman he has met. He says she is a relative of Lorenzo.

What do you know of Alessandra?

Lodovico is not yet sixteen.

Need I worry?

May the Lord bless you.

Mathye

Feast of Saint Catherine of Siena, under seal.

DIARII
Venice
May 10, 1494

Isabetta says the Cavalcanti is a sterling family – yes, that's the word she used, 'sterling' – that Lodovico is in good hands.

I don't want my fifteen-year-old son in anybody's hands.

I bank on the fact Alessandra is an only child. Her parents will want to keep her close for another while.

I bank on it!

Feast of Saint Gordianus.

Venice
May 12, 1494

Dear Isabetta,

The beautification of Venice proceeds apace.

I've been to see, in progress, Gentile Bellini's latest painting – *The Miracle of the Cross at the Bridge of San Lorenzo* – on the wall of the albergo, at the Scuola Grande di San Giovanni Evangelista.

Some months ago the Scuola ran out of money for this project, and had to take up subscriptions. Bellini is using the faces of all contributors.

Some of the richest women of Venice have made contributions, including Queen Caterina. In the painting the women are lined up along the ri.

I declined, in favour of Nurse; her birthday is on the Feast of Saint Hildegard.

A surprise for her.

Bellini has painted her in the foreground – her charge in front of her. Nurse is kneeling, most of her face covered but no mistaking who it is.

Five of the Collegio are to the right, on a temporary bridge, sons behind them.

Members of the more prominent families can rejoice to see

themselves on public display – testimony to their large contributions, their place in Venetian society.

Cynicism aside, it is a striking painting.

Blessings,

Mathye

Feast of Saint Domitilla.

DIARII
Venice
May 14, 1494
Sent Luigi to supervise the stonemasons working on the small ri touching two of the houses at San Iachomo de Lorio.

Ignored Guido's dark looks. He considers Luigi only fit to work in the garden.

Checked the finished work – Luigi reported accurately to me.

Vigil of the Ascension.

Venice
May 15, 1494

My darling husband,

You know it is not my habit to take my seat in the Bucintoro. Today, the Feast of the Ascension, I did.

The Bishop of Cyprus is here. Doge Barbarigo, ever conscious of the oil that greases the wheels of trade, made him his chief guest.

To honour His Lordship, His Serenity paid me twenty-five ducats for a Te Deum. It was sung at San Marco's when we returned from the Marriage of Venice with the Sea. I wrote it in the few months after Lodovico left. It might have been a dirge. It isn't.

For the occasion, our sons and servants – in our flotilla of gondolas – escorted me to the Bucintoro. Adriana was seated when I stepped aboard. She gave me a saucy wink.

The Doge, Bishop, ambassadors, Doge's musicians, all in

full canonicals, were a pretty sight as they made their stately way down the Piazzetta.

The Canal teamed with Scuole, children, families; every foreigner was on the water in every style and form of dress.

Trumpets, drums, fifes blared.

From the Arsenal cannon boomed. The racket sent the ravens on the chimney pots squawking into the air – you know the scene.

The Bucintoro moved out into the Adriatic.

The Doge hurled his gold ring one more time and performed the ceremony of wedding the sea.

This is a pagan ritual. Yet we all participate, year after year, or at least approve.

During the return sail, the Companion of the Hose enacted the Battle of Rovigo from their barge.

The Doge was annoyed.

Later in the day he summoned the head of the Companion and told him he would outlaw the Organisation if they ever again dared to remind the people of Rovigo of their defeat – yesterday's enemy, today's citizens of La Serenissima.

Our Scuola di Sant' Orsola, in their three barges hired for the occasion, sang one more time of the ten thousand virgins slaughtered by the Huns. It rent my heart. It always does.

When the Bucintoro returned to the quay, the Doge sent one of his servants to invite me on the walk to San Marco's.

Donna Barbarigo placed me on her right and all along the route, in a louder voice than she ought, told the Bishop and me racy stories in her beautiful Greek.

The Doge was left to smile on the crowd.

We were met at the door of San Marco's by the chief priest, wearing his mitre, carrying his crosier. He greeted his Prince and guests, invited us inside.

As we proceeded up the nave, my Te Deum rang out. What I would give to conduct, just once, the choir of San Marco – their voices were glorious.

Halfway through, I found myself murmuring: Thank you, God, it works.

My darling husband, I am free. We go to Montebelluna until the eleventh Sunday after Pentecost.

I am taking Sancio's tutor. Both Sancio and Sebastian will study during the morning hours.

When we return, Sebastian will spend his last term with the Dominicans, then he is off to Sagres.

I must prepare another son to leave home!

My dear, my dear.

Your wife, who would rather have you with us at Montebelluna than all the ducats in the public deposit of the mint.

Mathye
Feast of the Ascension.

Bristol
June 29, 1494

My darling wife,

I am getting impatient with these Bristol merchants. They will not give me a date for the voyage.

I do not intend to stand around waiting on their will.

I have convinced Thomas Canynges to give me a caravel to take to Iceland to trade.

This is the opportunity I need to get further information about Nicolas of Lynn's Norse settlements in Greenland and beyond. You may be sure, my dear Mathye, it is the 'beyond' settlements I am interested in.

If there is an opportunity I may go on to Greenland.

I have written to Lodovico. I wish I had been there to make it easier for you. But I must turn to that land under the stars of the great bear, rather than where my heart is.

Jesus hold you and our sons in his loving care.

Your husband who loves you,

Giovanni
Feast of Saint Peter, under seal.

My darling wife,

I have news.

I have met an old mariner here in Iceland who lived, as a young man, in Greenland; he heard there a story of a Bishop Eirik, who in the time of Pope Paschal II voyaged to a Norse settlement 'beyond' Greenland.

The name of the settlement is VINLAND.

If I can confirm that this Bishop Eirik was actually in Vinland, can you imagine what that would mean to my backers?

Will you ask Canon Leonardo when Pope Paschal reigned, and if the Holy See has a record of a Bishop Eirik?

This is the second time I have heard of Vinland. Nicolas of Lynn, the Minorite monk, wrote of a voyage there in 1355.

My dear Mathye, how I hope to find your reply at Bristol when I return.

May the wisdom of the great Creator be with you, my dear wife.

Your husband, who loves you,

Giovanni

Feast of Saint Swithin, under seal.

My darling wife,

I will not go to Greenland.

The merchant who trades there has told me there is a small colony of people at a place called Herjolfsnes on the west coast – otherwise the country is uninhabited, ice-bound and unapproachable for most of the year. The winds are rarely calm, the sea is strewn with ice and his ship is always in danger.

Within a few years, he expects it will no longer be profitable for him to go there; they have very few items of real value to trade, except the white falcon used in hawking.

This merchant told me he had heard of a pleasant land somewhere further west. He thinks that if such land exists, it will have to be to the south, as the currents around Greenland flow over ice-packs and nothing much can grow in that latitude.

This man had many practical experiences of northern waters. I was impressed with his knowledge and good sense.

I am inclined to believe all he told me. We talked for hours on this subject. His story never wavered. He did offer me a berth on his next voyage in 1495. I will not take his generous offer.

This is my last voyage to Iceland; this country has nothing more to offer.

I will be leaving within a week. I will send this letter out on a cob that will depart for Bristol in the morning.

Have you heard anything of Bishop Eirik?

God be with you and our sons.

Giovanni

Eighth Sunday after Pentecost, under seal.

Iceland
July 19, 1494

My darling wife,

After I put my last letter on the cob to Bristol, I went up to the cathedral to pray for my father's soul. Today is the anniversary of his death.

In the square in front of the cathedral a festival was in progress. Men were dressed in the most outlandish costumes, with horns on their heads. They were shouting their lines in the harshest tongue. I will not say it sounded like dogs barking but you will understand what I mean.

I asked a bystander what feast they were celebrating. He started to tell me something of the story that was being played out in front of us.

Do not think me mad, my dear Mathye, when I tell you that what these players were shouting was a saga of settlement in VINLAND, founded by their ancestors in the year 1000 after the birth of Christ.

I laid hands on that man and demanded he tell me where I could get a copy of the play they were performing.

He had never heard of a written copy.

And the players were speaking an old Norse tongue!

I wanted to drag that fellow off the square and shake the words out of him.

I questioned everyone around me, including the players. No one knew the story in detail. Yet they all seemed to know the words by heart.

I rushed off to the priest's house.

The priest was old and not much interested in a mariner looking for a copy of a Norse saga some wandering players were performing in the square. He sent me off to the convent. He thought the nuns might have a copy, as they make a living copying documents and binding manuscripts.

They did!

Yes, the nun I spoke to would translate the saga into Latin.

I wanted the work done on the spot! She hesitated. I offered three times the copying price!

No, Holy Rule prevented her from taking more than the work was worth.

No, she couldn't put my request ahead of other work she was doing.

Yes, she thought she could have it done by Easter 1495.

By Easter 1495!

My darling wife, on that sunny afternoon, Easter seemed a lifetime away, but I paid my money, and come the Resurrection I should have the story of how Icelanders in the year 1000 went across the Western Ocean and settled in a place called Vinland.

I am a happy but impatient man.

May Jesus and His Holy Mother be with you.

Giovanni

Feast of Saint Rufina, under seal.

DIARII
Venice
August 19, 1494

Played lute for three hours – fingers galled on left hand.

   Imagining ice:

   A mountain of ice.

   A land of ice.

   A sea of ice.

   Iceland.

   Have a new piece of music I can adapt to the Dies Irae.
Friday after the twelfth Sunday after Pentecost.

DIARII
Venice
August 20, 1494

Piero is leaving for London on the Feast of Saint Monica. He and Paola came to hear Giovanni's letters.

   Her uncle Rufin will be whispering the story of the Norse saga to the Doge at dinner tomorrow.

   He'll be whispering only parts of it!
Feast of Saint Bernard.

Venice
August 20, 1494

My darling husband,

   Canon Leonardo has written to the Holy See for information on Bishop Eirik.

   One of his priests, recently returned from Rome, reported there is a great deal of chaos at Pope Alexander VI's Court. The French King and his army are on the march. They plan to come down into the Peninsula and take control of Naples, which the Pope considers a part of the Papal States.

   Whether any of this will interfere with clerks looking for information in the Pope's scriptorium is difficult to say.

   Queen Caterina says the Pope wants Naples for his son,

the Duke of Gandia, who is even now trying to raise an army to march north and stop the King at Savoy.

The Pope has no love for this Christian King, who has some claim to Naples through his mother.

Of course all this may be French rumour or Papal intrigue.

But if the French do come they may take the route through Florence. It would stop my heart.

Blessings on you.

Mathye

Feast of Saint Bernard, under seal.

Florence
August 21, 1494

My dear Mother,

The people of Florence spend a great deal of time talking of prophets and prophetic events. They expect Divine intervention to deliver them from the sins of the flesh.

Friar Savonarola is encouraging these ideas.

He hints Charles VIII of France will be the scourge from God that will cleanse the Church and the people of Florence – will set up a Holy City in our midst.

The Friar weaves these ideas into his sermons.

Friar Brugnuli says this talk of divine intervention has nothing to do with reform. If the clergy and the people are to mend their ways they must do it themselves.

He says if the French come, they are coming to take and not to give.

Brugnuli is showing me a side of Friar Savonarola I didn't see when he was at Venice.

Your devoted son,

Lodovico

Thirteenth Sunday after Pentecost.

Post Scriptum

Are there rumours in the Piazza of the French King and his plans?

My dear son,

Our ambassador at Paris has advised the Doge that the French King will take his army through Florence on the way to Naples.

My beloved son, I do not want you in a foreign State with an army of French soldiers on its soil.

You went to Florence to be a part of the Church renewal you believed Friar Savonarola would bring about. The good Friar appears to be losing his way, if Friar Brugnuli understands the situation correctly.

You have had eight months; it has been good for you. It is time to return home, prepare for the University of Padua in October.

Hear me now.

May the Blessed Mother and her Divine Son be with you and guide you.

Your Mother

Feast of Saint Stephen, Apostle of Hungary, under seal.

DIARII
Venice
September 2, 1494
My child leaves home, 35,000 soldiers threaten!

And I do not have the comfort of my husband's arms . . .
Feast of Saint Stephen.

My dear Mother,

I have your letter advising me to return home before the French army arrives. While I agree that all you say is right and necessary for my future, I hope you will not be offended when I tell you I plan to start my university studies next May.

I know this is a time of difficulty and I should not cause you alarm, but I want to spend a little while longer with Alessandra, to be absolutely certain our relationship will survive our separation.

My darling Mother, and this will be a disappointment to you, do you mind terribly if I attend the University of Pisa? That university has some of the most eminent masters. Messer Lorenzo says many have world reputations.

At Pisa, I will be nearer Alessandra, and will be able to visit her on the few university holidays.

I've not discussed any of this with Alessandra, or mentioned marriage to her parents, but if you agree, I will have a plan to present to her and them.

Your devoted son, who will be guided by you,

Lodovico

Feast of the Exaltation of the Cross.

DIARII
Venice
September 24, 1494
I pondered, on my knees, the idea of hitching up my horses, going to Florence, bringing Lodovico home.

I discussed it with Nurse. Wise old Nurse:

You bring him home, another plague comes down upon Venice, Lodovico succumbs, how will you feel?

It stopped me.

And this is the feast of Our Lady of Sorrows.

Venice
September 24, 1494

Lodovico, my dear son,

Of course I am disappointed; I would prefer you were safe at Padua. I would prefer you completed your university studies before you contemplated marriage.

You have chosen differently.

I need not tell you marriage is a legal and sacred contract. Since you won't be sixteen until December, I suggest you not speak to Alessandra's parents until after your birthday, lest they see you as too young and not take you seriously.

I understand the University of Pisa requires its students to be celibate for the first two years. Confirm this with Messer Lorenzo; he studied there.

Marriage then would be a number of years away, but it is a part of your future; you must be ready to meet it.

I will set out for you what you can expect by way of financial support.

My father's Will made provision for all my children, but only to a point. His money and property are entailed on the men of his family.

As my father's only child, I have use of both his property and one-third of the money in the Fraterna as long as I live. I cannot leave property or money to my sons; these stay in the Fraterna to be distributed to Piero's and Carlo's male heirs.

You and your brothers are provided for until you marry, finish university, or reach the age of twenty-five, whichever comes first.

There are no provisions in the Will to grant you or your brothers a house or any large sum of money.

As long as you are unmarried and at university, you can expect to live the life you are accustomed to. You understand why I prefer you to finish your studies before you marry.

I have an amount of personal money at the Pisani and Tiepolo Bank, which includes my mother's dowry and part of my own dowry. You can expect a stipend when necessary.

There is also my jewellery and my mother's, which I hope to distribute among my daughters-in-law at some future time.

Your father has put some small properties in my name, including three salt works.

All of this is dispersed in my Will.

I am telling you now so that you will know exactly where you stand.

Should you decide to speak to Alessandra's parents before you leave for Pisa, let me know soon after, so that I may confirm your financial situation to them.

I will send a copy of this letter to your father. He has also made provisions for you and will want to write you.

In the meantime, much of what I write is, I suspect, far in the future.

God bless you, my son. May you be saved from all disquiet.

Your Mother

Feast of Our Lady of Mercy, under seal.

Florence
October 5, 1494

My dear Mother,

Thank you for not insisting I come home and go to the University of Padua.

Thank you for your generous letter giving me advice and information on the money I may expect.

Before Father left for England he told me he had set aside one thousand ducats each, for the three of us. He said I could have my portion when I finish university. At the time the information meant nothing to me. Now I am grateful.

I will do as you say and wait until I am sixteen before I speak to Alessandra's parents. But I must tell you, Mother, while we have not used the word 'marriage', Alessandra and I talk as if we will spend the rest of our lives together.

Mother, please don't worry about me. I am young, but I am honourable, like Father. And I am lucky, for I have the best of mothers.

May the great Saint Clare bless you all your days.

Your son, with due obedience,

Lodovico

Feast of Saint Foy, Gallic martyr.

My darling husband,

Last year I worried Lodovico was too young to be sent to university.

You will see by the enclosed letters he has taken all our plans, tossed them in the air, rearranged them in a pattern I could not have imagined.

I would have preferred he go to the University of Padua. Alas.

Isabetta says Alessandra is the pride of her parents; they will certainly not want her married before she is eighteen – now precluded by Lodovico's decision to go to the University of Pisa.

I thought our house would ring always with voices of the young; that they would give me headaches.

Neither Lodovico, and certainly not Sebastian, will take holidays at home.

I painted the wrong istoria.

My dear, I've long since schooled my heart to patience but it is more than two years since you left home and this day seems like the first you left my side.

Bless you, my husband. Bless you profoundly.

Mathye

Fourteenth Sunday after Pentecost, under seal.

DIARII
Venice
October 16, 1494
I want now – my husband – now!

Venice
October 18, 1494

My darling husband,

The French King and his army are on the march, as expected.

They will take the road through Florence. The King's envoys are already there.

The French are demanding safe passage and more: men, arms, galleys. Queen Caterina tells me the Signoria of Florence will not give it.

I am staying close to Caterina as the Doge has set up a constant relay of messengers from Florence, and Caterina is briefed by her brother, Zorzi, each day.

I worry less about Lodovico when I know exactly what is happening.

I had a letter from Lorenzo, written on the Feast of Saint Pelagia. He has not moved his family – nor our son – out of the city. He says Florence is a trading partner of France, and while the French King is making demands on the Government, they do not expect belligerence from the French army.

I will write to you as often as I have news, although this terrible business will likely be settled by the time you get this letter.

May you be in the hands of the Living God.

Mathye

Feast of Saint Luke, under seal.

Venice
October 21, 1494

My dear son,

You can be sure I pray for you constantly in these confusing times.

Please do not leave the house without your servant, even to go as far as Alessandra's home.

I tell you this only to set my heart at ease; I know you would do nothing to put yourself at risk.

Be sure you follow to the letter directions given by Lorenzo, who grew up in Florence and knows the city intimately.

Today, Sebastian, Sancio and I went to San Marco's; we each lit a candle for you.

We lit one for Alessandra too. Then Sancio thought we

should light one for Marco. By the time we left we had lit one for everyone in Isabetta's family, including the servants.

Tell Isabetta.

Sancio says he will light one for you each day until the danger has passed.

My dear son, you can imagine how you are on our minds at every hour.

Within the hour I will walk in the procession in honour of Sant' Orsola. Sebastian has joined the Scuola and will be with us for the first time.

Yes, he will carry a banner.

Please send your letters under seal. In these distressing times you cannot be too careful.

May the love of Jesus surround you and keep you safe.

Your Mother

Feast of Sant' Orsola, Patron, under seal.

Florence
October 30, 1494

My dear Mother,

You mustn't worry I will have difficulty. Messer Lorenzo and Donna Isabetta are being very cautious with Marco and me. Each time we go outside the neighbourhood they send two of their most trusted – and largest – servants with us.

How lucky I am Alessandra lives so near!

I will follow your request and take my servant when I go there, which is almost every day.

Messer Lorenzo goes to his work at the Mercato Nuovo and is undisturbed by all the rumours. He insists we live a normal life and not be fearful until we have cause.

I follow his advice, carry on with my studies and pray the marching French will pass us by.

Thank you for the lighted candles; I told Donna Isabetta. She sends her blessing.

She wrote to you five days ago.

Sebastian owes me a letter. Would you tell him his funny epistles are welcome in these interesting times?

Mother, to allay your concerns and assure you of my safety, I will write to you often.

I am, my dear Mother, your son, with due obedience,
Lodovico
Twenty-fourth Sunday after Pentecost.

Florence
November 3, 1494

My dear Mother,

The shops and factories are starting to close and hundreds of people are on the streets all hours of the day and night, and rumours, and rumours of rumours, are flying. You can't walk in the Piazza without someone grabbing you by the sleeve demanding the latest news.

Alessandra is very brave. Not once has she wavered. Her mother told me she comes out of her studio shouting '*Aut vincamus aut vincamur!*'

Each evening, with her parents, we walk in the Piazza to catch the latest news.

Alessandra greets her friends with:

It is only the French who are coming. Courage, courage.

The Signoria will not give the materials the French are demanding and there is rumour they will sack the city. Friar Savonarola has been sent as envoy to the French King to bring that Monarch to his senses.

I was with the large crowd at the gate when the Friar left the city. He went on foot, a small sack on his back. As he trudged out of sight, the wind whipping his habit, the crowd fell silent.

I wonder what will become of him?

Your loving and devoted son,
Lodovico
Feast of Saint Rumwald, under seal.

I hear the post will get through even if the city is occupied; you should receive my letters.

Florence
November 14, 1494

My dear Mother,

Friar Savonarola has returned from the French camp. He didn't get a written agreement but he has a commitment that the French will pass peacefully through this State.

Last evening the Friar went back to his preaching.

Alessandra, her parents and I went early. When we arrived, people were already standing outside. Only by pushing and using our elbows did we get in.

The Friar was late.

Head bowed, he walked from behind the high altar into the sanctuary, mounted the pulpit and stood for a long moment. Then he lifted one arm to the heavens and a piercing cry echoed and reverberated in the rafters:

Lo, I shall loose over the earth the waters of the flood!

He continued on that subject for almost an hour. The vein in his throat bulged and pulsed. I thought it would burst. At one point he rested on the pulpit steps. Tears ran down his face.

We were so affected that some wept silently, others swayed on their feet, still others staggered out.

At one moment the hair of my head lifted.

Alessandra, too, was affected. When she returned home, she wrote down what she remembered; here it is, in part:

Vox dicentis clama. O Florence, for your sins, for your brutality, your avarice, your lust, your ambition, there will befall you many trials and many tribulations.

O clergy, who are the principal cause of so many evils, through your evil-doing comes this storm; by your sins have been prepared so many tribulations; woe, woe, I say unto thee who bear the tonsure! *Vox dicentis clama*, a voice still calls.

We were a subdued crowd that wandered back to our homes, distracted by visions of our most private sins, and the army of the French marching in the night.

The sculptor Michelangelo had told me he was disturbed by the Friar's sermons and didn't think he could live here anymore. The sermons reverberated in his head; he couldn't sleep.

Yesterday, he left for Venice without saying goodbye. If he calls on you I suspect he will still be distracted.

Donna Isabetta and Messer Lorenzo have lost faith in the Friar; they think he is wrong to try to make the people believe the invasion of the French army is because of our sins.

Messer Lorenzo says the King of France has come to the Peninsula to grab the Kingdom of Naples and has no interest in Florence beyond using our roads.

I hope he is right.

With respect, dear Mother,

Lodovico

Feast of Saint Laurence, under seal.

Florence
November 17, 1494

My dear Mother,

The French are here!

They arrived today!

With Alessandra and her parents, I was at the Cathedral of Santa Maria dei Fiore when they arrived.

The Signoria had ordered the population to welcome them. Most of us were dumbstruck.

King Charles was at the head of his army, astride a ferocious black horse, lance at his hip.

Four of the tallest knights carried a silken baldachin above his head.

He wore a jacket of gold over his armour.

He was followed by trumpeters, fifers, drummers – the music was clamorous. Every bell in Florence, including La Vacca, was clanging.

A monstrous number of monstrous military pieces were trundled over the bricks, adding to the din.

Wave after wave of Swiss Guards, black plumes flapping about their helmets, passed in front of us. They were followed by archers so horrifyingly tall they seemed hardly like men at all. The cavalry, each soldier mounted on a black horse, carried every variety of banner.

I don't know if I was terrified or thrilled.

When the King was helped from his horse, we saw one of the smallest men who could call himself a man. And he was ugly: large head, hair like straw, bulging eyes, thick lips that hung half open. I saw his lolling tongue. On his feet he wore a kind of velvet boots that looked like horses' hoofs. He, with his officers, who were similarly shod, padded up the nave of the cathedral and gave their thanksgiving at the high altar.

We were so astonished at the sight of this odd little King, a hush spread over the crowd.

His prayers said, he and his officers cantered through the streets to Via Larga, where they took over the de' Medici palace.

The army has spread out around the city looking for their billets. From my window I still can hear the tramp of feet. There is a low rumble of voices, as thirty-five thousand men swarm the streets.

My dear Mother, this must seem disturbing, but you must not be unduly concerned. Isabetta's house is at the bottom of the street and there is no reason why any member of the French army should find his way down here.

Your loving and devoted son,

Lodovico

Feast of Saint Gregory, mover of mountains, under seal.

Post Scriptum
Have you had a visit from Michelangelo?

DIARII
Venice
November 26, 1494
A full afternoon of choir practice.

Without these hours away from myself I would not get through the days – my son in the path of a marauding army, my husband on the rim of the world.
Saturday before the first Sunday of Advent.

Bristol
November 27, 1494

My darling wife,

Richard Americ has just come down from the English Court and reports that the French King is not interested in making war on the Peninsula but wishes only to claim Naples.

Pray God it is so. Pray God our son is safe.

I have come from another endless meeting with the merchants who say they will back my voyage to the East.

They now tell me they are waiting for some proof of the Bishop Eirik story. Will you ask Canon Leonardo to write again to Rome?

I have given those merchants an ultimatum: if they give me no certain date by Eastertide, I will no longer look to them for hope.

When my mind is not fixed on this voyage, be assured, my darling wife, it is fixed on our sons. It is fixed on you.

I do not persuade myself this is the best way to be a husband, a father. I know what this has cost you; has cost us, our sons.

May the Mother of God hold her hand over you and our sons.

Your husband,
Giovanni
First Sunday of Advent, under seal.

My dear Mother,

We are safe!

The French have taken the road to Siena and on to Naples.

Messer Lorenzo didn't go to his office the whole time the army was in our midst.

We always felt protected.

Before each meal, the family knelt and said the Salve Regina that no harm would come to Florence.

Three times a day Messer Lorenzo sent a servant to the Piazza for the latest news or rumour.

Donna Isabetta was intrepid. She set out two tables and put 200 quattrini in the pot. We played scartino and buttino every day for the week.

We became zealots.

Donna Isabetta is a master.

Her knuckles rattled the table every time she laid a trump.

Beat that!

And that!

She won most of the money.

I won forty quattrini.

When we heard the French were leaving the city, the whole family, with all the servants, went to the Piazza for the first time since the day they arrived.

The place was crowded. Rumours were rampant: the King was here, there, everywhere. People were swarming in all directions.

We went to the Cathedral of Santa Maria dei Fiore.

The King and his officers were inside. We could hear the shouting of 'Francia! Francia!'

The news that the King had placed the Peace Treaty with Florence on the altar spread like a sweet breeze.

We thought he and his army would leave that very day.

They stayed three more.

Finally, Monday, after the first Sunday of Advent, they did leave, with the same clatter with which they arrived.

The gates of the city were locked.

No one remembered, or cared, it was Advent. La Vacca and all the bells rang out.

With Messer Lorenzo, Donna Isabetta and all the servants, we joined the rest of Florence in the streets.

There were fireworks, bonfires and merrymaking into the night. Rocks were thrown, windows were broken, the injured were picked off the streets in the morning.

Friar Savonarola, who is much praised for our deliverance, is again giving us visions of hell and damnation from the pulpit of Saint Mark's.

I go less frequently.

We are all exhausted. Alessandra and her parents are going to the Mugello valley for a week. They have invited me. Donna Isabetta has given me permission to go.

Your son, with deep respect,

Lodovico

Monday after the first Sunday of Advent, under seal.

Venice
December 5, 1494

My darling husband,

Lodovico is safe.

King Charles and his army have finally left Florence. They were there ten days.

All the inhabitants escaped unharmed. There was very little damage to the city.

But the King has done a great disservice. He gave the Pisans their freedom. Florence has now lost access to the sea; you can imagine the indemnity Pisa will exact.

The French King is on his way to Naples.

Piero de' Medici is no longer in Florence and the people have set up a republic based on the Venetian model. The friar,

Savonarola, has his own political faction – a grave error for a member of the Church. Lodovico has moved away from him. The canon lawyer he is working with has shown him the good friar's clay feet.

Our son is sadder but wiser.

Bless you, my husband; may the Great Christ be with you.

Mathye

Monday after the second Sunday of Advent, under seal.

DIARII
Venice
December 8, 1494

Days when nothing but the underside of life fills the Piazza. Yesterday – one such.

A lovely morning to be alive.

Dawn – I turned into the Piazzetta, to San Marco, to hear a sung Mass I wouldn't have to direct.

A small knot of people was standing between the columns.

Someone was hanging by his neck!

His face wasn't covered.

It was Natalin di San Giorgio, who knew my father – and told me so every time we met.

No one could tell me what happened.

Natalin was wearing his long-sleeved official gown.

My stomach, empty – I planned to go to Communion – began to betray me. I turned back.

I spent the rest of the day in bed. In the evening Piero came – told the story.

Natalin, who worked in Chancery, gave State secrets to the ambassador of the Duke of Milan.

Although he had a family at Chioggia, Natalin, who must have been sixty-five, was living with Laura Ponte, who has a home at Santa Trinita.

The meetings with the ambassador took place in her house. She overheard the conversation – which was in Latin. Natalin didn't know she knew the language.

Laura told a friend.

The Collegio held the trial in secret and at night. When Natalin was presented with the facts, he fell silent.

He refused the last rites.

The Collegio left his body hanging until late in the day. It was finally cut down and buried without a Requiem Mass.

The ambassador of the Duke of Milan has been imprisoned for life on the Isle of Crete.

There is a pall over the city.

I am still sick to my stomach.

What will the Collegio do to someone who diverts our trade to another country?

Now I feel sicker!

Feast of the Immaculate Conception of the Blessed Virgin Mary.

DIARII
Venice
December 12, 1494

I have entertained a number of unusual guests in my home, but Michelangelo Buonarroti is the most peculiar: he pads about the house on those short and sturdy legs, glowering at everyone he meets, as if we are in his way.

Whenever we are in a room together he looks at me as if in the next breath he is about to shout 'Avaunt!'

He can find no work in this wealthy city. In a few days he leaves 'for the bogs of Rome, to taste the corruption at the Imperial See.'

If he were my son, I would sit him down – have a long talk.

Monday after the second Sunday of Advent.

Venice
December 15, 1494

My dear Isabetta,

How do they raise sons down in Florence? Michelangelo

Buonarroti, a sculptor and friend of Alessandra and Lodovico, is here looking for work, which he hasn't found.

He was staying at a scruffy inn. I invited him to my home. With your place empty next door and only two sons left in mine, I was, I suppose, nostalgic for the days when a half dozen young people were running in and out of our doors.

He spent the first day in his room. At sundown I thought I should see if he was sick. I walked along the hall, making as much noise as possible, tapped at his door; there was no answer. I called his name – no answer. I opened the door: he was sitting in the middle of the bed, cross-legged and staring into space. I spoke his name twice before he shook himself and turned; the look, I thought, was of hate, mixed with astonishment.

He jumped off the bed.

I treated him like one of my sons, told him to join us for meals and come at the first bell. He scowled, then agreed. I could see he wasn't used to being told what to do.

At the end of the first week, he presented me with a small painting of San Nicholas, asked me to give it to Giovanni. I hardly knew how to thank him; the face of the saint has the most tortured look.

Blessings on you and your family.

Mathye

Thursday after the second Sunday of Advent.

Post Scriptum
I sent you two letters when the French were in Florence. Did you get them?

Venice
December 20, 1494

My dear Lodovico,

Your friend Michelangelo came to visit. He was lodged at the White Lion; I saw no reason why he should spend his money on a bad inn.

Yes, he was despondent, and remained so throughout his visit. In fact, he made no effort to be agreeable. I was surprised.

He went round looking for work, but no work was offered.

At the end of the first week, he presented me with a small painting of San Nicholas, patron saint of mariners (if you have forgotten), to give your father.

He spent a great deal of time at San Marco's. The last thing he said as he was leaving was:

Maybe it's good I go to Rome. In Venice I'd spend half my time on my back gazing at the mosaics.

May the Spirit of God guide you, my son.

Your Mother

Tuesday after the third Sunday of Advent.

Florence
January 2, 1495

My dear Mother,

I am sorry Michelangelo was morose when he was in our home. He is generally a lively fellow. I admit he is a bit more boastful of his work than he ought to be.

Alessandra had a habit of saying to him:

Michelangelo, you need to gloat today, do you?

Michelangelo would then look at her with those intense eyes, yet every day he came again.

For a while I thought he might be my rival, but his affections are in another direction.

As well, his teacher, Domenico Bigordi, who signed his work 'Ghirlandaio', died recently and he was feeling bereft.

He does have another side, my dear Mother. I want you to see it. We have a letter from him written at Venice. I am enclosing a copy.

Your loving and devoted son,

Lodovico

Feast of Saint Basil the Great.

Dear Alessandra and Lodovico,

I slunk away from Florence under the cover of darkness. Had I done the rounds of my friends I would have lost courage.

To be truthful I could no longer stand the hammer of Fra Savonarola's voice; it was haunting my sleep. My sins, as he named them over and over in those damnation sermons of his, worked on my imagination until I felt I had already arrived in the City of Dis. I had to get away. Nor could I stand watching Piero de' Medici kicking a ball outside his palace when he should be sitting with the Signoria deciding how best to stop the French.

Your mother, Lodovico, is very kind. She took me in, introduced me to Canon Leonardo and the two Bellinis, but I have not been successful. The Bellini brothers have the work of all the Scuole under commission for the next five years and these seem to be the only major works that anyone knows of.

I expect I will have to move on to Rome. I hear the Borgia Pope is interested in painting and sculpture.

The first time I attended Mass at San Marco's I climbed to the choir loft and was overwhelmed by the dome of the Pentecost. I went back again and again. The mosaics are dazzling. Surely it must be the most beautiful church in Christendom. Maybe it's good that I move on. I could imagine spending half my life looking at the work of those Byzantine mosaicists. Are you Venetians never homesick for all that beauty?

No, you are not!

Not once did I see anyone raise his eyes to look at that glory.

Alessandra, you must insist that new friend of yours bring you to Venice; every artist must see the Piazza at dusk – and witness how this city, with the most divinely designed streetscape in Christendom, floats like a lily in its pond.

You must see what the Bellini brothers and Carpaccio do

with narrative and the way they place the action of the piece right in your face.

The walls of all the public buildings are covered with their paintings. I intend to steal their thunder and bring it to Rome.

Unless a miracle happens, I will be off to the Imperial City before Ash Wednesday, in search of the Pontifex Maximus.

I hope your plans for the Sacrament are proceeding.

Alessandra, give my regards to your parents and thank them for their kindness to me. I will write to them when I arrive at Rome.

Christ keep you.

Michelangelo

Venice
January 7, 1495

Beloved,

The harshness of your absence sometimes breeds tyranny in my heart, but you must not worry about our sons. They are progressing as they should. It is the Venetian way to have a father at sea.

Lodovico has come through the French invasion without apparent scars. He is continuing his studies.

His friendship with Alessandra continues apace. He is a happy young man.

We still miss him lamentably.

I have hired a Greek teacher for Sancio. He comes in the afternoon, a Franciscan, a fine scholar. In May I intend to take our son out of the priory school and put him full-time with this tutor. Our other sons at his age were further advanced in their languages, although his master told me he knows more geometry than any at the school.

Sebastian is doing well, though never as well as he should. But we have known from the beginning Sebastian will never apply himself to his studies as he should, unless of course he finds a subject he likes. He has read everything available on hydrology, and his chart-making has improved a hundredfold.

But may the Great Spirit of God protect you and all our sons and bring you home safe.

Your loving wife,

Mathye

Feast of Saint Ambrose, under seal.

DIARII

Venice

February 4, 1495

Invitation from Queen Caterina to her pre-Lenten frolic.

Feast of Saint Andrew.

DIARII

Asolo

February 7, 1495

Caterina says Zorzi has settled four properties on his son in anticipation of the Pope making the young man a Cardinal.

Piero's and Carlo's sons inherit six houses in Campo San Giacomo de Lorio, three houses along the Canal, three villas, three farms and God knows the amount of money.

My sons – nothing.

It hurts that Carlo, who is a natural son of Uncle Clemente – God rest his soul – will leave my money to his children.

Is not justice one of the Cardinal Virtues?

Feast of Saint Raymond.

DIARII

Asolo

February 9, 1495

I have never heard of a Will broken in favour of a daughter.

No, that is not what I want.

I have more than I need. I want my sons to have the right to what I own.

Is there a lawyer who would defy every nobleman in Venice, and the security of every family Fraterna, to take the case?

We shall see.

We shall see.

Feast of Saint Apollonia, deaconess.

DIARII
Asolo
February 10, 1495
I asked Caterina if she knew an honourable lawyer.

Honourable lawyer?

She laughed.

She agreed to think about it.

Feast of Saint Scholastica, abbess.

DIARII
Asolo
February 11, 1495
Caterina says she would trust Marco Varchi.

Can I?

Feast of Saint Caedmon, poet.

DIARII
Asolo
February 13, 1495
Lecture on the rotation of crops by Caterina's ascetic cousin, Alvis. I almost fell asleep. But Marco Varchi was there. I suspect summoned by the Queen.

I walked him to the loggia. Danced around the idea of the lawyer being in the same position as confessor.

He agreed.

I asked my question.

He froze, stared off into space, bit his lip, turned pale.

Somewhere deep inside and far away came a desperate need to slap his white face back to health.

Where he was staring, I imagined a thorn-forest of black-robed Venetian lawyers arrayed in front of me.

You have a weak stomach, Messer Varchi!

I walked off.

He will tell Paola, Paola will tell her uncle, her uncle sits next to the Doge in the Maggior Consiglio . . .

I have made a mistake.

Hell's fiery flames!

Monday of the sixth Sunday after the Epiphany.

Florence
February 13, 1495

My dear Mother,

You asked about our holiday at the Mugello. The village is ten miles north-east of Florence. We sauntered there.

Messer Cavalcanti gave me his very good gelding; Alessandra rode a mare.

At one point the road ran straight ahead for about two miles. Without warning, Alessandra goaded her horse into a standing gallop and shouted to me. Her mother gave me the nod. I raced after her.

That fair-minded woman stopped and let me catch up. Then she offered two horse-lengths for the race.

I shouldn't have laughed.

The women of Florence ride like demons. I have seen them in the countryside mounted on those large horses, tearing up ground. It's a wonder there are any horses left in this Republic.

I nearly killed that big gelding trying to catch Alessandra.

She beat me by a whisker.

She whipped that young mare around and raced back to her parents.

I pounded after her.

Messer Cavalcanti said it was a tie. I'm not sure.

Other than the excitement of the road it was a quiet week.

We walked for hours. Often we set out in the morning with wine, bread and cheese and didn't return until dusk. We were burnished as the nut.

Occasionally Alessandra's parents let us make a trek into the wild and beautiful mountains.

The de' Medici have a castle there and a stable of prized horses. We skirted it in one of our rides, but saw no one.

I am writing this letter in Alessandra's garden. She is reading over my shoulder and sends her respects.

Your devoted son,

Lodovico

Monday of the sixth Sunday after the Epiphany, under seal.

Florence
February 14, 1495

My dear Mother,

The worst has happened: under the pain of excommunication, Pope Alexander VI has ordered Friar Savonarola to stop preaching, and the people of Florence to stay away from his sermons.

Only the faction that is against the Friar is obeying the edict.

Friar Brugnuli suggested as I work in his office, I should obey. Although I am disappointed, I have submitted.

Alessandra is under no such obligation and, like all Florentines, follows her own will.

Friar Brugnuli is trying to find a way to protect the Friar because the purity of his life has had an enormous effect on his fellow friars, as well as the people of Florence.

But because of his attacks on our dissolute Pope, he doesn't see how anyone can protect him.

I have written so much about the Friar because so much seems to be at stake for him and Florence.

We talk of little else.

Your devoted son,

Lodovico

Feast of Saint Valentine, under seal.

Dear Isabetta,

Giovanni has been here five days!

I heard his special tap at my study door.

I thought it Sebastian, the joker.

I heard his voice.

Joy!

He brought a caravel of Bristol Red cloth which he traded, first day, on the Rialto, for wine.

He brought me a bolt of brilliant blue!

My husband will stay in Venice to supervise the loading. No jolly times with the family at Montebelluna.

I have declared a holiday for Sancio and Sebastian. We keep Giovanni to ourselves – except for Adriana, who wouldn't take no for an answer.

You know how we always allowed Adriana to persuade us.

He will be leaving in a week, an event I try not to think of.

God bless you, bless all of yours.

Mathye

Monday after Septuagesima Sunday.

DIARII
Venice
February 25, 1495
Adriana's dinner.

The wines, from their vineyards, would inspire a choir of cherubim.

It was our children who were inspired.

In faultless Greek, their mouths dripping irony, they gave a performance of *Oedipus*.

Giacomo – Oedipus

Maria – Jocasta

Sebastian – Creon

Sancio – Teiresias

Whoever wasn't centre stage played all the other parts.

Sancio did something clever with blind Teiresias: he turned his head slightly to the left, dropped his voice, affected a monotone, which gave to his speech a detached and cruel significance.

It warms the heart to know your own are finer than you were at that age.

Feast of Saint Walburga, medical doctor.

DIARII

Venice

February 26, 1495

Told Giovanni if he goes across that western sea I will make a pilgrimage to Jerusalem for his safety.

Go! Yes! Go!

Adventure quickens my husband's imagination – even when it is not his adventure.

Sexagesima Sunday.

DIARII

Venice

March 3, 1495

Giovanni left Feast of Saint Macarius.

Head under the pillow three days.

This morning I made myself get out of bed – go to San Zan – sing a dirge for the souls of the dead.

Another year of celibacy.

Gr-rr-rr-rr.

Tomorrow Adriana and I will go to the stables to ride two of our wildest horses.

Feast of Saint Cunegud.

My dear Mother,

A year ago I came here full of excitement, eager to hear what I then thought was the bravest and wisest man of the age.

I am disillusioned.

Friar Savonarola is now meddling deeply in politics. He is no longer just a friar with a cowl, calling for a scourge against sinful people, wicked clergy, and a bad Pope.

It is said he has written to all the Christian monarchs requesting they call a Church Council for the purpose of dethroning His Holiness.

Alessandra has ceased going to his sermons. She tolerated the screen he put up in the middle of the church to separate men from women; and being a modest woman, she overlooked the scorn he heaped on people who wear jewels. But when he ordered men and women to hear his sermons on different days, and one of those sermons attacked the writing of poetry, she walked out of his church and hasn't returned.

I am very sad.

Your devoted and respectful son,

Lodovico

First Sunday in Lent, under seal.

Post Scriptum

Thank you for all the letters during Father's visit. I did miss not being home.

My dear son Lodovico,

I had a conversation with Canon Leonardo. He thinks Friar Savonarola's chance of surviving is slight.

When I told him the Friar is calling for a General Council

of the Church to dethrone the Pope, he took the belt of his cassock and wrapped it around his neck.

If half what is said about Pope Alexander VI is true, the hangman is already on the road to Florence.

My dear son, your time in Florence is getting short. I know you have left Friar Savonarola behind, but do be careful when you return to visit Alessandra.

May the Great Spirit of God protect you in all you do.

Your Mother

Feast of Saint Patrick, patron of Ireland.

Florence
March 27, 1495

My dear Mother,

I am leaving Florence a happy man.

I have spoken to Alessandra's parents. The first question from Messer Cavalcanti was:

How do you intend to support my daughter?

I talked about the stipend you promised and the money Father has set aside for me. I told him I intend to get both an arts degree and one in canon law.

Donna Cavalcanti then took over the conversation; I was glad. I had used up all the breath in my body.

But I shouldn't have worried; Alessandra has a large dowry and will inherit her parents' money. Already she has income from her painting. Nevertheless, as Father would say, a man wants to support his family.

Messer Cavalcanti asked me to finish my arts degree and let life proceed as it will.

I would imagine Alessandra's parents will be expecting a letter from you.

When I told Alessandra of my conversation – it was 'my ordeal' – she announced she was sixteen; she will talk to her parents.

Mother, I am pleased she will protest the long wait.

However, I am more prepared to wait now than when we first met. We know each other better and are deeply committed.

Donna Cavalcanti asked me to consider returning to Florence when I finish my canon law studies. As that is what Alessandra wants, I agreed.

Dear Mother, I know it will not warm your heart to have both Sebastian and me living away from Venice, but don't mourn too long: the future is not yet here.

I will leave for Pisa on the Feast of Saint Mark.

Your son, with respect and devotion,

Lodovico

Feast of Saint Rupert, under seal.

Chapter Four

Bristol
March 27, 1495

My darling Mathye,

I wrote to Amerigo Vespucci some months ago hoping for information about Columbus. I sent copies to both Florence and Seville, but have received nothing.

I wanted to confirm a story from João Gonsalves. João is a friend from Huelva, here with a caravel of wine and oil.

Over a tankard of warm sack, at a bad inn, he told me:

Christopher Columbus, on the return voyage from that new land, made all his mariners take a solemn oath to say they had reached India.

João is often at Seville but has met Amerigo only once – in the Spring of 1493. Each time he called on Amerigo after, he was away. More he does not know.

I am beginning to believe there is some mystery surrounding Amerigo's activity. He always kept himself to himself, but this is passing strange.

If he is working for Columbus, then of course he is no longer of use to me.

Giovanni

Feast of Saint Rupert, under seal.

Venice
April 5, 1495

My darling Giovanni,

Guido was in Campo San Giacomo de Lorio, Feast of Saint Venantius. He is certain he saw Amerigo. He was dressed like a Saracen, had grown a beard. I trust Guido; he would take care to size up his man. He is as curious as we are to discover what Amerigo is doing on these furtive visits.

I have enquired. None of our friends have seen him.

Maybe it is time to give up on our friend Amerigo Vespucci.

God bless you on this lovely morning.

I hear Sebastian and Sancio playing calcio in the meadow.

Your wife,

Mathye

Feast of Saint Isidore, under seal.

DIARII
Venice
April 7, 1495

Canon Leonardo here with a report and chart for what appears to be land to westward – put me through the greatest temptation of my life.

Twice I went to the fireplace, twice turned away.

What stayed my hand was no mention of fabulous wealth.

Piero leaving for the London trade – gave him the Bishop Eirik report to have sent on to Giovanni.

He turned it over – saw it was sealed.

I believe my beloved cousin will not tamper with my letter to my husband.

Friday after the fifth Sunday in Lent.

Venice
April 7, 1495

My darling husband,

I know you have already seized upon the enclosed chart.

I have had Canon Leonardo for two hours telling me how he managed to induce his friend at the Holy See to compel three seminarians to work for a week in one of the Pope's dungeons in search of traces of Bishop Eirik Gnupsson.

Little attention is given to records of past pontificates. All are thrown into cupboards, helter-skelter, without regard for the century they refer to; if you want something from the twelfth you have to dig among the dust.

The young clerics, two Norwegians and a Venetian, had done their week's work and found nothing.

The friend to whom the Canon had written sent the seminarians back into the dungeon for one more day; they found the enclosed chart and the following information:

Bishop Eirik Gnupsson was consecrated Bishop in 1113. He was Papal Legate for the area of Norway, Iceland and Greenland; he was given the extra responsibility of preaching a mission to the Skraelings at Vinland.

He went to Vinland in 1117 and spent a year there. His report of that year states he made very few conversions, as the idea of one God is foreign to those people, and all their ceremonies are based in the harvest of the sea and animals.

They do not bury their dead immediately but place them on platforms in trees and when the flesh has been eaten by birds, the bones are put in the ground.

Bishop Eirik returned to Rome after the death of Pope Paschal II, in 1118, for the election of the new Pope.

He made a second mission to the Skraelings in 1121 and died there. The date of his death was not recorded.

The chart accompanied one of the Bishop's reports.

So the Icelandic mariner was right: there is a place called Vinland. If the chart is correctly drawn, it is nearer Greenland than we imagined. But will there be a passage through or around that land that will lead to the East?

Canon Leonardo said the Holy See has no record of a bishop having gone to Iceland or Greenland in this century, although the Pope still makes a titular appointment for that area.

The light of the Light guide you always, my own.

Mathye

Friday after the fifth Sunday in Lent, under seal.

My darling wife,

I am astonished at the chart drawn by Bishop Eirik. I am looking at it as I write; I can't let it out of my sight. If this is as accurate as it appears, then it is certain that by sailing directly across the fifty-second parallel I can reach Vinland.

Already the unknown is known.

Where Vinland is, that is where I will find the eastern coast of the great spice lands.

This is an astounding find; to have a chart detailing the coastline of Vinland and made by someone who was actually there. It confirms the charts of Nicolas of Lynn.

As I write, I am drinking a skin of Pellestrina wine. I planned to keep it for the day I landed on the shores of that eastern land, but this day is a new day in the world, and I celebrate it.

I am holding this information close to my chest. There are Portuguese here, as in every port, and if they hear the vaguest rumour, they are not above coming up to your face and demanding what you know.

My dear and beloved Mathye, you have sent me the greatest piece of news I may ever get. I thank you with all my heart.

Please convey my thanks and respect to Canon Leonardo and tell him he and his friend at the Holy See have made a large contribution to my work.

Blessings on you and our sons who are more precious to me than the wealth I seek.

Giovanni

Feast of Saint Athanasius, under seal.

Bristol
May 2, 1495

My dear son Sebastian,

This letter is to repeat our many conversations on the subject of your future.

In a month you will be on your way to the Portuguese Royal School of Navigation, at Sagres.

For three years you will devote yourself to astronomy, geography, cartography and navigation.

Your teachers will be both Jewish and Arabic; these are the people who have written the most accurate treatises on the subjects you will be studying. The King of Portugal, unlike the Monarchs of Castile and Aragon, has kept these wise men in his Court.

You will spend four months of every year on the open sea. You will certainly sail to the Azores, to Guinea, and maybe to Iceland. I did when I was there.

You will learn a cosmography needed only by men who sail beyond the closed Mediterranean Sea. At the end of your three years' study, you will join a select group of navigators who roam the unknown waters of the world.

Your mother and I have already selected from my stock the astrolabe, compass and navigational charts you are to take. Guard them well: they are your most precious possessions.

Do not take your grandfather's charts or navigational instruments; they are prized by your mother. Besides, the ones you have are more accurate.

Once at Sagres you will be assigned a servant.

You will be initiated into the Order of Christ and will take an oath that you will never divulge any sea-route the Portuguese hold secret. I have not broken my oath. You will demand no less of yourself.

God speed you, my dear son.

Your Father

Feast of Saint Athanasius, under seal.

My darling wife,

I heard from the nuns in Iceland.

I have new information about Vinland. Tomorrow I will pin Richard Americ to his chair and review for him all my evidence.

I will have my voyage!

These learned nuns sent me ten pages of tightly written Latin prose that tell of a four-day voyage from Greenland to Vinland.

If this is correct, I should reach that land in twenty days from Bristol. A shorter voyage than Venice to Bristol.

Think of that, my dear Mathye!

The document states that the Vikings in the tenth century discovered three separate lands west of Greenland:

Helluland, which they reached first, and is ice-bound.

Markland, to the south of Helluland and heavily forested. The Greenlanders often went there for timber.

Vinland, to the south-east of Markland.

In the document it is called VINLAND THE GOOD.

There was regular shipping between Iceland, Greenland and Vinland. Settlements were made in Vinland.

Grapes and furs were brought from there as well as timber. There are many species of fish.

> There were salmon in the river bigger than they had
> ever seen. The country seemed so kind, no winter fodder
> would be needed for livestock; there was never any frost
> all winter and the grass hardly withered at all.

My darling wife, I am going in search of neither salmon nor furs, but these stories confirm there is a great land just where I knew it would be. I will leave from Bristol and sail across the ocean seas to that land. I will sail southward along its coast until I reach the port inhabited by those who grow the spices.

I will!

I am copying the Norse saga for you and will enclose it

with this letter. There are many amazing stories therein; not the least is Gudrid's vision.

My brave Mathye, because you are my wife, in five hundred years they will say your name. They will.

The Holy Mother be with you and our sons.

Giovanni

Saturday after the third Sunday after Easter, under seal.

Bristol
May 7, 1495

My darling wife,

It has begun!

Richard Americ has agreed to invest in the voyage!

He is a man of some learning and has read widely in cosmology and geography and understands it is possible to reach the East by sailing west. This is my man.

He says he will bring in other patrons. In fact, he intends to take responsibility for that part of the venture, and I am to concern myself solely with getting the right ship and crew.

Because Richard Americ is the first person to commit to this voyage, I promised I would give his name to the first land I found. He is not a modest man; his eyes danced.

My spirits soar.

Your husband,

Giovanni

Fourth Sunday after Easter, under seal.

DIARII
Venice
June 3, 1495
Giovanni's spirits are soaring.

I can engender no such excitement.

If I had not music, the faces of my sons, Venice in the falling light – there would be no joy.

Vigil of Pentecost.

My darling husband,

You will not be surprised that I say the rosary all hours of the day and night.

But there is happiness, too.

Sebastian is dancing a gigue in your honour.

There is no doubt our son plans to accompany you over that western ocean. It is the spur I use to keep him at his studies.

On the Feast of Corpus Christi he leaves for Sagres. Already he has all his books and instruments packed.

My darling Giovanni, our sons are slipping away.

May the Spirit of God descend upon you.

Mathye

Pentecost Sunday, under seal.

Bristol
June 7, 1495

My darling wife,

Richard Americ has brought in Thomas Canynges and Edward de Gaunt, who is a cousin to King Henry; they, with myself, will form the partnership.

Getting the Letters Patent seems not to be a concern for them.

The King comes to Bristol on occasion and is seen with his de Gaunt cousins.

Canynges gave me access to his large stock of charts. I have found among them one drawn by John Jay, who left this port for the Isle of Brazil in the Summer of 1480 and spent many months searching for that place, but found nothing.

I have spoken to John Jay's son. He told me his father ran into many storms on his voyage. If he had gone again he would have left earlier in the Spring, as he believed the ocean seas, westward, are calmer at that time. Another small nugget to add to my tidy store.

I am living a joyous life! My dear Mathye, I wish I could share it with you.

I hope soon to share it with our son.

On the way to the Bristol quay there is a fine church – Saint Mary Redcliffe. I go there every day and pray for you, our sons, the success of the voyage.

Giovanni

Wednesday of the Pentecost Ember Week, under seal.

DIARII
Venice
June 10, 1495

Trinity Sunday, at the home of Cassandra Fidelis, Pietro Pomponazzi gave a reading from Dante's *Divine Comedy*.

Since, I have been under a foreboding.

When Giovanni started his search for a patron, I had a recurring nightmare.

Giovanni, me, all our children are brought to the Tower of Hunger, at Pisa. Through a slit in the door I see Count Ugolino, his sons and grandsons lying across each other, dead of starvation – Ugolino's punishment for having betrayed Pisa.

In the dream I am beside myself, afraid one of our sons will tell the gaoler their father is about to betray Venice.

This nightmare recurred for years. Then it left.

Now it haunts my waking hours. Except our children are grown. One is at Pisa.

Feast of Saint Margaret, Saxon Queen.

Montebelluna
June 12, 1495

My dear Lodovico,

You missed one of the great parties – farewell to Sebastian.

Your brother brought ten friends; with all our relatives and other friends there were over a hundred.

We hired extra servants.

Almost everyone stayed two nights; I used Donna Barozzi's villa for the overflow.

Montebelluna was resplendent.

Pasquale had trimmed the trees to geometric precision.

I have let the labyrinth grow, now that all my sons are taller than I am. Sebastian encouraged his friends to get lost in it – it was a great attraction.

The first night – a full moon – Sebastian and his friends performed a sea battle on the river. Your brother hired a man from the Arsenal who knew how to handle gunpowder. In the noise and confusion the explosions appeared to come from the occupied boats.

The battle went on for three-quarters of an hour. Halfway, they received reinforcements from down-river. I wasn't sure if it was boys from the village or some of our party.

It was ten of our young women, in costume, Maria and Lisa among them.

They were welcomed with rousing cheers and the tide of the battle was turned.

For the rest of the two days, every performance had a nautical twist.

Sebastian brought many of his charts, had them put up in the public rooms.

I remarked on his self-aggrandizement.

Mother, never too much!

You know your brother's laugh.

We drank your last cask of Trebbiano wine. I had it sent to Sebastian's table. I heard your health being drunk on a number of occasions. Once at Sebastian's insistence – the room was brought to its feet, you were toasted as 'my missing comrade'.

Your brother has his books and nautical instruments packed already. A more eager student will not appear at Sagres.

Jesus and his Holy Mother be with you.

Your Mother

Monday after Trinity Sunday.

Venice
June 15, 1495

My darling husband,

This morning we put Sebastian on the galley to Sagres.

I sent Guido with him.

Getting him ready and out of the door was a storm.

He took all his books and charts and wanted to take many of yours. I warned him off. He wanted me to promise he could go to sea if he knows as much as his teachers.

Our son is in for a surprise when he rubs shoulders with the older scholars; it will be good for him; he will have a yardstick to measure his learning and that will settle him to the work he has to do.

The house is quiet, except for an occasional thump from the back room were Sancio is building another piece of furniture or dismantling one.

Last week, in the meadow, he diverted the stream by the rock wall, and built a small stone bridge over it. I told him to leave it until you return. It looks impressive for the work of a thirteen-year-old.

I have given him permission to put a second floor on one of the rooms at the top of the house that has never been finished or used. He assured me he had consulted Brother Chrysogonus at the priory and he had approved his drawings.

He can't do much harm.

May the Divine Heart be with you.

Mathye

Feast of Corpus Christi, under seal.

Venice
June 18, 1495

My dear Isabetta,

It's a bleak life we mothers sometimes have of it.

Sebastian is on his way to Sagres.

Sancio, Nurse, all the servants went to the Piazzetta to see him off. Most of his friends were there, so was Adriana.

We sang him down the Canal.

Adriana came back to the house. You can be sure I drowned my sorrow for an hour or so. She stayed for supper. By the time she left I was as merry as I know how to be.

But today?

Today I have only one son in my home. I go drooping about the place.

May the Spirit of God be with you and your family,

Mathye

Second Sunday after Pentecost.

My darling wife,

A mariner from Castile accosted me in a public house with the startling news that Pope Alexander, for the purposes of exploration, has cut the world into equal parts. He has given one half to the Catholic Monarchs, the other to the King of Portugal.

I had Richard Americ enquire at Court for knowledge of this. But not even King Henry has heard of it.

I must know exactly what has transpired between His Holiness and these several monarchs.

Would you ask Canon Leonardo to write to the Holy See for a copy of any such Treaty? Or, if the Canon is reluctant, as we have been asking a lot of him lately, would you approach the Patriarch?

Best of wives, I ask much of you.

Blessed may you be with our sons.

Giovanni

Feast of Saint Alban, under seal.

My darling wife,

We are striding forward.

We will victual one ship with a crew of eighteen for eighty days.

Richard Americ is still looking for sponsors, but mainly to spread the financial risk. Anyone with as little as two pounds can take a share. Richard, now that the voyage is secure, is having a great deal of fun gathering in those smaller sums.

I spend my days talking to mariners, gauging their ability. I have already selected six I have previously sailed with; they are courageous and hard-working.

I am looking at two vessels. One I have taken as far as Land's End to see how she takes the water. The other will be available within a few weeks.

My dear Mathye, the news has spread that a voyage is being prepared, and I am surrounded each time I step into the street.

May the Spirit of Pentecost be upon you and our sons.

Giovanni

Feast of Saint Theobald, under seal.

DIARII
Montebelluna
July 27, 1495
Not even the Saracens could destroy the trade of Venice!

And yet if Giovanni finds a short route to the East and shifts the trade from the Mediterranean to the Western Sea, Venice will die as a trading nation.
Feast of Saint Pantaleon.

Venice
August 1, 1495

My darling husband,

The Guild of Singers was here last night; there were eight of us. Only Deacon Garofoli and Ana Carpaccio were absent.

He was on a sick call and she was caring for her ailing grandmother.

We had a very good meal: we started with pears matured in wine, followed by roast perch, wild boar, and green salad. The wine too was better than average. Cook had bought a number of jars of *aithôpa oinon*, which gave a neat kick to the back of the palate; there are a few jars left, which I am saving for your return.

After supper I took out my new madrigal.

It is in the Ionian mode.

The first line of the verse starts with one voice – the descant; the second – two, flowering into three voices on the third line, and breaking into full bloom on the fourth, and on to the end when the verse is repeated with the male voices joining in the same sequence as the female.

I work on a piece in my study, delighted to have an idea that allows me to begin; I wrestle with the ensuing problems, bring it to my friends and they pour life into it, as I never imagined.

Agustin had a new madrigal which he left for another night.

My darling husband, it was a lovely evening of music. You would have enjoyed it so.

I am working on a second Petrarch madrigal. I will keep its unveiling until you return so you won't miss all the fun.

May Our Lord and His Mother have you in their Holy care.

Your own true wife,

Mathye

Feast of the Holy Maccabees, under seal.

DIARII
Venice
August 1, 1495
Guido is back.

A disturbing letter from Sebastian.

Commemoration of Aghia Sophia.

My beloved son,

No doubt everyone who conducts the Sagres School of Navigation knows who you are; who your father is.

You must not be surprised, then, if one of the Holy Princes seeks your company; he may be assigned to you.

What you will remember, and you have been often reminded, my dear son, is you never make your father's work or any of his ideas, a topic of conversation, most particularly not with a Portuguese Prince.

I need not repeat to you that Portugal is a rival to Castile and to any other country in search of the short route to the East.

Hear me, my son! Keep your counsel. Remember you are at Sagres to study and practise the science of navigation; do that and only that, and all will be well.

My dear son, begin sending your letters under seal.

God be with you.

Your Mother, who loves you better than herself.
Feast of Saint Stephen, Pope, under seal.

My darling husband,

There is great consternation: the Venetian galleys were attacked by the French in the Bay of Biscay. They were forced to run into Southampton for shelter, where the Collegio have ordered them to off-load their cargo.

Our galley is a part of the convoy.

Piero has been made Captain of the fleet for the homeward voyage.

All this is secret, but when family is involved nobody thinks of secrecy; an hour after the ballot was taken by the Collegio to compensate the galleys for any loss, all the family knew.

You can imagine the anxiety. Masses are being offered for a 'special intention' in half the churches at Venice.

You are near Southampton, you may already have used your good graces, as titular ambassador, to free him and the other crews.

Do write immediately.

May the Spirit of the Great Creator descend upon you.

Mathye

Feast of Saint Dominic.

Venice
August 6, 1495

My darling husband,

Another messenger has arrived from Southampton.

The news is grim.

The heavily armed French ships followed our fleet into the harbour and have set up a blockade.

The Donado galley was attacked and Francisco, one of the sons of Toma Donado, was wounded by a shot from a falconet.

There is now a ransom of 550 ducats on the head of each captain.

You can imagine the activity in the Collegio with our trade threatened and our mariners in peril.

Messengers leave the Doge's Palace every day for the courts of France or England.

Paola is paler than fresh wax.

I visited her last week, brought Cyprus malmsey; she pretended to drink, cried all the while. She keeps the worst of the news from Giacomo, but Piero's name is heard everywhere in the Piazza.

We spend half the day on our knees.

God go with you.

Mathye

Ninth Sunday after Pentecost, under seal.

DIARII
Venice
August 8, 1495
Had I not music to gladden my days, even Venice would not be enough.

This morning, at Mass, I wept for Piero.

In the last three hours I composed the music for the first verse of Psalm 67.

All the world is sunny.

What a blessing.

Tuesday after the ninth Sunday after Pentecost.

Pisa
August 15, 1495

My dear Mother,

I have written to Sebastian.

You worry too much about old Sebastian. His eye is always on the main chance; he will, I am certain, do all the right things; he does have a way of getting on with those he meets.

The first time I saw this, I was about five. The two of us were in the meadow and the three little Foscari girls from across the campo wandered over – they were standing there in a row, and I remember looking at them, maybe staring. Then they moved together toward Sebastian and pulled him off the grass and the three, one after the other, kissed him.

Sebastian must have been four. He smiled, he laughed out loud, he gave them the top he was playing with; they each took a turn spinning it; they never looked in my direction. At the time, I remember thinking – he's the youngest, that's why they went to him.

I had left home before I realised it wasn't because Sebastian is younger than me, it is because he has the royal jelly.

Sebastian knows people are attracted to him. He knows he is as much at home in the hold of a ship as he is with theologians and he enjoys them both equally. He's like Father in that way.

You mustn't worry about Sebastian.

In the letter I wrote, I told him Father had given me advice about the value of putting my head down and not losing the best chance, and I wanted him to have the advantage of that advice, and that's what a brother was for.

I got a wonderful letter ribbing me about being a lawyer to lawyers, that he would certainly take such expensive advice and on in that vein. No, Mother, I don't worry about Sebastian, but I can understand how you see around more corners than any of us.

Your devoted son,

Lodovico

Assumption of Our Lady into Heaven, under seal.

Sagres, Portugal
September 1, 1495

Dear Mama,

This is your beloved son who loves you. In other words, and as Nurse would say: I love you, God love you.

Study is wearing me down, but that good brother of mine, the future canon lawyer, has written me a nicely worded treatise on the praise I owe Heaven and you, and Father when he's home, for this sound education I'm receiving. And I have replied to that good notary in whom you are well pleased – so am I – and in a profound genuflection position I told him that, as woolly-headed as he believes me to be, as woolly-headed as I am sometimes, I know why I am here and my woolly-headedness is a bit of a ploy that is intended to accrue to my benefit. I see that it does.

A man has to have something to get along in this world: Lodovico has the brains, Sancio has the beauty, Sebastian has the . . . woolly-headedness.

My dear and sweet mother, that Papa of mine promised if

he goes cavorting over the western seas this year he will take me with him, and Mama, I mean to hold him to that promise. The man said, and you were there:

Son, when you are sixteen you can come on a voyage of discovery with me.

I am, Mother, in my sixteenth year.

On the pure blue waves I will be safe from all my temptations.

Dear Mother, I know how you furrow your brow over this son of yours. I remember that, and keep my wits about me.

We have had a sparse evening meal which is no doubt good for my soul. There is still light in the sky and I will take a turn around the quadrangle before I light my candle and do what students must do.

Good night, dear Mama.

Your loving son,

Sebastian

Feast of Saint Giles, abbot, under seal.

Bristol
September 7, 1495

My darling Mathye,

Every time I meet my backers we have to dance around the international situation: if it is not Isabella and Ferdinand asserting their claim to half the earth, it is the King of France threatening shipping.

I was not able to get away to Southampton.

I did the next best thing: I sent a knowledgeable messenger with the swiftest horse, charged him to survey the situation, talk to the right people, and give me a detailed report of the Venetian galleys and their crew, with special attention to Piero's situation.

Here is the report I received:

A French bark and a French barge, both heavily armed,

have captured our three galleys in the harbour of Southampton. Other than Francisco Donado, no one else has been injured. There is some damage done to their galley.

One of our sous-ambassadors from London is aboard Piero's galley.

Negotiations for a settlement are underway.

Richard Americ says this English King grew up in the courts of France and Burgundy. He has many French cousins. Richard thinks this close relationship will encourage the French to negotiate a settlement without further bloodshed. An envoy from the King of England left for France on the Feast of Saint Hedwig.

I know, my dear wife, you expected me to go to Southampton but, in conscience, I could not do it. I am deep in discussions with my backers and cannot be seen to abandon my post.

Be with me, now.

Richard Americ told me there is suspicion at Court that this attack on the Venetian galleys is aimed at England, with the intention of bending her mind against joining the Holy League.

No one here seems to know the terms of the Holy League. Do you think you can get information without bringing suspicion on yourself?

My dear Mathye, it is a difficult time for Piero, you, and all your family. I know it.

But it is my time of good fortune and I have to force my will to remember you are all anxious.

You will bear with me.

May Jesus and His Holy Mother be with you.

Giovanni

Thursday after the eighth Sunday after Pentecost, under seal.

DIARII
Venice
October 2, 1495

My only real cousin in the world is in the hands of the French.

Giovanni sits in Bristol.

How can he fail to use his good graces as ambassador of the Republic of Venice?

No, I will not understand!

Now I have to tell Paola that my husband considers his own affairs above Piero's life, her happiness – mine.

How to live through this misfortune?

Feast of the Holy Guardian Angels.

DIARII
Venice
October 5, 1495

Piero is home! The convoy arrived safely!

The whole family gathered at San Zan Degolla yesterday morning – joined by half the parish.

We sang a Te Deum.

Canon Leonardo celebrated a High Mass in thanksgiving.

At Piero's house – every member of the Collegio came. So many in purple, scarlet, blue – all wearing black or red velvet sashes. It looked like a marriage.

Paola had hung the tapestries. The house was awash with garlands, flowers.

All the silverware was brought out – like a wedding feast.

No one mentioned Giovanni's name!

Feast of Saint Placidus.

DIARII
Venice
October 6, 1495

I have to write to my husband, keep the fury out of my letter.

Days I have to remember I chose him!

Giovanni,

I guess you are aware the convoy left Southampton safely.

Every time I mention your name, Piero and Paola change the subject. I've stopped!

Mathye

Feast of Saint Bruno, under seal.

Giovanni,

Your letter arrived today requesting information about the Holy League. There is no secrecy surrounding it.

Its aim is to encourage the French to leave the Peninsula.

It consists of Emperor Maximilian of Germany, the Duke of Milan, Isabella and Ferdinand, the Pope, and ourselves.

The Agreement was signed on Friday after the fourth Sunday in Lent. It was read at noon from both the Edict Stone and the Hunchback – for three days running.

Leading up to the Signing – we had delegations from the English, Milanese; three came from the Pope. We had the French once, also one from Florence – every time I went to the Piazza another delegation was marching up the Piazzetta.

Following the signing there were bonfires, processions and banquets for a week.

In spite of the Holy League, Charles VIII has had himself crowned King of Naples. With his army, he is now on his way to Rome, seeking an investiture from the Pope.

Pope Alexander, I hear, has no intention of putting the crown of Naples on the head of that little King.

Mathye

Feast of Saint Osyth, under seal.

DIARII
Venice
October 8, 1495
Piero, Carlo and I were summoned to meet the Collegio, to discuss indemnity for our galley.

The Doge greeted us with:

I want the French wiped off the face of the earth! How dare they attack our galleys.

How dare they!

Piero told the story of the capture, added gruesome details of injuries suffered by Francisco Donado and other crew members, spoke of insults to himself and the other captains.

After some mysterious clicking of tongues and waving of hands, it was decided the Republic will award each galley one thousand ducats; this will cover time lost at Southampton, less valuable cargo loaded from that small port.

We had expected less.

The Doge wants Piero to leave again for Flanders within a few months.

Paola is livid.

Feast of Saint Bridget, visionary.

DIARII
Venice
October 10, 1495
At the Tron home last night was Doge Barbarigo with a snarl in his voice:

Where was your ambassador husband during the blocade of Southampton, Donna Caboto?

In Bristol! Do you know where Bristol is, Principe?

Donna Barbarigo catching our tone, if not our words, wheeled, put her arm through mine, walked me away.

She has had a lot of practice at the farce of public good manners.

I smiled beatifically on her.

I wanted to spit tacks.

Feast of Saint Victor.

My darling wife,

Already the negotiations for the Letters Patent have begun.

The King attended our first meeting with his lawyers; we with ours.

I presented my ambassadorial documents. I explained my sphere, presented my charts, twice traced my proposed route along the fifty-second parallel to the East. I cited the ancients, told the Viking saga, and the stories of Toscanelli and Nicolas of Lynn.

The King looked grave all the while. There is no doubt he understood everything. This Monarch directs his own foreign policy and will attend all future meetings. He is plain-spoken and has a keen mind for the cost of everything.

He informed us he has advised the ambassadors and envoys of the interested States.

I told the Monarch of the secrecy the Portuguese maintain in these matters; that the Portuguese and Spaniards consider all but themselves to be trespassers on this Western Ocean.

The King was courteous but I believe he will not be persuaded.

Everything is spoken of openly in this country. Edward de Gaunt goes up to London and comes back with the latest news from the continent. I know more about the court of the King of Portugal than when I was at school in that country.

My darling wife, my life is moving in the direction I planned for it.

May the Great Lord Jesus be with you.

Giovanni

Feast of Saint Wilfred, under seal.

My darling wife,

As I told you in an earlier letter, which I hope you now have received, I was unable to go to Southampton when Piero was held.

King Henry has since sent an envoy of high rank to France and there is now an understanding between the two countries. There should be fewer incidents in the future.

In August a number of Englishmen were involved in the murder of two Venetian merchants in London; the King had the culprits brought to Southampton and hanged in full view of the Venetian galleys. This King seems to be a man inclined to sue for peace; when crimes are committed he responds in a swift and public way.

Every time France, Portugal or the Catholic Monarchs make a political move we have to consider whether it has any bearing on when or how the voyage will take place. I try to let my patrons worry about these things and concern myself with the practical matters: men and materials. But we never sit down without the international situation being discussed.

My darling wife, forgive my not going to Southampton. I must be seen to be concentrated on the goal.

Light of my eyes, be with me now.

Your husband who dedicates his life to you,

Giovanni

Nineteenth Sunday after Pentecost, under seal.

Post Scriptum
I have received no letters from you since Piero was embargoed. I expect a packet any day.

DIARII
Venice
October 20, 1495
I start a letter to Giovanni. Write what I will regret.

Stop.
Friday after the nineteenth Sunday of Pentecost.

Bristol
October 30, 1495

My darling wife,

We were near closing the negotiations for the Letters Patent and would have already done so, but this King wants to be present for every session. He is much distracted just now with a pretender to his throne, who styles himself Duke of York.

It seems this Duke has convinced Holy Roman Emperor Maximilian he is the late King's true son and the Emperor is supporting him. This pretender made a foray into Kent.

As well, Ireland is in turmoil and the chief of that place, the Earl of Kildare, has been arrested and brought to London.

All these events take the attention of a King who must have all his fingers in all his pies. This leaves me pacing the quayside with nothing to do but worry my fingernails.

I meet with Richard Americ and my other partners almost daily but they tell me we must await the King's summons. I tell them that the King is only a man and can be persuaded, but I get nowhere.

Your husband, my dear wife, is an impatient man and wants to knock heads, including the one who wears the crown.

I have written to Sebastian and told him to be in Bristol the first week in May.

God bless you, my own true wife.

Giovanni
Feast of Saint Marcellus, under seal.

DIARII
Venice
November 11, 1495
Patriarch Donato was at San Zan for Confirmation. When Mass was over he complimented my Choir, asked about my sons – no mention of Giovanni.

I was so angry I walked away in a blind fury.

To Luigi's alarm I had him land me on the other side of the Canal.

I stalked home through the mud of the back streets.

Used my elbows and an occasional shoulder on the throng.

Greeted no one.

It cleared my head.
Feast of Saint Clement.

Venice
November 12, 1495

Giovanni,

Hear this. How can I write you letters when daily I have to accept insults on your behalf?

I am not used to my husband's name being anathema.

Tell me what you will do about it.

One evening I was at the Tron home. The Doge sidled up to me, irony draining from his lips, wondered where you were during Piero's crisis. It wasn't a pleasant moment.

Even the Patriarch doesn't ask for you.

Mathye
Feast of Saint Martin of Tours, under seal.

Bristol
November 25, 1495

My darling wife,

I have my ship and mariners.

All but the final clauses of the Letters Patent are complete.

I tried to urge its completion but the King could not be made to sit down to it.

To compound my disappointment, this King has sent Richard Americ to France on some urgent Royal errand. He will be away at least three months. Negotiations cannot go ahead without my chief backer.

My dear Mathye, you can imagine how I want to place this King under discipline.

I cannot walk the quay at Bristol and do nothing. To stem my frustration, Thomas Canynges has given me a caravel of wool stuff to take to Bruges. I will be back in Bristol by the middle of December.

My dear wife, you must pray that I will not lose patience with these people who hold my destiny in their hands.

I have written you many letters but have received none of yours since Piero was held.

Your husband who loves you as his life,

Giovanni

Feast of Saint Catharine of Alexandria, under seal.

Bruges
December 5, 1495

My darling wife,

We arrived at Bruges yesterday morning. We took on a load of stockfish. It took forty-eight hours to load. We are ready to leave port now. I have given my mariners just one hour shore leave.

I still have no letter from you.

Were we to stay another night I would have had to tie myself to the mast, so great is my urge to take horse for home.

I must be in Bristol when Richard Americ returns from France. I must keep his mind bent to the work of getting the Letters Patent.

However, Domenego Cozzi is in port. He told me he

greeted you and Sancio on the Grand Canal on the feast of Sant' Orsola.

My darling wife, be with me in these bold times.

God be with us and our sons.

Giovanni

Feast of Saint Sabbas, abbot, under seal.

Venice
December 6, 1495

My dear son Sebastian,

Yes, negotiations are going ahead with the King for Letters Patent.

Your father has written to you. He will take you with him. Be at ease.

Sancio and I spent a few days at Montebelluna and rode all the horses; they are getting fat and lazy. I decided to sell six of them and keep only the favourite of each.

I am keeping your stallion.

The stable boy assures me he can handle five with the sometimes help of Giorgio whom Pasquale has put to work in the fields.

Sancio is getting ready to leave for the University of Padua. Giacomo is going too.

My dear son, I am certain you will be on this voyage.

May Jesus and his Holy Mother guard you.

Your Mother

Feast of Saint Nicholas, patron of mariners, under seal.

DIARII
Venice
December 6, 1495
I assure my son of a berth on the ship that will voyage over the Western Sea, as if every word did not rip my heart.
Feast of Saint Nicholas.

Dear Isabetta,

You are right, I have been neglecting you.

There appear to be some months of quiet ahead. The French army is wintering at Naples, the Holy League seems uninterested in routing them.

Lodovico is settled at Pisa; Sebastian has begun his studies at Sagres; my wandering husband is trading between Bristol and Bruges but that's a story of another kind.

Caterina Cornaro and Asolo are flourishing. Her Thursday entertainments are amusing. Often she invites a small party for supper. She is wonderfully adept and has the art of repartee and can entertain a table of wits.

Giovanni and I are always invited.

My husband is never home.

Caterina starts the evening by trailing us around her formal gardens to see the latest exotic plant, from God knows what exotic land. Musicians stand around and play and sometimes sing as we pass. Certain musicians are hired for the evening and others are chosen from the live-in group; she treats them all like favoured servants.

After dinner she has the doors of her large ground-floor room thrown open and whoever is standing outside becomes the audience. Once in a while you see a few members of the rabble stray in. As long as they are quiet and don't smell too badly, Caterina lets them stand along the wall.

Last Thursday, Lord Nicolas of Frankfurt gave a lecture on the craft of printing.

He recently arrived in Venice and publishes Bibles. He has a shop near the Bridge of San Lio.

He brought a number of his beautifully illustrated books and had them on display.

This Thursday, the San Marco choir will be there. Violante Picorina will sing. She has a glorious voice, and is living in one of the houses on Caterina's ground.

All this adds to the excitement of life in Venice and gives

Caterina, whom everybody addresses as Your Highness, a chance to play Queen again. She does it with some grace.

When you come home – it is time you visited your parents, not to mention your parents' neighbour – you must be a part of this happy addition to our lives.

God bless you and your family.

Mathye

Feast of Saint Ambrose, doctor of the Church, under seal.

Venice
December 10, 1495

Dear Isabetta,

Caterina has a writer living on her estate.

Do you remember Marin Sanudo? He's about seven years younger than we are, handsome and learned. He is writing a history of Venice. He gave a reading last night – lively. There were only twelve of us, including the Doge and his wife. Caterina didn't open the doors, which I suppose was in deference to the Doge.

I look forward to Marin's book; it promises to be amusing.

We had a long conversation; he told me he has been given access to State papers and secret documents up to 1440. He has spent the last few years at the Chancery taking notes. He hopes to have a first draft in two years – now that he has isolated himself from the distractions of Venice.

He will give a reading once a week while he is at Asolo which, he says, is the goad he needs to keep at his writing.

Blessings,

Mathye

Second Sunday of Advent, under seal.

Dear Isabetta,

I have been to a second reading by young Sanudo.

Caterina's room was overflowing.

Marin read a piece about the way Venetians were housed fifty years ago, in comparison with today: the cost of material, land, labour, which everybody in the room seemed to have an opinion on, including Caterina; he mentioned one of her family's palaces as an example of the upper range of housing and priced it at a resale value of 20,000 ducats, today's specie.

And Messer Sanudo, have you priced the cutlery?

Young Messer Sanudo blushed. But he is still occupying the house at her estate, so I assume he wasn't thrown in the street with his quill and one sock.

I find young Sanudo quite amusing. He tells me juicy bits of Venetian life that will never see the light of day. Exempli gratia: our family was saved from shamefaced poverty in the thirteenth century by marrying into the Tiepolo family.

And you, my dear, had a natural great aunt who was stuffed into a convent by her father at the age of four; the eight hundred ducats given to the convent for her upkeep was taken back when she died at fifteen.

I look forward to Caterina's Thursday evenings more than usual; I now have the raffish side of my nature satisfied, which of course I will give up for Lent.

Blessings on you and your family.

Mathye

Friday after the second Sunday of Advent, under seal.

DIARII

Venice

December 19, 1495

I told Marin Sanudo's servant to come the third hour of the afternoon to pick up the manuscript of *The Tartar Relations*. I left it with Gemma.

It was Marin who came.

Why isn't he at Asolo?

Why is he running errands like a servant?

Do what you will, says God, and pay for it.

Tuesday after the third Sunday of Advent.

Venice
December 20, 1495

Dear Isabetta,

The Doge and his wife gave a supper to celebrate Carpaccio's completion of *The Reception of the Ambassadors*. The painting – big, bright, brilliant – wonderfully animates the south wall of Scuola di Sant' Orsola.

After the dinner, Hieronymus Beolco and his troupe put on a mummery in the Ducal courtyard: a dozen knights and their ladies mistook a sleeping draught for wine; when they woke they didn't know where they were, or to whom they were married.

A lot of falling about and going off with the wrong spouse as they came to their senses at different times.

There were four new dances by the Dancing Master's troupe from Mainz; they were dressed like Saracens; the music had an Eastern ring. They carried lighted torches, wonderfully effective in the softened light.

Adriana and Maria were with me. Adriana dripping pearls.

God bless you and your family.

Mathye

Wednesday after the third Sunday of Advent, under seal.

DIARII
Venice
December 21, 1495
Last evening, during the performance, Marin came and stood near Adriana, Maria and me.

He spoke to Adriana for several minutes. Bowed gallantly, invited us to his next reading. Cantered away.

Adriana harrumphed and wondered why she couldn't take Maria in public without being accosted by young men.

When did I learn the value of silence?

Feast of Saint Thomas, Apostle.

DIARII
Venice
December 23, 1495
Last choir practice before Nativity Mass.

Put out more wine than I should.

Young Claudio Tiepolo staggered down the stairs. I sat him down. Sent for Luigi.

Claudio was silly drunk.

Donna Caboto, you're lovely.

So are you, Claudio.

No, that's not what I mean.

You're lo-oov-e-ly.

He started to giggle.

Luigi got him out of the house. With help from his gondolier they eased him into his gondola.

He went up the Canal singing my new Alleluia at the top of his voice.

And we have three sons . . .

Saturday before the Vigil of the Nativity of Our Lord.

DIARII
Venice
December 27, 1495
The Queen of Cyprus has invited me to join her for winter frolics.

I will.

I will.

Her guests won't quiz me about Giovanni and Southampton.

No, they won't!
Feast of Saint Fabiola, scholar.

DIARII
Asolo
January 3, 1496
Marin seems to have the run of Caterina's castle, unlike other artists.

Maybe she sees him as a son. Last evening he fetched a chart she wanted.

Blessed with good looks and charm, he must be pleasant to have around.

Nevertheless, at the end of the evening, he sat with me, told me he discovered that in the fourteenth century one of the Cornaro's natural sons was exiled from Venice for two years, having divulged secrets of the Republic to a Papal Legate.

We had a glass of mellow wine together.
Feast of Saint Genevieve, prophet.

DIARII
Asolo
January 5, 1496
Riding every day for the last three. The weather is bracing. Yesterday, Marin and I left the main group and veered off to see a herd of wild boar some two miles away.

Ugly creatures.

I was happy to turn away.

Along the road we came upon a piglet.

I jumped from my horse; Marin urged me back on – the dam might be near and charge.

I was anguished to leave it mewling in the road.
Feast of Edward the Confessor.

DIARII
Asolo
January 6, 1496
Caterina has a glassed-in loggia. Delicious in these brisk January days.

Yesterday afternoon we were waiting for her guests, enjoying the warmth, sometimes talking, sometimes not; after an unusually long silence she said:

I don't have to invite Marin to any event you attend.

If I wasn't sitting I might have staggered. I looked at her. Looked away. I wanted to turn over the table; at least throw the rest of my wine in her face. I did none of it, but replied in the same measured tones.

No, it's fine. I'll see that all will be well.

I am not particularly interested in the Queen of Cyprus feeling responsible for my virtue!

I know the teachings on adultery! Like her, I can repeat them in the three languages of the Church.

I would let the fires of hell singe her skirts before I would offer such advice.

Queens should mind their own business!
Feast of the Epiphany.

DIARII
Venice
January 8, 1496
Lorenzo's mother is ill. Isabetta believes she's dying.

Spent all afternoon comforting Donna and Ser Barozzi – comforting myself.

Donna Barozzi thinks Isabetta and Lorenzo will not return to Venice!
Monday after the first Sunday after the Epiphany.

Dear Giovanni,

I have sad news.

Alvise Querini drowned on the Feast of Saint Raymond. His body washed ashore at Chioggia.

Adriana, as you can imagine, is stricken.

It's a bleak time.

Mathye

Tuesday after the first Sunday of the Epiphany.

Dear Isabetta,

This is not a happy letter. I must tell you that Alvise died on the Feast of Saint Raymond, tragically; he was returning from a banquet at the Doge's palace. While no one has told dear Adriana, at least one of the Collegio has said Alvise was more drunk than usual.

You and I know that since he was sixteen Alvise has been coming home 'more drunk than usual'. I expect that Adriana is as good at guessing as the rest of us.

It happened on the Grand Canal, about the third hour of the night.

Their gondolier said Alvise was inside his gondola humming away, and without warning came out and tipped into the Canal.

Alvise was always happy in his cups.

The gondolier shouted for help, jumped overboard. Alvise was nowhere to be found.

Gondoliers spread out along the Canal and trolled all night.

The tide was out and running.

Adriana immediately came on the Canal. I spent the first night with her. She wasn't crying, she wasn't tearing her hair; she was just sitting there. Suddenly that laughing, happy woman had turned to alabaster.

Maria joined her mother when I left.

The boats made a little island of space around their gondola; it looked pitiful.

A day later, Alvise's body washed up fifteen miles away, on the shore at Chioggia.

The wake was held in the Sala del Maggior Consiglio. All of Venice, it seemed, lumbered up the stairs and passed the bier.

I happened along just at the moment the Doge, robed in his glitter, and a number of the Collegio were preparing to mount the stairs. The Doge was on about the sixth step when some sense made him turn – Antonio Loredan was passing a note to Zorzi Cornaro. The Doge's face lined, went a deeper shade of grey.

It is rumoured that Zorzi wants to be the next Doge.

At a funeral for one of their own, intrigue proceeds apace.

The Patriarch sang a High Mass in Office at San Marco's. The Doge was enthroned, the Collegio around him. The Sanctuary was full of bishops, canons, and at least a hundred priests. Large contingents from all the Scuole, with their banners and candles, filled the church.

The Doge had the relic of San Marco brought to the Piazza, and half the sick and lame in Venice passed under it.

When we left to follow the corpse to the Dominican's chapel of SS Giovanni e Paulo, where his body was entombed, it took an hour for the procession to form and pass out of the Piazza.

Alvise would have enjoyed it all. You know how he loved pomp. Adriana used to say that the only reason he got himself elected to the Collegio was his love of wearing his purple toga.

We buried him with all the ceremony the Church could muster, and that was a great deal.

Adriana often said she would be given a splendid funeral because Alvise was a member of the Collegio. I was unkind enough to remember the Church doesn't bring out her glitterati for widows, not even rich ones.

Widow – a grey word.

I have not seen Adriana since the funeral; I'm waiting until the formal visits are over. She's taking it hard, as you can imagine.

Adriana is the first of the three of us to have been hit by tragedy. I suppose we have been lucky. We are all over thirty and have escaped two waves of plague.

I lost my parents before I was old enough to realise, but you and Adriana were blessed. And you, my dear Isabetta, most blessed. I hope it lasts for many more years. And it may. It may.

But my dear Isabetta, this has been a dolorous week.

Mathye

Wednesday after the first Sunday of the Epiphany, under seal.

DIARII
Venice
January 11, 1496
Two of my sons are in separate States.

My husband is in disgrace.

Alvise is dead!

I have had two consoling notes from Marin which on this day appear ridiculous.

Thursday after the first Sunday of the Epiphany.

Venice
January 30, 1496

My dear Isabetta,

I visited Adriana last Sunday. I sent a note.

Was shown to her glassed-in altana, the wind had dropped. It was warm.

She was looking off into space and fondling that little white Maltese, that ugly, hairless Maltese that is always trying to bite my ankles. Adriana got up to greet me, it snapped at my hand.

The big bloodhound bounded in, growling. It tried to eat

the little one. Adriana kept him off with a stick which he chewed savagely. Had you been there, you would have had both dogs slobbering over you in an instant.

Maria was near the rail, flapping a white scarf at the numerous birds: doves, pea hens, crows, all cropped-winged and squawking. Jocko, their new dwarf, was racing around trying to stuff them in cages.

Maria had removed her shoes – startling red ones, four inches of platform, the latest fashion the young in Venice are hobbling about on. She never bothered to put them on again.

Widowhood has not been kind to Adriana – she has sunk into it.

Is widowhood kind to anyone?

Suddenly, from one visit to the next, her back had enormously bulked. But she was wearing her jewellery: gold necklace, rings on those lovely Visconti fingers, and her still wheat-coloured hair was in place, her cap at the proper angle.

Her eyes, when I looked into them, were vacant.

Jocko had got himself and the cages off the balcony and relative quiet had settled on the lovely day.

I read her your letter, the one that told about the Sforza dinner. I saw a smile flicker over the mask she now presents to the world.

There was a letter on the floor, near her chair, which she didn't bother to pick up; if I had bent, ever so slightly, I would have seen who had written it. I imagine Adriana has been sent greetings by half the eligible men in Venice, and Maria the other half.

Maria was wearing the black pearls, which alone must be worth the Doge's hat. She had the same bruised look as her mother. I agree something must be done. Maria was to go to the University of Milan in May; now cancelled.

I am angry with Alvise. I shouldn't be angry with the dead.

Alvise was so careless. Such devastation. I cannot believe his death was the Will of God.

Ah well.

I invited them to Montebelluna. Adriana said it has too many memories.

What has happened to the happy six, Isabetta? Adriana and I are the remnants in Venice. Giovanni will return. You and Lorenzo – sometime. But how do we start again without Alvise? How does Adriana? How enormous the loss for her! For us.

She said she received your invitation but she has never travelled without her husband and wouldn't know how to begin. (What a fortunate statement; I have rarely travelled with mine. I didn't tell her – you get used to it.) But Maria showed real interest.

I will visit again next week and press the idea of a holiday. You may yet have them, and their entourage, riding up your long lane.

I can do nothing to make it better for Adriana. Another reason why I am angry. Were you here, Isabetta, you would think of something. I feel so useless in these circumstances.

But I will do what you ask. I will repeat your invitation each time I visit.

Bless you and your family.

Mathye

Feast of Saint Martina, martyr, under seal.

Venice
February 5, 1496

My dear Isabetta,

Adriana is going to Church again.

She visited Sunday. We spent an hour on the altana. The sun was warm; that fierce wind that sometimes takes our heads off had died down. We consumed some fiery *aithôpa oinon* wine.

I wish I could say she was looking better.

Alas.

We have the bad times.

Blessings,

Mathye

Feast of Saint Agatha, under seal.

Most dear and singular beloved wife,

Your last few notes, which I have just now received, seared my heart. I have caused you a great deal of pain.

I know it is difficult to believe I could not have taken a few days and gone to Piero's rescue.

It was my best judgement that I stayed in Bristol.

The enclosed letter is a copy of one I sent to Piero and Paola. I hope it makes things right.

If there were time I would come home.

My darling Mathye, do not waver in your faith in me.

I would make my voyage to the East with a heavy heart if I believed you had not forgiven me. Be with me, I beg you.

And Alvise's death is tragic.

There are seven chantry priests at Blessed Mary Redcliffe. I have had seven Masses said each morning for a week for the repose of his soul.

Dear Adriana. Bless her. I have written to her.

It has been a sad time.

Your husband who loves you above his own heartbeat,

Giovanni

Feast of Saint Romuald, under seal.

Post Scriptum
Did you get information about the Holy League?

My beloved husband,

I have received the copy of your letter to Piero and Paola. My, but you did exaggerate!

Piero has obviously forgiven you.

So have I, in biblical measure: pressed down, shaken together, running over.

But you were in the wrong, my darling husband; you must not call half-good good enough.

It has been a difficult time.

But that is behind us.

We must go on.

I shall not fail you. Be at ease.

I wrote to you last October about the Holy League. Attached are the significant points of that letter.

May the Spirit of God protect you.

Mathye

Friday of Ember Week in Lent, under seal.

DIARII
Venice
March 1, 1496
Piero is prepared to forgive and forget; the corners of Paola's mouth still droop when she hears Giovanni's name.

My husband – half across the world – I give him half the story.

Friday Ember Week.

DIARII
Venice
March 2, 1496
San Marco's was crowded – a mind's Mass for Alvise.

I was comforting Adriana on the steps – waiting for the crowds to move off.

Adriana stepped aside to speak to her cousin.

Marin was at my side.

How are you, Mathye?

Maybe it was his hand on my shoulder.

Maybe it was the review of my life that passed in front of my eyes this last while.

Maybe none of these.

I'm going to England to visit my husband.

I felt his hand leap off my shoulder. He fell back into the crowd.

I have no intention of going to England.

Sometimes I confound myself.

Saturday Ember Week.

DIARII
Venice
March 3, 1496

Started to compose a Requiem Mass this afternoon.

Worked ferociously – when I looked at what I had written I could hardly read it – had to make a copy.

I have the music for the Gradual – it has a wonderful dirge-like ring.

I will work on this Mass the rest of my life.

Second Sunday in Lent.

DIARII
Venice
March 4, 1496

Third hour of the afternoon Paola and I were at the Scuola di Sant' Orsola distributing corn. People had come and gone.

Paola, it's Lent. It's time to forgive Giovanni.

My husband could have died.

The French don't kill citizens of Venice. They need our friendship.

I have forgiven Giovanni.

You never mention his name.

Then I will.

But she doesn't.

And I will not beg.

Monday after the second Sunday in Lent.

My darling wife,

The Feast of Saint Lucius, March 5, was a great day in my life. The Letters Patent was signed at Westminster. There was to be a reception but the King was called away to Sheen. When Richard Americ, Edward de Gaunt and I arrived, only the King's Chancellor, Archbishop John Morton, was there to witness my signature.

My spirits were high. I don't remember the walk back to Sergeants Inn.

I have named our three sons in the Letters Patent and all profits from lands discovered, save one fifth for the King, shall accrue to me and them. As well, we or our deputies may conquer, occupy and possess all towns, castles, cities and islands discovered.

This Letters Patent is as well-drawn as reasonable men can make.

There are no further obstacles to my voyage. I will go.

I will return. You may be sure of that.

And you, my brave wife, will go to Jerusalem, as you promised, to pray me safely home.

God go with you.

Giovanni

Wednesday after the second Sunday in Lent, under seal.

DIARII
Venice
April 1, 1496
This day has been slouching toward me from my first meeting with Giovanni.

No amount of forewarning staved off the clutch at my heart.

Now! Jerusalem!

But Jerusalem with whom?

Isabetta and I talked of a pilgrimage to Jerusalem for the whole year we were seven.

Or was it for a week when we were seven?

One afternoon we escaped our nurses – started out. Some man, smelling of fish, recognised us on the Piazzetta, brought us home.

Isabetta is in Florence comforting the dying.

Paola wants to go to Jerusalem with me.

I am astonished.

How can I go to Jerusalem with a woman who no longer mentions my husband's name?

I didn't believe she would leave Lisa with the servants.

But she will.

She's determined.

Feast of Saint Macarius.

Venice
April 2, 1496

My darling husband,

When you sail into the stars, know your wife will be placing her lamps on the Holy Sepulchre in your name and that of our son.

Yes, I have set my face toward Jerusalem. I will keep my promise to you.

Paola is coming with me.

She is still having Masses of thanksgiving for Piero's escape from the French. It will be a gloomier time than it might, with Paola along, but there is nothing to be done.

I have asked Friar Cucholino to say a Mass each day from the Feast of the Ascension to Lady Day for your safety and Sebastian's. Canon Leonardo will say one every Wednesday for the success of the voyage. It will be a High Mass. Keep strict count of the days.

Events are tumbling ahead. I can just keep them within my compass. I am preparing Sancio for the University of Padua.

Sebastian will press to stay in Bristol at the end of the voyage.

He has already written of it to Lodovico. I know you will be firm.

Beloved, I am becoming a pilgrim for your safety and that of our son.

Mathye

Tuesday after Passion Sunday, under seal.

Bristol
April 4, 1496

My darling wife,

I have your letter of forgiveness. I am a man with a glad heart!

Best of wives, on the Feast of the Ascension we will leave Bristol and turn into the Western Sea. With our son, I will be heading into our future.

I have written to Sebastian again and expect him in a few weeks.

Here are my plans: I will sail to Dursey Head in Ireland, pick up the fifty-second parallel off that coast. Given perfect conditions, I should make one hundred miles a day.

In twenty days I shall travel two thousand miles; that will bring me to the land of the East. I have no doubt of it. On the return voyage I will use up another twenty days. That leaves forty-three days for coasting and, hopefully, a landing. Of course, I don't expect perfect conditions. However, I am prepared for whatever comes.

I have a flag of San Marco, a papal banner, and the red dragon of King Henry VII. I will plant them in the first new ground I reach.

Be certain you will be with me, for I carry your image always before my eyes.

The enclosed letter is for Sancio.

Your husband who holds you as dearly as his heart,

Giovanni

Holy Thursday, under seal.

My darling husband,

To say Godspeed to Sancio and Giacomo, I had a family gathering at Montebelluna.

Your cousin, Asher Romano, came with his father and son. I watched them strolling the grounds. It is a rare sight to see three generations of Venetians after so many waves of plague.

In all, there were sixteen adults and twenty children.

I had the labyrinth closed. The younger children amused themselves all afternoon running through the cloisters.

We ate outdoors in the large loggia.

There was music as usual. Sancio manfully took over Sebastian's place on the bellows of my organ, and did it with confidence.

I had many hours of anxiety on account of Sancio. Anything out of the ordinary seemed to make him tremble. He has got over it.

It is always somewhat of a miracle to see one of our sons move from child to adult. Sancio did it one day when I wasn't looking.

Because it was Lent, we didn't have general dancing but Sancio with Giacomo and Maria did a lovely ballo, learned for the occasion; they performed it with such an air. I was wildly proud of our son. He has become quite tall but is still rather thin. He will never have the sturdiness of Lodovico or the strength of Sebastian.

Everybody brought a lute, even the youngest. We managed a frottola with a polyphony of four voices, which, if you had drunk enough wine, didn't much hurt the ears.

On the Feast of Saint Zeno we will put Sancio and Giacomo on the road to Padua.

Our home will soon be empty of sons.

Lodovico will not return to Venice, nor do I expect Sebastian to be content to ply trade from Venice to Tana.

My darling husband, how did it all end so soon?

The enclosed letter is for Sebastian.

This is the last letter that will reach you before you leave for the unknown, but I will continue to write, give you details of my first steps on the road to Jerusalem.

Hieronimo Ziliol, who is leaving for Bristol on the Feast of Saint Athanasius, will carry the letters I write after today.

May the Spirit of God sweep over the face of the waters and guide you safely back to shore, to me.

Mathye

Vigil of Easter, under seal.

DIARII
Venice
April 6, 1496
Carlo was astonished when I broke the news I am going to Jerusalem.

Wanted me to tell him who would take his place as master of the galley to Constantinople while he replaced me as supervisor of the Fraterna.

He fully expected me to change my mind.

I stood in silence until he reached his own conclusion.

Vigil of Easter.

DIARII
Venice
April 8, 1496
Paola has asked the Patriarch for permission to make our pilgrimage to Jerusalem.

Easter Monday.

DIARII
Venice
April 12, 1496
Sancio and Giacomo off to the University of Padua – in high glee. Paola and I went as far as the stables.

Our sons protested one more time the four servants we sent with them – the stable boys with their extra horses.

When we returned we took a jar of wine, lingo bread, cheese to the altana.

Replenished our supplies!

Didn't raise the general gloom.

Feast of Saint Zeno.

DIARII
Venice
April 15, 1496

I spent the morning finishing a Kyrie for Ascension Day.

I sent Luigi running through the streets with it to Ana. She has barely three weeks to practise.

Monday after the second Sunday of Easter.

> *Padua*
> *April 18, 1496*

My dear Mother,

I have settled in.

The week of 'yellow beaking' is over. The senior students are not allowed to beat the younger ones, as at other universities.

There is a book of regulations. During yellow-beak week they charge a fine for every infraction. I lost two lira.

On the Feast of James the Less, two students from Regusa marched across the quadrangle with their swords brazenly at their sides. They were hauled before the Rector; their swords were forfeited and broken. They were fined five ducats each.

Another student, from God knows where, punched a senior in the head and was made to eat by himself at a small table in the centre of the Hall, for a week.

You can imagine I walk carefully among such public forms of punishment.

In the Hall, there is a strict rule of silence. At meals one of the senior students reads from the Bible or some other assigned book. Latin is spoken at all times, even in the garden.

My servant is a poor student studying the Grammar degree; I am obliged to hear him read Latin for a half-hour each day. He is a good fellow, a little older than me. I pay him seven lira a month for his services.

All junior students are expected to share rooms. I couldn't stomach that. I pay an extra ten lira a month and have a rather large and beautiful room. Giacomo had no such qualms and shares with a fellow from Naxos, who is so young he was brought here by his mother.

Dear Mother, pray for me at Jerusalem.

Your respectful son,

Sancio

Thursday after the second Sunday of Easter.

DIARII
Venice
April 19, 1496
Who will attend the Masses for Giovanni and Sebastian?

I will have Masses said at the Church of the Holy Sepulchre in Jerusalem!

Feast of Saint Alphege.

Chapter Five

My dear Mother,

I had a memorable Easter holiday in Florence, but I could not distract Alessandra from working each morning on an Annunciation – a commission from the Sisters of the Poor Clares.

I amused myself by riding Martino's horses.

Amerigo Vespucci's uncle, the learned Ser Anastasio, was a guest one evening while I was at Alessandra's. I overheard him tell Messer Cavalcanti that Christopher Columbus went on a second voyage to the new land, from where he sends back slaves. Amerigo, who is now working for the Berardi family, sells them.

Ser Anastasio was gravely concerned; there is a long-standing papal bull against slavery, though they seem to get around it in Venice.

I have sent this news to Father.

Messer Lorenzo's mother is still very ill. Every time I went to visit Donna Isabetta, the doctor was there.

I am, my dear Mother, your devoted son,

Lodovico

Friday after the second Sunday after Easter, under seal.

DIARII
Venice
April 20, 1496
Will take Nurse with me to Jerusalem.

A buffer against Paola.

Is anything ever what it seems?

Saturday before the third Sunday of Easter.

My darling Giovanni,

When you receive this letter you and Sebastian will have returned from your great adventure.

I from Jerusalem.

I will leave Venice on Wednesday Rogation Day.

I am taking Nurse with me.

It will be hard for her, especially the thirty-seven-mile donkey ride after we disembark at Jaffa.

But she will go.

I tell her we are to go as pilgrims. She is not to wait on me. If she does I will not get the grace of being a pilgrim. She looks at me from under her pale brows and has thoughts I do not ask about.

We will be with two Dominicans: Friar Christofaro Venier and Friar Zacharias Pivello, from San Marco's, who will accompany us to the holy sites.

Paola has asked the Patriarch to provide us with credentials.

We have bought our pilgrim's garb and staff.

I am quickly turning into a pilgrim – people I hardly know ask me to pray for them in the Holy Land.

Go on your journey in the hands of the Living God, and with our son return safely to me.

Mathye

Feast of Saint Agnes of Montepulciano, under seal.

My darling husband,

The five of us went to the Piazzetta today and bargained for passage.

We were given detailed instructions about what we may bring on board: bedclothes, live hens, and such. We got a copy of the rules of travel, including what we can expect from the Saracens.

I bought a phrasebook for the multiple languages spoken in the East. Our Dominican Friars speak Greek and Arabic, and I can still get my tongue around Hebrew and Greek.

Did you know pilgrims bring their belongings aboard wrapped in their bed blankets, tied with rope? I expect you did something similar as a young mariner.

We were told not to wear jewels.

We have a receipt for the belongings we will leave on the ship.

We are going on Agostino Contarini's galley.

When Agostino saw my name on the manifest he sent a servant round with an invitation to go first class, for the same price. I told him I was 'making my soul' and would stay with the rest of my fellowship, in the great cabin, below deck.

We have to bring wine, as the Saracens don't drink – but you know that.

Now that the word is around we are going to the Holy Land, we have been told stories of stale bread, tainted meat and other unsavoury tales. We have laid in a store of biscuits and Lombardy cheese, a half dozen laying hens.

Your kinsman, Asher Romano, who went to Jerusalem last year, told me that at Jaffa we will spend one or two nights at the stables known as St Peter's Caves, used to stable horses and donkeys. I hope my stomach can stand it.

When we reach Remleh we will stay at a hospice, recently built by the Duke of Burgundy; and in Jerusalem we will live with the Franciscan nuns. So, except for Jaffa when we are in the clutches of the Saracens, we are housed pretty well.

It is the lack of baths that will be my greatest trial, but we are going on a pilgrimage; this is the last you will hear of baths.

I hear that money in Jerusalem is the colour of the language the pilgrim speaks. Nevertheless, we went to the money-changer on the Rialto and bought aspers.

We each will take an extra three hundred newly minted gold scudi; the Saracens won't take used coins.

The galley will leave on the Feast of Saint Hervé.

My darling husband, it is for you and our beloved son I make this pilgrimage that even now I am beginning to enjoy.

Mathye

Fourth Sunday after Easter, under seal.

Venice
May 2, 1496

My dear Isabetta,

Remember when we used to pray to be allowed to go on a pilgrimage to Jerusalem? Remember how we thought we would never sin again if we could get the plenary indulgence given to Holy Land pilgrims?

I'm going – to pray Giovanni back from that sea of darkness.

I will certainly get the plenary indulgence.

Alas, the bit about never sinning again . . .

I regret you will not be with me.

There are five of us in our fellowship: Nurse, Paola, two Dominican Friars and myself. The galley is supposed to leave in a few days – if the pilgrims have arrived from Germany.

We will be a month travelling and spend three weeks there. We should be home by the eleventh Sunday after Pentecost.

Today we went to the Piazzetta to buy aspers. Ahead of us at the table were what I took to be two Greeks. They both wore tight chokers of pewter beads; the younger had on a blue alb, not girdled, and a large red stocking cap rolled off his face, forming a diadem of cloth.

The other wore an orange jerkin, belted. His full sleeves were bound at the wrists by metal cuffs; on his head was a huge cap of green stuff with a bow of the same hanging over his left ear.

Both men were arguing sotto voce with the money-changer.

Finally they got their scudi and were off. Friar Venier said he thought they were actually speaking Armenian.

Having witnessed the trouble the two ahead had, we presented our scudi as if we bought aspers every day and knew the rate of exchange.

My dear Isabetta, there will be prayers said aplenty for you and your family while I am in the Holy Land but think how happy the days if you were among our fellowship.

Mathye

Feast of Saint Athanasius, under seal.

DIARII

Venice

May 4, 1496

I have written my last letters to Giovanni, Lodovico, Sebastian, Sancio.

I have given the servants their final instructions.

Like Sancio I am shivering in anticipation.

Feast of Saint Florian.

DIARII

Venice

May 5, 1496

I understand why it didn't break Giovanni's heart to leave Venice – to leave home.

Had I known the high heart of the foreign traveller – might have arranged my life differently.

How long does this high heart last?

Fifth Sunday after Easter.

DIARII

Istria

Aboard the Pilgrim Galley

May 9, 1496

Last night, hatches up, a patch of sky and two stars visible, I snuggled down in my blankets. Felt like the first night at Montebelluna, after the winter winds of Venice.

The sails slapped; the rhythm of the oars lulled.

A woman, sleeping just at my feet, started great rolling snores – sounds the galley's groans could not drown.

No sleep!

Thursday after the fifth Sunday after Easter.

DIARII

Off Zara

May 10, 1496

Third day at sea.

It's hot.

Paola and I have removed our stockings, put on our pilgrim sandals.

The oarsmen are stripped to the waist.

Nurse looks at our bare feet.

Feast of Saint Gordianus.

DIARII

Pilgrim Galley

May 11, 1496

Fourth day at sea.

Noise of men fighting went on and on last night. A woman near the curtain raised the edge, in the dark could see only shadows.

This morning I expected to hear of murder. It was the meanest of common fights: a man had stolen a jar of wine.

The culprit was hauled to the poop deck. Agostino Contarini had him placed in stocks for the day. The poor wretch fainted in the heat.

He is just set free – had to be helped below deck.

The ship's doctor is attending him.

Feast of Saint James the Less.

My darling husband,

I will not bore you with the harshness of life shipboard. I will tell you the interesting bits.

Two days out of Venice, off the Dalmatian coast, we were becalmed. I had expected wind, I had expected storms, I would not have been surprised had we had hail; becalmed, I did not expect; it lasted half the day. A number of pilgrims I had not noticed before heaved themselves up to the gunwales; they were in a miserable state.

The heat was so intense the Master removed oarsmen in shifts for respite. The galley crept along at about two knots.

Nurse is holding her own. She hasn't been seasick, as she had feared. But one of the Dominicans has. A few hours out of Venice there was a sea swell. He turned green. The poor man lost his supper. While we were becalmed he got his colour back and his sea legs. He has been as merry as a cricket ever since.

I promised myself I wouldn't get seasick. I did feel a little queasy in the swell. It didn't last.

God bless you and our son as you prepare for that lonely sea.

I will pray you safe. I will.

Mathye

Commemoration of Saint Boniface.

My darling husband,

We have a fellowship from England travelling with us. There is with them a middle-aged woman who causes them a lot of grief; she has a great devotion to the Passion of Christ which she talks of constantly. Sometimes she falls to wailing about her sins. All this is very embarrassing to the English.

After the third day her fellowship would not eat with her. She and her servant were abandoned in a corner. I asked Nurse to invite them to eat with us. Of course I had an ulterior motive, will get no grace for doing this: I wanted to practise my English.

Her name is Jane Percy. She told me she has visions, talks with Jesus and His Mother. She speaks so feelingly of this and weeps floods of tears telling it, I am inclined to believe her. Nurse thinks she was putting on a show for the pilgrims.

When she discovered that you were a navigator and an explorer she told me her husband had studied at Oxford and has a copy of Nicolas of Lynn's *De Inventio Fortunata*. He used to read it to her when first they wed. She wanted to know if that is the kind of exploring you are doing. I had to confirm my almost total ignorance of the book but conceded you might be following in the wake of Nicolas.

My dear husband, I was amazed to hear the story of Nicolas of Lynn from the mouth of our visionary.

God bless you, my husband, God bless Sebastian.

In the Holy City I will pray you safe.

I will.

Mathye

Vigil of the Ascension.

Pilgrim Galley
May 15, 1496

Dear Isabetta,

For my sins I have taken on an English woman who is a visionary and has metaphysical fits. She eats all her meals with us. She is a good person, just hard on the nerves.

I behave like a true pilgrim and sleep in the great cabin, in the hold. There are fifty women separated by a leather curtain from some hundred and fifty men.

In the first class section, in the sterncastle, there are about thirty pilgrims.

I have six feet of space by three feet, marked off on the boards. When I get up I am obliged to tie everything in my bedclothes and hang it from a peg in the ceiling above my bed space. I empty my slop-pail overboard and wash it with sea water.

You would have made a thousands jests.

It would help if I could take a bath in the sea. When it rains everybody puts out pots to catch it.

I have learned to sleep among the snoring and caterwauling. I have astounded myself. Only my stomach rebels.

We eat our meals on deck. The food is no better than it ought to be. Sometimes Nurse and I go to the galley and boil eggs; we squeeze in among the other pilgrims.

Sometimes the cooks are in a foul mood and throw us all out.

The Dominicans are below deck with the rest of us. They never complain. In fact our fellowship tries to see all the torments of the body as cause for merriment. It's the only way.

Bless you,

Mathye

Vigil of the Ascension.

DIARII

Somewhere off Ithaca

May 16, 1496

Ninth day at sea.

This is the day Giovanni and Sebastian sail out of Bristol – head their ship into the dark.

Found a spot behind the ship's boat, meditated an hour.

Ascension Day.

My darling husband,

I have a portolano chart with me, will track you across the open sea. At the end of every week I will draw a ship on the chart to mark your progress. I used to do that when we first married.

It kept me hopeful.

Blessings on you, my dear husband; blessings on our son.

Mathye

Feast of the Ascension of Our Lord into Heaven.

DIARII

May 17, 1496
Tenth day at sea.

I want to wallow in a warm bath.

God, your pilgrim is groaning toward Jerusalem.

Friday after the fourth Sunday of Easter.

DIARII

Pilgrim Galley
May 18, 1496
Eleventh day at sea.

In the sterncastle there are a dozen professional pilgrims, hired to make the pilgrimage in the name of their employers.

All the spiritual benefits go to those who hire them!

These pilgrims stay to themselves, never participate in daily prayers or hymn singing, are often seen grinning behind their hands at some act of piety by a true pilgrim.

Poor employers!

Another group – pilgrims for the sake of seeing the world – withdrawn, silent, try not to see the dirty, noisy, smelly pilgrims who swarm the ship.

I am one of the smelly pilgrims. No real bath since home – won't get one until Jerusalem.

Paola, reserved and cheerless at home, enthusiastically joins the praying, singing, dancing.

Nurse has not lost her Venetian dignity, yet.

Feast of Saint Venantius.

DIARII
Pilgrim Galley
May 19, 1496
Twelfth day at sea.

Nurse and Paola no longer smell the unwashed bodies.

My stomach churns every morning.

We will take passage in the sterncastle on the return voyage.

Nurse is pleased.

Paola laughs at me. Tells me I just can't live without the comfort of first class.

But she will join us.

First Sunday after the Ascension.

DIARII
Modon
May 22, 1496
Fifteenth day at sea.

Fresh supplies!

Drinking water was beginning to look and taste like bilge.

Modon – Eye of the Republic – halfway to every land we own on the trade routes to the East.

The Galley contingent from Constantinople is here. All six of them.

I see Ser Tron posturing on his poop deck.

In two weeks they will be spilling furs, hides, enamelware, icons onto the Rialto; sending it over the Brenner Pass – along the Barbary Coast to Flanders, London.

There are in this harbour at least a hundred other ships from all parts of the Mediterranean, the Aegean, the Black Sea – all heading home to Venice.

I saw on the Cornaro galley Frederico, one of Queen

Caterina's young cousins, out from Cyprus. Caterina may be at Asolo – Cyprus is still providing wealth for the Cornaro family.

There are clerics, soldiers, merchants, whole families, en route – some of those families have been away from Venice for three generations yet, all are taking ship for 'home'.
Feast of Saint Julia, patron of Corsica.

DIARII
Coron, aboard the Pilgrim Galley
May 23, 1496
Sixteenth day at sea.
Many of the first-class passengers have gone ashore in search of an inn for the night.

We found a convent run by the oldest Franciscan nuns. They provided us with baths, a fine supper of lamb, a green salad of twenty-six ingredients, sublime muscat, the memory of whose taste will sustain me through the desert.

I feel like a queen.

The abbess invited us to their oratory. We joined them for Vespers.

We returned to the galley.

Rumours are flying.

Everybody is whispering it: there is no reason to stop at Coron. The Captain went ashore. He has a home here – another family.
Feast of Saint William.

DIARII
Off Crete
May 27, 1496
Twentieth day at sea.
Last night, the sea running high, sails rattling and groaning, between waking and sleeping, I had a – what? a vision? I saw the galley go down under us, people tumbling into the waves.

My body went cold.

I raised my head. Nurse was awake. We spoke a few commonplace words.

The moment passed.

Today something of that disconnected feeling persists.

No pilgrim ship to Jerusalem has foundered in living memory.

It is not of this ship I am thinking!

Whit Monday.

DIARII
Rhodes
May 28, 1496
Twenty-first day at sea.
Paula singularly cheerful since she stepped on the galley to Jerusalem.

Can even manage a merry face when Nurse and I talk about Giovanni.

Whit Tuesday.

Rhodes
May 28, 1496

My darling husband,

I am getting tired of the wailing and weeping of Dame Percy.

My English is considerably improved. I should be more grateful.

Yesterday, just in the middle of supper, the good lady started to roar out her sorrow for her sins; threw herself on the deck and rolled around, moaning of her love for the Passion of Jesus.

Now I understand why her fellowship turns their faces from her. I will not abandon her, but I will have nothing to do with her once I leave the galley.

I hear there is a man in the sterncastle who is affected the same way.

Today, when we arrived at Rhodes, Nurse, Paola and I left the ship and found a peaceful meal, without floods of tears.

Paola has surprised me – she has remained constantly lighthearted.

I am keeping a record of my pilgrimage for our sons. I expect Lodovico (and maybe Alessandra) will want to make this trip as soon as he is finished his canonical studies. In a letter I had from him before I left he gave all kinds of advice and wished he could accompany me. All of a sudden our son sees his mother as needing protection, now that I no longer feel I need to protect him; I am amused by this, but don't mention it to him as he is very earnest.

We leave Rhodes as soon as provisions have been loaded, which should be at sundown.

God keep you and Sebastian.

Mathye

Whit Tuesday.

DIARII
Famagusta, Cyprus
June 3, 1496
Twenty-eigth day at sea.
Letter from Sancio – dear Sancio.

The mail bag came aboard at each port we stopped.

None of our fellowship got letters. We didn't expect any.

When my name was called, I froze.

Nurse had to retrieve it for me.

Feast of Saint Kevin, hermit of Glendalough.

Padua

My dear Mother,

University life throws up interesting bits of knowledge.

Yesterday, I attended a lecture given by Simon de Cartagena, a senior from Cadiz. He spoke on the subject of the voyages of Columbus. He had attended a public lecture given by the navigator just after he returned from that new land.

He said the man looked like a great navigator: confident, dressed like a prince, with liveried servants nearby.

But he had nothing to say about the science of the sea. No mention of latitude, currents, declination of the sun. No mention of even an astrolabe. No science at all.

Columbus talked of his voyage as if, by some miracle, he had been guided to that new land by the Holy Mother.

De Cartagena tried to question the navigator but his questions were brushed aside.

He said if he hadn't seen the two strange-looking men Columbus brought from that new land, he would have believed the great man was living a dream.

I have written to Father and told him this odd story.

Mother, I await your letters from Jerusalem. Each morning at Mass I pray for your safety.

Your son with deep respect,

Sancio

Fifth Sunday after Easter.

Famagusta, Cyprus
June 3, 1496

Dear Isabetta,

We have struck sail in one of the richest cities on the pilgrim route. There is a brisk trade carried on from the deck; the mariners have dragged from the hold barrels of Venetian glass, damask and satin; all the crew is involved, including the captain. The Master, Agostino Contarini, has left the galley and gone ashore. The famous Cyprus wine and malmsey is being loaded aboard.

And we were told the pilgrim ship was forbidden to trade!

Cypriots seem to be neither Greek, Saracen nor any other race, but a mixture of all.

Young men of wealth prance around on magnificent horses, the tips of their tails dyed all colours of the rainbow. There is a look of decadence about them – the young men, not the horses (well, maybe the horses too) – which is just beginning to show its face at home in the shape of the Companions of the Hose.

Prostitutes go about weighed down with jewels. I have been told they own houses as richly set up as any Cornaro palace. Obviously men pay dearly for their favours.

When I lift my eyes I see in every direction evidence of the crusaders; they left massive forts they handed off to the unfortunate Lusignan Kings.

Somewhere to the south-west is Nicosia, where Caterina Cornaro buried the last of those kings; buried her infant son and shed her crown and adopted country at the insistence of the Collegio, and with the help of her brother Zorzi.

Did you know Caterina has kept her title as Queen of Jerusalem? And uses it!

Later in the day:

We promised ourselves we would stay aboard ship and be true pilgrims, as the Friars are doing, but after a few hours in the stinking harbour of Famagusta, Paola, Nurse and I agreed we were courting illness and went in search of an inn for a bath, meal, a good night's sleep. All are to be had at the rate of fifty scudi per night, which includes our clothes washed, but it is a great scandal of a price.

In the morning we are off to Jaffa. Maybe there I will become a pilgrim and not run away, every chance I get, from the dirt, noise, rancid food.

Bless you, my dear Isabetta. Bless your family.

Mathye

Monday after the second Sunday after Pentecost.

Off Jaffa
June 6, 1496

My darling husband,

Two hours ago the crow's nest called down: *Land ho!*

Everybody raced to the gunwales. No land could be seen, but the entire ship erupted in the Te Deum; musical instruments of all shapes were dragged from the hold; we danced, sang, prayed; some of us threw ourselves on our knees and wept; the professional pilgrims looked the other way.

The music and dance is still going on. Like a few other cautious souls, Nurse and I – Paola is still in the dance – pulled ourselves away to make sure we have our belongings packed.

We will take a few changes of linen and a pillow for the donkey ride. We have had no rain since Famagusta and everything we carry with us has been worn at least twice.

In anticipation of stepping onto the soil of the Holy Land we have put on our pilgrim robes, which give the impression of cleanliness.

There is another mad dash to the gunwales. I believe our pilgrimage is about to begin.

Dearest Giovanni, it is you and our sons my voice will name before all the holy shrines.

Mathye
Feast of Corpus Christi.

Jaffa
June 7, 1496

My darling husband,

We have arrived at Jaffa.

We tried to kiss the holy ground but the Saracens kept prodding us forward. We were made to line up in the boiling sun to have our names written down and be given a ticket we must keep with us at all times.

St Peter's caves really are used for stabling donkeys; we had to clean the dung from our sleeping area. Job sat upon it; we sleep in the smell of it.

We had not finished making a space when the Saracens started to arrive in droves; they set up a regular bazaar outside the doors. We could have bought anything and everything to make the night more pleasant: rolls of muslin, soap, fresh water, and fresh food prepared on the spot.

A Saracen cooked us a supper of goat's meat and greens.

They slaughtered the goat before our eyes. With a good meal in our stomachs we were ready for the first night stuffed in the caves.

Once inside, we were not allowed out. I heard that some people crept out during the night and were screamed at, had to pay five scudi to get back in – there are worse things than sleeping in a donkey byre.

Today the Saracens have returned, again the bazaar is set up. The Saracens are fond of grabbing us by the cloak and demanding we buy whatever it is they have in their stalls.

Although donkeys are provided as a part of the cost of our ticket, today the place is overrun with drovers who want us to hire their donkeys which, they tell us, are fat and nothing like the hungry ones we will be given tomorrow.

We did not buy.

My darling, we are so far from each other.

May our Lord and His Holy Mother have you in their care.

Mathye

Friday after the Feast of Corpus Christi.

Jaffa
June 7, 1496

Lodovico, my dear son,

We have been in Jaffa a night and a day.

Jaffa: the home of Tabitha, disciple of Jesus, friend of Saint Peter.

The Bible states that when Tabitha died, friends went with the sad news to Peter who left his mission just down the road at Lydda, and came here, 'straightaway'.

He walked in on the women gathered round the body of Tabitha, admiring and weeping over tunics and other clothes she had sewed: a gentle way to mourn the dead.

Peter knelt and prayed. Rising, he called Tabitha's name. She opened her eyes and he helped her to her feet.

With his friend again among the living, you would have

thought he would have gone back down the road to Lydda –
he tarried a while at Jaffa – stayed at the home of Simon the
Tanner. I like to imagine he stayed for Tabitha's sake; to comfort
her, to reassure her.

I believe there is not a gentler story in the Bible than this.

My dear Lodovico, the city that was Jaffa has disappeared;
there are a few walls, a few ruins; there are Peter's caves where
we pilgrims wait for our guides to make ready for the journey
to Jerusalem.

These caves are all that is left of the home of Simon the
Tanner.

Last night, as I cleaned dung from the few feet of space I
was given for my bed, I tried to imagine Simon and his wife
taking their evening meal with Peter – where I was about to
try for a night's sleep.

My imagination failed me.

When I had spread the sweet-smelling rushes, bought from
the Saracen for five scudi, I hardly had my head on the floor
before I slept.

I dreamed Simon the Tanner came into the room and looked
around in the most quizzical way – as if wondering what the
crowd was doing in his home.

Simon wore an apron, like tanners at home.

My dear son, may Saint Peter strengthen you.

Your Mother

Friday after the Feast of Corpus Christi.

Jerusalem
June 9, 1496

My darling husband,

Oh blessed day!

Outside Jerusalem we were ordered off our donkeys.
Christians are not allowed to ride past Saracen cemeteries.

At the Fish Gate we removed our shoes, crossed our arms

over our hearts, bowed our heads and, singing the Te Deum, we passed into the Holy City.

Tired though I was, and hot after the long journey through the desert, my heart lifted; I all but ran up the long road leading to the Church of the Holy Sepulchre.

In the forecourt of that sacred Church our group threw ourselves on our knees; some lay in a swoon, others wandered around beating their breasts; even the professional pilgrims went down on one knee.

You can be certain you and Sebastian were in my mind as I trod that holy ground.

The power of the place was extreme; I wanted to remain prostrated on the cool white tiles. There was no possibility of staying; we were rounded up by our guides who were contracted to deliver us to our lodgings before sunset. They were obviously tired of us and all but harried us through the streets.

The Convent of the Franciscan Nuns is just beyond the Dome of the Rock. We were one of the first groups to be enveloped in kindness – and warm baths. We had sent our clothes ahead by our drovers; they were already washed.

There are only eight other pilgrims at this Convent. We have been given cool rooms with balconies, on the second floor.

I will go to bed in clean sheets.

The meal, this first night, was veal served with the most delicious local wine.

Will it be possible to hold on to my plenary indulgence in the midst of a luxury I now appreciate?

Be assured, my dear husband, it is you and our son who will be in my mind during this holy time.

Mathye
Third Sunday after Pentecost.

My darling husband,

Yesterday we stayed close to our beds.

The trundle through the heat of the desert was more exhausting than I expected.

In the evening, accompanied by the Friars, we went back to the Church of the Holy Sepulchre.

We spent the night in vigil, locked in that hallowed Church. The Saracens lock the doors to control the collection of the entry fee.

The interior of the Church is under the supervision of the Franciscans who give the homily and set the rules for the vigil, including a warning not to chip pieces from the shrines or to carve our names on the posts.

Not all pilgrims are Venetians, after all!

We lit our candles and, singing hymns, followed the Franciscans from shrine to shrine. I held the rosary beads I am bringing to you, our sons, the servants.

The crowd jostled and shoved, Paola and I put Nurse between us to keep her from getting crushed; Friar Venier went in front and Friar Pivello behind. In that holy place I often found myself sticking out an elbow.

There are numerous side-altars in the Church of the Holy Sepulchre, and Mass is said continuously by priests of all the Christian rites: Maronites, Romans, Byzantines, Greeks, Nestorians – others I didn't recognise.

The pillar where Christ was bound and whipped is worn away by the lips and hands of earlier pilgrims and is now enclosed by an iron railing; this didn't prevent people from sticking their hands through, and howls were heard as those behind pushed forward.

We heard Mass and received the Blessed Eucharist where the soldiers cast lots for Christ's robe. The Mass was almost ruined for me – two young priests of the Maronite rite were arguing vociferously about which of them was assigned the altar; it finally got sorted out by our Franciscan and some measure of peace and sanctity was restored.

At the spot where Christ appeared to Mary Magdalene after His resurrection – when she mistook Him for the gardener – we met our English Pilgrim; she was in a high state of ecstasy. She asked us where we were staying; holy as I think she might be, and holy as the place was, I faltered in reply; I could not have survived had she shown up at our convent.

The last shrine visited was the chapel of the True Cross where Saint Helena, mother of the Emperor Constantine, was supposed to have found the Cross on which Christ was crucified.

The pillars are covered in drops of water, in eternal grief, it is said, at the scenes they have witnessed.

My heart wrenched.

The doors of the Church of the Holy Sepulchre were thrown open at first light. We were unceremoniously herded out by the Saracens. After a night reflecting on those sacred events, it was disorienting to be tumbled so suddenly into the day.

We three went back to the convent. The Dominicans, hardy souls, went on to other sites around the city.

At each Mass I pray to God for your safety and that of our son.

Mathye
Feast of Saint Barnabas, disciple.

DIARII
Jerusalem
June 12, 1496
The nun who runs this convent told me she was here in 1452 – during the Muslim persecution. She was in hiding for five years.

Convents, monasteries, churches were desecrated. All Christians went in hiding, fled, or were massacred.

The Religious Orders have been trickling back and are tolerated – in small numbers – to care for pilgrims.
Wednesday after the third Sunday after Pentecost.

DIARII
Jerusalem, Convent of the Franciscans
June 13, 1496
My husband and son are on the Western Sea looking for a shortcut to the wealth of the East.

I am in Jerusalem praying they do not find it!
Feast of Saint Anthony.

Jerusalem
June 13, 1496

My darling husband,

Our Franciscan convent is on Mount Zion. From the balcony I see the Dome of the Rock.

I faltered at the first sight of the mosque raised on the site of Solomon's Temple.

Last night the dome danced in light; it is the one great architectural wonder in Jerusalem; even seeing it from this distance dazzles. The Abbess told me it was built by a Greek Master.

The forecourt has a white marble pavement and appears to stand in a pool of bluish milk.

We, the infidel, are not allowed near, unless prepared to bribe and take the consequence. You here, you would have wrapped on a turban, strolled inside, and no one would have noticed your blue eyes. I, who could easily disguise myself as a Muslim woman, would never dare such a feat.

My darling husband, I was so affected by a mosque on the site of Solomon's Temple – where Jesus lived so much of his public life – I wrote this poem to console myself.

CANTICLE OF ANNA THE PROPHET

Listen, it was an ordinary day:

For no reason, I put on my violet dress, my green cloak, my red shoes; left my house, pushed through the throngs still flooding into the Temple.

As I passed near the pillars I saw there a young couple doing for their son according to the Law. The two turtle doves cooed pitifully.

Moved by so meagre a gift, I stopped and looked into the delicate face of the child about to meet his first tribulation. As I contemplated his sweet features, a voice within me cried out:

This is the One who will go before the Face of the Lord for the redemption of Israel.

This is the One who has been proclaimed from ancient times.

This is the One who will make the early and later rains come down on us.

Rejoice, daughters of Zion, shout Israel and be glad, for the Desired of nations has come, and this House is filled with glory and peace.

Marvelling at what I had heard from my own mouth, I left the startled young family and went into the Temple and, from that day, remained there, in contemplation of that Voice that proclaimed the knowledge of the Living God.

My darling husband, to be a Jew in Jerusalem and be barred from the Dome of the Rock must be an exquisite form of perpetual mourning.

Your wife who loves you,

Mathye

Feast of Saint Anthony of Padua.

DIARII
Jerusalem
June 14, 1496
Have placed the last caravel on my chart.

If Giovanni's calculations were right – winds with him – he has reached the land of the East.

I try to imagine the strange sights he is seeing.

I imagine only water.
Feast of Saint Methodius.

DIARII
Jerusalem
June 16, 1496
Jerusalem without my husband?

Jerusalem because of my husband!
Fourth Sunday after Pentecost.

Jerusalem
June 17, 1496

My darling husband,

As used as I am to seeing families of Muslims in the streets of Venice, I know very little of the way they live. My knowledge is improving: I can see the flat roof of a home from my balcony; in the evening the family comes there for their meal. The women, without their veils, do a ritual dance when the meal is over. All the women join in, old and young.

They are accompanied by the most wild and piercing pipes, but the dance is dignified; sometimes it goes on for an hour.

The men sit cross-legged on the floor and watch, or do not watch. Afterwards, the family spreads their bedclothes and sleeps on the roof.

That event, so familial, I wept the first time I saw it.

The Great Spirit of God protect you and our son and bring you safely home.

Mathye
Monday after the fourth Sunday after Pentecost.

My dear son Sancio,

I know you have opened the enclosed set of drawings even before you read my letter. Let me tell you what they are, and how I got them.

Yesterday, we went to Ramat Rachel, outside Jerusalem, to hear Mass at the Hagia Zion, a synagogue from the time of Christ, although much repaired and now used as a church.

When we came out, there was a young man making drawings. In the crush of people I almost fell over him; I stopped, apologised.

He told me he was making a sketch of the synagogue; he was going to build a similar one in his home town, in Macedonia. He said he had borrowed the original plans from the priest, had copied them, that this was his last set of drawings.

I asked him if he would make another set of the originals; I would pay him well. He agreed.

My dear son, you have the plans of one of the earliest built synagogues in Jerusalem.

I pray for you at each of the shrines, and at the most famous ones I light a candle for your intentions.

Your Mother, who holds you in her heart
Feast of Saint Alban.

Jerusalem
June 22, 1496

Dear Isabetta,

There is a criminal trade in relics going on here. Neither Nurse, Paola nor I have bought any, but the Friars are bringing home a great stack. We had a small quarrel: I indicated the good Dominicans were being naïve.

Naïve! Don't we study for years before we are let out of the priory? Don't we preach to the multitudes? Don't we speak all the languages of the universe?

I suggested none of these things had anything to do with the fact they were buying human parts from grave robbers. I did make them see, and they did concede that yes, the Saracens make a business of it. The quarrel died down.

They let us know they would be looking for more relics, we might as well go on our own.

We enjoy seeing the holy places at a slower pace. The three of us formed a safe fellowship. Often we meet other pilgrims from the galley who are visiting the same shrines and travel a while with them.

Be assured I pray for you and your family.

Mathye

Saturday after the fourth Sunday after Pentecost.

Jerusalem
June 23, 1496

My dear son Sebastian,

Among the many adventures we are having at Jerusalem is a daily visit to the wonderful markets, at the behest of cousin Paola. After a number of such forays, I too am caught up in the fun.

Nurse frowns.

These markets are crowded, dirty, noisy, but wonderfully joyful.

I have found a musical instrument of rare beauty for you. It is a monochord, but one that has never been seen at Venice. It is made of ebony; the pitch is controlled by a horn-shaped attachment at the end of the staff. When I asked the mercer, I was told a caravan leader brought it across the desert with the spices.

I have played it. It has a sound not heard in our world – very high-pitched, but sweet.

It unscrews into three parts and fits neatly into a cedar box.

Dear son, I pray your journey will be a joyful one.

Your Mother

Fifth Sunday after Pentecost.

My darling husband,

The Dominicans, who are interested in collecting relics, have gone off on their own; we are reduced to a merry band of three.

The nuns assured us it is safe. The Saracens depend on pilgrims for gold. And the penalty for harming a pilgrim is severe – the loss of a finger, a hand or a head.

We start each morning with our list of shrines.

We have been stopped only once. Three young Saracens, on the road to Ramat Rachel, suddenly appeared out of a ditch. They formed a line across the road. I started to walk up to them as if to walk through them. Nurse uttered a sound I recognised as a warning. I stopped.

As usual, they wanted money; any time or any place we may be halted by Saracens with a demand for a fee.

So we wouldn't be fleeced by such robbers, the three of us devised a scheme: we each bought the poorest and smallest of purses; we keep a few aspers in them. The rest of our money we keep inside our pilgrim robes.

We planned, if stopped, Nurse would produce silent tears, which I discovered she can do on demand, and we would pull out these mean little purses, with our little bit of money.

This time we rummaged for the two aspers each of the robbers demanded. I found mine after digging in the lining. Paola produced hers. Nurse had only one in her purse. The robber who took it threw it back at her.

They disappeared into the countryside.

Nurse picked up her coin.

We joined a large fellowship from Pest for the return trek.

My beloved husband, be safe.

Mathye

Feast of Saint John the Baptist, son of Elizabeth.

DIARII
Jerusalem
June 25, 1496

Isaiah wrote four thousand years ago: *As a mother comforts her child, so will I comfort you; you shall be comforted in Jerusalem.*

Yes, yes I am.

Feast of Saint William, abbot.

Jerusalem
June 25, 1496

Lodovico, my dear son,

We have been ten days in the Holy City. We have visited all the holy places; we have seen the important sites.

Today we were at Ein Kerem, the town in the hill country of Judea, where Mary visited her kinswoman, Elizabeth, after the Angel Gabriel told her she was to become the Mother of the Messiah.

We could not persuade the Friars to come with us.

The nuns packed us a lunch of figs, dates, almonds and quinces.

The three of us took our pilgrim staffs and trudged up the hilly road. We got pointed at by a family of Saracens; they did us no harm; we went on our way.

As a young girl, I used to think Mary must have been uneasy, alone, on that road. Maybe she was; Jerusalem was an occupied city, then as now; there must have been Roman soldiers everywhere. When we walked the three miles today, chatting all the way and enjoying the lovely country air, it seemed just a pleasant stroll.

Ein Kerem is also the place, tradition has it, that Elizabeth hid with John the Baptist when she was fleeing from Herod's soldiers, who were killing the boy-babies.

As I prayed for my sons in the church built on this site, though much damaged by time and the recent Muslim persecution, I thought how terrified Elizabeth must have been, trying to hide herself with a young baby who might cry at any time.

It was dark and cool inside. My mind was flooded with thoughts of the events that have taken place there. I wrote a poem. It is for you and Alessandra – you will know when to give it to her.

ELIZABETH
There was no shade;
All day there was no shade;
I sat in the doorway – limp.

Why did I look to that spot in the distance,
Where the light flickered and weaved in the dust,
 moved with purpose?
It was my young cousin coming to me out of the light,
Carrying the light,
Being the light.

My soul shivered.
My body, fused with a resurrection joy, rose off the
 ground.
The child in my womb leapt.

While still far off I called out:
 Blessed are you among women
 And blessed is the fruit of your womb.

In a swirl of green light she came to me singing.
I clapped my hands; we met in a dance of joy.
In that moment I thought I looked into the Mind of
 God.

My dear son, I pray for you and Alessandra at all the shrines.
  Your Mother
Tuesday after the fifth Sunday after Pentecost.

My darling husband,

I have bought you a gift.

After the Friars left us, Paola, who has discovered a great fondness for markets, insisted we stop at one a day. Nurse is appalled and scolds us about bringing home other people's cast-offs.

We go anyway.

I found an astrolabe – not just any fifteenth-century astrolabe, but an elliptical one with large elliptical circles bearing the signs of the Zodiac.

A star chart is attached to the sphere with pointers for nineteen fixed stars. I have never seen the like of it. The Saracen I bought it from said it was new and made in Azerbaijan.

Isn't that a grand find?

May the Holy Trinity guide you, and our son.

Mathye
Feast of Saint Maxentius, hermit.

Jerusalem
June 26, 1496

My dear son Lodovico,

Today, my penultimate in Jerusalem, I have found a gift for you.

We came upon a small store run out of the front of a house by a very old Saracen.

I was looking at some parchment fragments of the Gospels, written in Greek. They looked old.

The man got up from his stool.

What are you seeking?

My son is studying to be a canon lawyer. I am looking for a gift.

He went to the back of his shop and returned with a small parcel wrapped in leather. He opened it before me.

When I raised my eyes and looked into his, he knew I knew the value of it.

I doubt if I can afford it.

Name me a price.

I said what I thought it was worth.

Then you shall have it.

No, I don't have that kind of money with me.

How much do you have?

I emptied my purse. I had only half the value.

For your son the canon lawyer.

He wrapped up the gift.

I thanked him as best I could and walked away with my treasure.

Open it, my beloved son.

You will see an exquisite illuminated copy of the Gospel According to Saint John, in the Greek language.

I asked the old Saracen where it had come from.

He told me Constantinople, that it had been in his family since that city fell to his people in 1453. Saracen though he was, he loved it and knew the value of it.

And so will you.

Now I will have to borrow from Paola to pay the various bribes on the way to Jaffa.

My dear Lodovico, I have made this pilgrimage to this City of God that your father and brother may come home safely to us.

But you too have been in my thoughts and prayers, constantly.

Your Mother
Feast of Saint Maxentius.

My darling husband,

My last day in Jerusalem.

I visited all the shrines commemorating the life and times of Our Saviour. I heard many Masses. I lit candles – all for your safety, for the safety of our son.

Paola and Nurse were the best of companions: Nurse, stolid and determined; Paola, cheerful, drinking more wine than she might, taking part in any frivolity – a different woman than at home.

I occasionally scribbled a line as we rested on a wall, in the shade of a tree.

Each evening we arrived exhausted at the convent, ate our supper, washed off the dust of the day, wrote our letters, fell into bed.

We leave for Ramleh first light.

Nurse, Paola and I will each take a berth in the sterncastle on our return.

I have to confess, I can't take the smell in the great cabin. The heat I can put up with, the noise I can bear – the arguments, the fights.

The smell makes me sick.

Paola says she will take first class accommodation as a penance and come with us. Nurse, of course, never believed we should have been below deck.

So it's to first class.

I have a sizable packet of letters to send off to you when I reach Famagusta. They will serve until we tell our news in each other's arms.

May the Spirit of God guide you and our son.

Mathye

Thursday after the fifth Sunday after Pentecost.

DIARII
Jerusalem, the Franciscan convent
June 28, 1496
Venice!

We leave for Venice!
Feast of Saint Irenaeus.

DIARII
Pilgrim Galley
July 7, 1496
More water for washing in the sterncastle than for drinking in the great cabin.

How quickly forgotten the rigours of the outward voyage! The creature comforts satisfied; the air fresh; I am lulled.

I think of my life, my dear ones, with the fondest feelings. My head swims with music.

Paola is bored. She enjoyed the rough and tumble of the great cabin.

Nurse is at ease.
Seventh Sunday after Pentecost.

DIARII
Off Negroponte
July 26, 1496
Flutterings of unease visit me as we near home.

Where is my husband?

Where has he taken our son?
Feast of Saint Pelagius.

DIARII
Off Corfu
July 31, 1496
How will I live without sons at home?

Will Venice be enough?

Will music save me?
Feast of Saint Neot.

DIARII
Off Zara
August 4, 1496
I've added it up – in our twenty years of marriage, Giovanni
and I have spent less than six together.

   We had no daughter.

   Giovanni said he will leave the sea in 1500.

   He will be 45. I will be 41.

   Tempus fugit.
Eleventh Sunday after Pentecost.

Chapter Six

My darling husband,

Yesterday we sailed up the Grand Canal – sun glinting off houses, spires, golden cupolas.

Sublime!

Everyone on the galley seemed to be playing a musical instrument. The Doge was on the Piazzetta with his musicians.

A grand cacophony.

Half Venice was out to greet and touch us. Every relative was there, all the servants. Nurse, Paola and I were squeezed within an inch of our lives.

It was good to be home.

There were at least a hundred Dominicans to welcome Friars Venier and Pivello.

The procession to San Marco's – the pilgrims directly behind the Doge, the rest in order of ecclesiastic rank – took a half hour to form and go off.

We sang the Te Deum all the way – repeated it three times.

All the relatives were at our house after the thanksgiving Mass. I stayed up half the night telling my story, giving presents.

My darling husband, I have made the pilgrimage to the Holy Land for your safety.

I have returned to Venice. Everyone I love dearly is not here.

How anxiously I await your letters!

May the Spirit of God be with you and our son.

Mathye

Feast of Saint Xystus II, philosopher, under seal.

DIARII
Venice
August 10, 1496
Time grinds slowly.

More anxious in Venice than I was at Jerusalem.

Paola reverted to her cheerless self.

Adriana grieves.

Feast of Saint Lawrence.

My darling husband,

I haven't seen you in a year and a half; it is a great torture.

It is a torture to walk by your picture.

How to bear it?

Lodovico is gone.

Sebastian is gone.

Sancio is gone.

Isabetta is gone.

Alvise is dead.

Have you my letters from Jerusalem?

God keep you and our son safe, wherever you are on the sphere.

Mathye

Twelfth Sunday after Pentecost, under seal.

My darling wife,

Ecce homo!

I arrived back at Bristol on August 9th.

And, my brave wife, you have been to Jerusalem!

Brava!

I have none of your letters from the Holy Lands. I yearn for them.

On August 12th, King Henry came to Bristol. I had to appear before him to explain myself.

I did not have a short route to the East in my pocket, but

had certain knowledge that the Eastern land I am seeking is there – almost exactly where I have forecast.

This is what happened:

We left Bristol on May 20th, put in at Dursey Head, Ireland, on the 26th. We left Dursey Head the 29th and battered our way along the fifty-second parallel for thirty days with wind and rainstorms almost every day. My mariners were beginning to wear down with the constant struggle to keep the caravel from foundering.

When we passed the halfway mark of our food rations, the men began to grumble.

I went among them and ordered that we sail westward for two more days. If nothing showed on the horizon, we would turn for home. They could count as well as I and knew we would be on short rations before we reached Bristol. They weren't happy but I believed I could trust them.

The next day the winds dropped. We were almost becalmed. About noon the crow's nest spotted something off our starboard quarter. We turned, saw it was the trunk of a large tree, larger than any I have seen anywhere in these northern lands. I sent one of the mariners overboard; he got a rope around it, dragged it in.

You can imagine the excitement.

The wind didn't freshen for six hours. I paced the deck like a wild man. I kept a mariner in the crow's nest for six watches. No land or anything else was sighted. I asked for another day.

There was not one man among them prepared to continue the voyage.

I gritted my teeth, ordered the helmsman to turn the ship and, with the wind on our stern, we headed home.

On the Feast of Saint Radegund I was invited to supper with the King. Sebastian and my chief backers were with me. The King was at Saint Augustine's Abbey. I had the tree-trunk delivered that day. After we ate, and I gave an account of the voyage, we went to view it.

You can imagine it was not what I had planned to present to the King, but he is a practical man – if he was disappointed, he did not show it.

In fact, he turned to me before the assembled group and told me I was to go again next year – find what is out there.

My dearest wife, my future is sealed for another year.

Another year without you. How I long for you.

Sebastian left for Sagres on the Feast of Saint Lawrence. He conducted himself bravely on the voyage; he will not have many trips that are rougher. If I ever doubted he was destined for the sea, this voyage convinced me otherwise.

He knows his seamanship and practises it wisely. His one weakness is a flaring temper.

I hope maturity will take care of that.

May the Divine Light surround you and bless our sons.

Giovanni

Vigil of the Assumption.

DIARII
Venice
September 23, 1496

Thanks be to the loving and Holy Mother of the Infinite God, Giovanni and Sebastian are safe; they haven't found a short route to the spices and silks of the East.

Every hour of the hard pilgrim's way to Jerusalem was worth it!

Feast of Saint Linus.

DIARII
Venice
September 24, 1496

Carlo made no decisions while I was away. Rii walls need repairs. Guido asked him three times.

Money sitting in the Monte Vecchio not invested, three months' interest lost.

If Carlo weren't named in my father's Will, I would fire him.

Feast of Our Lady of Mercy.

DIARII
Venice
September 25, 1496
Guido – with an odd little story.

At the White Lion Inn sometime in July, having a peaceful glass, he was approached by a stranger asking about Giovanni.

Guido – suspicious – told him he knew nothing of his master's travels.

The stranger kept insisting.

When he left, Guido asked the innkeeper where the man was from, was told – Castile.

I will tell this to Giovanni – he will push it aside.

Feast of Saint Finbar, patron of Cork.

DIARII
Venice
September 26, 1496
I have started to compose a Jubilation Mass – postponed the Requiem – already a draft for the Kyrie Eleison is ready.

The Credo will be plain chant. The Alleluia polyphonic, maybe six voices.

The voices of the Jews in the synagogues at Jerusalem still ring in my ears.

Had forgotten Christianity is an Eastern religion. Our plain chants echo the voices of the Temple.

Yesterday, I worked five hours without rest. When I raised my head I staggered, fumbled my way from the room.

This morning worked another three.

I haven't been asked for a Mass. After all these years, after all my sins, after Jerusalem, I am ready.

If I keep this pace, it should be finished by Easter.

Yes, it will make a triumphal Easter Sunday Mass.

Feast of Saint Justina.

My dear brother, the lawyer,

Your brother, the sailor, has been consorting with kings – at least with one king – at least I was in the room with him. I shook his hand.

He confirmed for me I was the Navigator's son.

You, young man, are the Navigator's son.

In my best Venetian-accented English, and a smart little bow:
Sire!

Our fortune, I thought, as I looked into his crafty eyes, is in the hands of this man. I put on display all my flashy teeth.

He moved on.

Do you think this will get me a line in the history books? Or will it be you – labouring over some illuminated manuscript from the tenth century with all the modesty you are famous for – who will shed light on some obscure clause in some obscure canon law, and grab the footnote, and poor old Sebastian with the wealth of the East in his coffers, forgotten.

No, I'm to be the famous Caboto! After the Navigator! You're the scholar; so mind you keep producing scholarship, modestly!

Fame hasn't come from this voyage. We beat our way up and down the fifty-second parallel for thirty days, storm-driven all the way.

Father was for going on, but the crew was already anticipating empty bellies for part of the return voyage.

Father said he could smell the land. I couldn't smell land, but on the one clear evening, I was sure I saw the reflection of land in the heavens.

Now here is the good news: Father has the King's command to go on another voyage next year.

Here's the tragedy: he won't take me!

He wants me to finish my studies at Sagres and doesn't want the constraint of having to turn homeward to get me on land in time to catch a boat to Portugal.

I spit fireballs!

But I put my tail between my not unmanly legs and hived off to Sagres, where the Portuguese King keeps his school for budding navigators.

This father of ours will, however, allow me to spend my summer holiday in Bristol next year.

I will go!

Give my most respectful regards to your intended wife when next you meet.

Your brother,

Sebastian

Thursday after the eighteenth Sunday after Pentecost, under seal.

Bristol
September 26, 1496

My darling wife,

Already the planning for next year's voyage has begun. Robert Thorne, one of my backers, will provide a new caravel.

He has given me the privilege of naming her and if you agree I will call her the MATHYE.

She is a proud ship. You won't be disappointed, my darling wife, to have your name on her. She should be finished by February next.

This new voyage will start in early May.

My darling Mathye, you have sailed to the Holy Lands; will you not consider coming to me in Bristol?

This city is not the trading centre of the world like Venice, nor does it have frequent religious spectacles in its public squares, but it has a rustic charm and you could be inspired to write a different kind of music here.

Mathye, you must think of it.

I pray each night you will be with me.

Giovanni

Thursday after the eighteenth Sunday after Pentecost, under seal.

My darling wife,

I hope you will come to Bristol. I would like you to be with me when I meet the King to receive my new Letters Patent – an event carried out with some ceremony. Do you think you and our sons can be here for a period before I leave?

I now have your letters from Jerusalem. They are full as a nut. I read them with great delight.

Richard Americ and his wife, Phillipa, invited friends for supper to hear them. I had to read many twice. Their children were there. I drew a rough mappamundo to give them a clearer picture of your pilgrimage route.

I will, my darling wife, enjoy your letters many times over during the long Bristol nights.

May the Trinity guard you always.

Giovanni

Feast of Saint Cosmas, under seal.

DIARII

Venice

October 22, 1496

We have come to it! Bristol! That wild northern land where everything shrivels and stiffens with cold.

How will I survive it? How will I survive another year without my husband?

Feast of Saint Salome.

DIARII

Venice

October 23, 1496

If I don't go to Bristol and Giovanni finds a short route to the spices of the East I will be found one day with a dagger in my neck!

DIARII
Venice
October 24, 1496

I will steel my nerve.

I will leave my home so full of all good things.

I will leave my choir – the balm of my soul.

I will leave Venice where my eyes are made glad with each bend in the Canal.

I will be with my husband.

I will be with my sons.

I will be happy.

Yes.

I will!

Feast of Saint Felix.

Venice
October 24, 1496

My darling husband,

Your letters inviting us to be with you in Bristol have arrived.

The seals were tampered with.

Whoever opened them read of a man inviting his wife and family to visit him in a foreign land.

Yes, I will come to Bristol.

I have written to our sons.

I plan to join our family galley for the February run to London.

I am honoured you will place my name on the ship that will take you into the future. Thank you, my darling.

We will be together at Paschaltide.

God be with you and bless you.

Mathye

Feast of Saint Felix, under seal.

Post Scriptum

Charles VIII and his army went back over the Alps early October after a few slight skirmishes, in which our mercenaries were engaged.

DIARII
Venice
October 27, 1496
When I think of being with my husband, Bristol seems tolerable.
Twenty-third Sunday after Pentecost.

DIARII
Venice
November 3, 1496
Told Paola I am going to Bristol – she appeared perplexed.

Have never known what to expect from Paola.
Twenty-fourth Sunday after Pentecost.

Bristol
November 22, 1496

My darling wife,

Your letter brought me great joy. Now all the world is mine.
I went out and rented a house.

I took all my backers for a feast at The Barbary Inn at Redcliffe Highway. Not a savoury area, but they have the best cook in Bristol. We drank a cask of good Cyprus wine in your honour.

I will be on sea trials in March and will bring the MATHYE to London to meet your galley.

And the astrolabe has arrived. It is a wonder. I can believe it came out of Azerbaijan, as that country has had an astronomical school for many centuries. Be sure I will take it on my great voyage to the East. Thank you for bringing it all the way from Jerusalem for me. It is a great prize.

God bless you, my darling wife, on this Saint Cecilia's Day, patron of musicians. You and our sons cannot come too soon.

Giovanni
Feast of Saint Cecilia, patron of musicians, under seal.

Dear Father,

Mother writes that you would like all your sons to be with you in Bristol for the start of your new venture. I have looked at my situation from every perspective with the intention of fulfilling your request. I find it impossible at this time in my life to go to England.

I have two and a half years of university work to finish at Pisa. I cannot afford to take even one week away from my studies.

As you know, I have asked a young woman to marry me. She and her parents have agreed. Our marriage will take place as soon as I have finished my arts degree.

Sir, I can hear all your suggestions for postponing our marriage, but Florence is not a city in which you postpone a marriage ceremony. I met there a crowd of educated and much too wealthy young men who spend all their money feasting and drinking, and Sir, they make sport of breaking up betrothals, though they take poor farm boys into their beds.

At least two of these men have asked for the hand of the woman I will marry. My intended wife will have nothing to do with them, but each one bears an ancient name, has great stretches of land and more money than a man needs. I have not grown to this age without realising that parents are very attracted by those things.

I do not forget, Sir, my mother's noble name, that I am seen as a suitable husband; yet I would be deeply concerned to postpone my marriage.

It is injudicious for a son to quote the Bible to his father, but it is written that a man must leave his father and mother and cleave to his wife.

I am sure, Sir, you will be successful on this new voyage. I will pray for you and your mariners.

I am, Sir, your respectful son,

Lodovico

Feast of Saint Cecilia, under seal.

My darling wife,

Has Canon Leonardo heard from Rome about the exploration treaty recently signed between the Catholic Monarchs and Portugal?

Thomas Canynges is as concerned as I am and believes we should know what this treaty contains.

How I await the galley from Venice!

May you be in the care of Our Lord and His Blessed Mother.

Giovanni

Feast of Saint Chrysogonus of Aquileia.

Venice
December 28, 1496

My darling husband,

The Treaties have been in Venice since August. Canon Leonardo forgot to tell me.

Yes, there are three of them. The Treaty of Alcáçovas, the Treaty of Toledo, and a new one: Treaty of Tordesillas.

The first two confirm what we know.

The new Treaty – Tordesillas, was signed in 1494; by it, a line was drawn 370 leagues west of Cape Verde, and everything to the east of that line belongs to Portugal, to the west – the Catholic Monarchs.

This Treaty was adjudicated by Pope Alexander VI. The Pope drew a line from pole to pole, as a knife slices an apple – he gave half the world to the Portuguese, the other to the Catholic Monarchs, for purposes of exploration.

But if all the unexplored land of the world and the water adjacent now belong either to the Catholic Monarchs or the King of Portugal, will these countries allow ships from other nations to sail in those waters?

My darling husband, will you be safe?

You must bring this Treaty to the attention of your King.

I keep you in my heart with my prayers as I turn my thoughts to being with you at Bristol.

Mathye

Feast of the Holy Innocents, under seal.

Bristol

January 26, 1497

My darling wife,

Thank you, my dear Mathye. You have reduced that dry treaty to its essence.

I have spent hours pondering why Portugal wanted their line of demarcation moved 370 leagues west of Cape Verde.

The only logical conclusion I have come to is that Portugal, which has been sending navigators in that direction for the past fifty years, suspects or knows of new land there or, as you suggest, they have found, or they know of, a sea route to the East around Guinea.

Pray God it is not a short route to the East they have found.

The Portuguese are like the grave on all matters of discoveries.

King Henry has responded to the Treaty of Tordesillas. He has written to both the Catholic Monarchs and the King of Portugal. He told them he recognises all lands already discovered by their countries, but lands not yet discovered are as much the prize of England as any other. My new Letters Patent will say that.

I am no longer concerned with the Treaty of Tordesillas.

I trust in the Lord that you will come to me shortly.

Giovanni

Third Sunday after the Epiphany, under seal.

My darling husband,

Sancio and I will leave for Bristol on, or about, the feast of Saint Polycarp. We will be in a convoy of three galleys. I hope the French keep their pirate navy at bay.

Sebastian will join you after the third Sunday in Lent. I expect you have already heard from him.

I have had no letter from Lodovico. I am sure he has written to you.

I will take Gemma and Guido and hire other servants when we arrive.

I look forward to our visit to London Town – the Royal Court.

I look forward to having our family together again – a joy I did not anticipate.

I look forward to you.

My love and the Holy Mother's be in your heart.

Mathye

Wednesday after the third Sunday after the Epiphany, under seal.

DIARII
Venice
January 30, 1497
Last meeting with cousins Piero, Carlo.

Carlo will take over as Captain General of the two galleys to London – no galley to Constantinople.

Piero takes my place: supervises the Fraterna, the properties, including Montebelluna.

His chance to take his seat in the Senate – Paola has always wanted him to swagger – wear the scarlet toga.

Under Piero's supervision, Luigi will be responsible for the upkeep of our home, the garden and the meadow.

Done!

Feast of Saint Martina.

DIARII
Venice
February 2, 1497
This day after Mass – gave over the direction of my choir to Ana.

She decided to have a practice right then – begin preparation for the Passiontide cycle.

I went down the choir steps, dragged my feet back to the Canal – Guido waiting.

I will take to Bristol the pieces of the Jubilation Mass I have completed.

I will finish it.

I will.
Fourth Sunday after the Epiphany.

DIARII
Venice
February 5, 1497
Giovanni has sent me Lodovico's letter.

This the son so meek and mild?
Feast of Saint Agatha.

Venice
February 6, 1497

My dear Lodovico,

I have your letter to your father.

You were invited to be present when he receives his Letters Patent from the King of England – a great moment in his life.

I was surprised at your refusal.

I was amazed at the tenor of your reply.

Hear my words, my son.

Consider if that is the letter you want your father to carry into the vast unknown.

I am disappointed. I had hoped my family would be together – one last time – before you went your separate ways.

How we shall miss you in England!

God be with you.

Your Mother, who loves you even when you disappoint.

Feast of Saint Vedast, missionary, under seal.

DIARII

Venice

February 9, 1497

I have given orders:

Luigi, Cook, Nurse will stay at Venice.

Justina and the rest of the servants will go to Montebelluna, help set out the crops, give the peasants a respite.

Nobody is happy with this – all faces are long.

Fifth Sunday after the Epiphany.

DIARII

Venice

February 22, 1497

Thanks be to God!

Sancio is home!

The gloom in the house has lifted.

I wanted the servants to be at Montebelluna when I leave – suggested they go today, their faces became longer.

We will have the harrowing at the quay, then.

Saturday of Ember Week in Lent.

DIARII

Aboard the family galley

February 28, 1497

Already into the Adriatic!

Behind us – Venice, shimmering.

I leave – sighing.

Friday after the second Sunday in Lent.

DIARII
Off Zara
Family galley
March 2, 1497
When will I go home again?

Ahead is my husband!
Third Sunday in Lent.

DIARII
Off Palermo
March 13, 1497
Fourteenth day at sea.
Moving at a fast clip.

The oars not used since we rowed out from the Piazzetta.

Impressed with Cousin Carlo. He shines on the galley. Runs a tighter ship than Piero.

Well now!

Carlo thinks we will do just as well if we keep two galleys on the Flanders–London run, forget Constantinople.

Will look at our profits – may consider it if the French have stopped their warlike habits.
Feast of Saint Nicephorus, scholar.

DIARII
The Galley
March 16, 1497
Seventeenth day at sea.
A fierce wind struck off Lisbon. Mariners brailed up the sails.

For two days the oarsmen fought to keep the galley on course.

In the wind and rain we lost sight of the other galleys.

I stayed on my feet; rather enjoyed the dip of the galley into the waves, the tons of water above our heads, the wildness.

Gemma and Guido stayed in their bunks.

Sancio up after the first day.

Carlo said it was a typical Lisbon blow; have lost all speed we had made.

Will spend Easter Week on the open sea. Had hoped to be with Giovanni.

The crow's nest has signalled the two other galleys are just appearing over the horizon.

Fifth Sunday in Lent.

DIARII
The Galley
March 23, 1497
Twenty-fourth day at sea.
My husband has always come home to me.

I am going to him.

Yes!

Palm Sunday.

DIARII
The Galley
March 25, 1497
Twenty-sixth day at sea.
Donna Tron once told me her mother – ten years married, no children – went to London on her husband's galley, came home with child.

Feast of the Annunciation.

DIARII
The Galley
April 1, 1497
Have arrived in the Thames.

Dawn – the harbour pilot came aboard.

A dense fog – the sails drip clammy dampness.

Below deck, I hear the three hundred oarsmen chanting the vessel forward.

Carlo says we will be at quay-side in an hour.

In an hour I shall see my husband.

Two years!

Tuesday of Easter week.

DIARII
The George Inn, near Powels-Wharf, London
April 2, 1497
Could see nothing as the great galley glided into the quay.

The gangplank was put down – there was Giovanni at the foot. He has a beard!

He leaped up the plank – swung me off the deck.

You, then, are my husband?

Madam, I am.

We chuckled.

Sancio had turned his head. I had to point him out to Giovanni. He did not expect this tall young man. Sebastian has put on weight, looks strapping.
Wednesday of Easter week.

DIARII
The George Inn, London
April 5, 1497
I arrived wearing layers of silk. Giovanni had bought me a worsted cape with a hood.

To wear in bed: a long flannel dress. He wears one. We both looked a fright. I laughed.

Men are so fragile.

How do the English make babies, wearing so many clothes in bed – the streets are full of children.

I like my heavy cape. I let it swing open to catch those lovely cool breezes.

I have bought laced boots – sturdy, warm – they shield my feet from those rough roads.

I often kick small stones. My husband says only children kick stones. I tell him I feel as free as a child.

I continue to kick stones.
Saturday in Easter week.

DIARII
The George Inn, London
April 6, 1497
I am in harmony with the universe.
Second Sunday of Easter.

DIARII
The George, London
April 6, 1497
The *Mathye* is splendid.

Smells of fresh varnish.

Can eat off her deck.

When showing me around Giovanni asked:

Would you like to stand watch on your caravel?

Yes, I would!

Done then.

I will not let him change his mind.

I have ordered a plain worsted dress – a hat that will stay on in the wildest wind.

I look forward to sailing up to Bristol.

I do.
Second Sunday of Easter.

DIARII
The George, London
April 8, 1497
Giovanni shaved off his beard. It was like wire. Burned my face.

My, but he looked handsome. And a bit fierce.
Tuesday after the Second Sunday of Easter.

The George, near Powels Wharf, London
April 10, 1497

My dear Lodovico,

I am writing in the public room of The George, a moderately good inn.

Your father knows more people in London than I imagined; we are often entertained. Today, with Sebastian and Sancio, we were invited to The Tower: the great Royal fortress that sits on the Thames and protects the city.

This residence is not much used by the present Queen; it was in The Tower, in 1483, where Richard, Duke of Gloucester, did away with her two brothers – twelve-year-old Edward V, and his younger brother, Richard, Duke of York.

We went there with John de Burgh, a knight of Bath, who seems to have the freedom of the place. He is one of the Londoners who has taken a share in the *Mathye*.

We hired a boat with six rowers and a master; we paid two pence per rower and five pence for the master: about nine scudi. I tell you this because of your request for details.

The Tower is about an hour's row down the Thames – the great river that flows through London Town. We entered The Tower through a drawbridge set down into the river. The gate was raised by some thirty men; the boat was rowed inside the walls, up to the stone steps.

It was Sunday morning. There was a Mass starting in the Royal Chapel; we decided to fulfil our Sunday obligation.

This chapel is of pale yellow limestone and was built by William the Conqueror. It is richly frescoed with scenes from the lives of the Evangelists.

It has an atmosphere of great serenity, but as Mass proceeded, I was oppressed with the thought that two young princes were murdered somewhere on these grounds. I pity the Queen who, on occasion, has to come to The Tower and pray in that Chapel. It must not be a happy trip downriver.

After Mass we went to the Constable's house for breakfast; he is responsible for the day-to-day running of The Tower.

We ate with his family and servants in a great hall; they served a kind of blood pudding which was fried – I liked it – and a wine made from fermented honey they call mead; it was too sweet, I drank little. Your father and your brothers ate and drank with gusto.

Later in the morning, your father reviewed the upcoming voyage for the Constable and his family. They brought him parchment, he drew a mappamundo. He and his wife insisted their six children stay and listen to the 'Great Navigator'. We insisted Sebastian and Sancio roam about the fortress.

The Constable, who is a munitions man and has never been out of England, can hardly imagine the coast of Normandy. He looked at your father as if he were describing the ante-room to the stars.

He kept repeating:

Can that ever be possible? Can that ever be possible?

Their children took it for granted.

The Constable and his wife went with us about The Tower grounds. It is really a small village with a moat and inner and outer walls.

The main building, The White Tower, is the tallest building in England and the official home of the Royal Family. The Constable told us the court is constantly on the move.

The Tower grounds has a mint, munitions buildings, hospital, and houses for the workers and their families.

The crown jewels are kept there. We were shown them; I stumbled out of the room – dazzled by their glitter. The guards, indifferent to our presence, lazed in an ante-room.

The Tower is also used as a gaol; it was there we came upon your brothers using their halting English with the gaoler.

There is a second chapel; in fact, it is two-thirds of a chapel, it has but a nave and a left isle. This chapel bears the unhappy name of San Petro ad Vincula; under the altar are thrown the bodies of the people whose heads are chopped off on a block installed outside.

English kings are much given to chopping off the heads of those who disagree with them.

The Tower is not a happy place.

I must stop now. Your father and I are about to walk down to the Thames; there is a cob there bound for Pisa; you will get this letter in good time.

God go with you, my dear son. How I wish you were with us!

Your Mother

Thursday after the second Sunday of Easter, under seal.

DIARII

The George, London
April 11, 1497

On the way to Mass at the Abbey – a nun plodding across a square, a sack of grain on her shoulder, the sack balanced with a hand on her hip.

She was wearing a coarse brown habit, blue veil.

How is it that a nun with a sack of grain on her shoulder, and any woman with a basket on her head, can go about freely?

As soon as a woman drapes her body in silk, all the world expects her to have a companion.

No silk on my body in this city, neither inside the house, nor out! I go about the town totally unattended – though Gemma frowns. Feel as free as at home. More free – I have no responsibilities.

Feast of Saint Leo the Great.

The George Inn, near Powels Wharf, London
April 13, 1497

Dear Isabetta,

London is a smaller town than I imagined. No more than forty thousand people, less than half the population of Venice.

It is not clean.

Yesterday we were invited for dinner at the home of Charles

and Clotilde de Gaurney. They wanted to invest in the voyage. I didn't want to go. I hear these English in the streets talking like the wind. I had promised Giovanni a great row when we returned if I had to sit there all evening with a smile painted on my face.

To my surprise, everybody spoke French and it was I who sometimes had to translate for Giovanni, as his French is hesitant.

One of the women had money. She told stories of how her many relatives have spent years trying to get control of her properties; how she has had them before a succession of Kings, including the present one, trying to keep her lands and homes in her name.

Someone called down the table:

And did you impress the stern Henry?

Yes, to do it I was not only adamant, but plastered myself with all the family jewels; he likes display, our Henry.

I could see how she would dazzle a sober King, used to doing business with ponderous lawyers, enigmatic churchmen.

This woman has taken a small stake in the voyage, the only woman to do so.

Later in the evening we were taken to see a morality play, *Everyman*, at the home of a very proper English gentleman and his wife who live on the other side of the Thames. After we landed we waded through a great deal of muck and scraped it off our boots in the grass near the door.

The play was staged in front of a wooden screen at one end of the great hall. We sat at the other end on a dais with the Englishman and his wife, while along the other two sides sat other guests.

At the break between the Summoning of Everyman and The Judgement we were served cold fowl and the mead those English are so fond of.

The play was well written – unified in situation and thought. Those English shouted their lines. I understood all of it.

Now I have run out of parchment and must go off in this clear northern air to buy more. When outside, I feel my whole body breathing this lovely coolness.

God bless you, Isabetta, and all your family.

Mathye

Third Sunday of Easter, under seal.

DIARII

The George, London

April 13, 1497

Whenever Giovanni speaks of the voyage in public, he never uses the words:

EAST

SPICES

SILK.

Third Sunday of Easter.

DIARII

The George, London

April 14, 1497

A letter from Paola – unexpected. Must compose one to her – say nothing.

Feast of Saint Justin.

London
April 14, 1497

Dear Paola,

I was sitting in the public room of this small but clean inn yesterday, waiting for Giovanni to return from one of his interminable meetings.

The door opened and in stalked a tall, thin, scarecrow of a man, bearded, maybe in his thirtieth year. He sat at a table at the back. The innkeeper brought wine. The scarecrow took a letter from his pocket, started to read.

Within five minutes a husband and wife arrived; the husband

was as tall as the first man, and the woman just as tall. This second man had an Eastern cast to his face; in Venice I would have said he was from Palestine.

The scarecrow greeted the woman so warmly, I thought I had been mistaken, that this was his wife. He turned and shook hands with the man and slapped him on the back.

More wine was brought. The three carried on an animated conversation, they laughed and burbled throughout. The scarecrow, it seemed, was intent on entertaining the woman, and the husband was left to the side, nodding and smiling, as if indulging the pair.

The door opened again. A red-haired man and his wife joined the others; he bounced in, throwing his arms about; she was sedate. There were kisses, and another round of handshaking and back- slapping by the men. I know this new couple were man and wife because they occasionally reached across the table and held hands.

More wine was ordered.

More animated conversation, more burbling.

Another woman appeared. I say 'appeared' because, so taken was I by this group, I did not hear the door open.

She sashayed in. I lost her for a second behind the pillars. She, too, was tall. When the others stood to greet her I got the impression that if I looked closely I would see stilts.

This newcomer sat facing me. Where the other two women were Saxon – blue eyes and yellow hair, and could have been sisters – this woman would pass for a Sevillian – high colour, black hair, beautiful by any standard.

The group lost all interest in each other and turned their attention to the beauty. They bent their bodies toward her. They smiled, they listened – rapt – to her story. If she had been a child I would have said they were childless and had this one favoured niece among them.

They left before Giovanni arrived.

Thus, my dear Paola, I amuse myself in this strange northern country.

God bless you, Piero, your children.

Mathye

Feast of Saint Justin, under seal.

London, The George Inn
April 14, 1497

My dear Brother,

Our father, the Navigator, has set about the task of making a 'man of the sea' of me. A task I have set to with a will. When my will is engaged, my dear brother, the mountains move.

Today I am writing from an inn in this great, not at all princely, London Town. Our father is across the room doing the business that goes with seeking new wealth. He has taken me with him, not to sit at the table and deal, but to observe, from afar, him sitting at the table and dealing.

We are on sea trials from Bristol. We have a mighty ship. She warrants her name.

But that father of ours cannot be moved from his decision not to take me on this second voyage.

However, while on the trials, he has given me charge of the sails, riggings and ropes. A man who controls that aspect of the work hugs the ship to himself as you would a good woman. A metaphor I use out of respect for your proposed new state.

The Navigator has given me advice that you, my dear brother, will never need, sitting as you do in your rooms studying dusty tomes:

When you arrive in a foreign port, son, find an inn some miles away from the harbour; walk there every day for a meal, a glass of wine. You will gain two advantages: your legs will be kept in shape for the rigging – a captain must always keep himself fit to run up the ropes.

You will meet another kind of man in those inns – the kind you will have to sit with, to make deals.

You will remember our father gives advice to his sons sitting straight-backed, in a straight-backed chair, his chin up, looking off into space.

Are you not impressed, my dear brother, with this grand learning I am engaged in?

Mother, as I expect you know, will sail with us to Bristol.

That lovely mother of ours was on that pilgrimage to Jerusalem and knows the hold of a ship intimately.

We rough sailors are presently sleeping in relative comfort and not strung out on deck as they will be when provisioned for the voyage.

I send my prayers to you and Alessandra who, when you have stuffed your head with canon law, will, no doubt, make a good man of you.

Your brother,

Sebastian

Feast of Saint Justin, under seal.

The George, London
April 15, 1497

My dear Lodovico,

Your father has gone to the Inn of the Sergeants, on the higher levels, to meet with a company of merchants, who at the last minute want to invest in the voyage.

He has taken Sebastian with him.

Sancio and Guido are exploring.

This afternoon, your father and the lawyers will meet again with the courtiers who are reviewing, for the last time, the terms of the Letters Patent.

The King is taking a particular interest in this draft of the document; he is anxious that the known territory of Their Highnesses of Castile and Aragon should not be breached, since negotiations for the union between the English Monarchs' oldest son and Their Highnesses' daughter, Catherine, are still in progress.

I am writing in the public room of the inn.

I was alone; now I hear behind me a number of unrecognisable languages. London, like Venice, at least in its public places, is Babel.

God bless you, my dear son.

Your Mother

Tuesday after the third Sunday of Easter, under seal.

The George Inn, near Powels Wharf, London
April 15, 1497

My dear Nurse,

Yesterday was so warm I went without my English cape.

At dusk Giovanni and I walked to the Thames to see the red-tailed deer that come down to drink; we saw none.

The wind came up. I knew I would have a cold today. I have.

This morning I went across the road to the convent. The nun, who is the apothecary, gave me a concoction of horehound, as well as a jar of rue and dill, boiled in wine. I must take a glass every four hours. I have to stay in bed two days. I told the nun I was too busy to stay in bed – she gave me a look.

We have only three more days in London, and I have to stay in bed! Today I am damp and sticky; bones I did not know I had ache.

The wife of the innkeeper brings my meals. This afternoon she moved me to a room with a fireplace. The heat is spreading, I can feel myself getting better.

I don't know how to live in this country. We should have had a fire last night. It's not cold outside but it is in our rooms.

We have to pay extra for the fire!

Every hour a young boy comes with wood. He tells me:

Missus, another yaffel for you! Don't worry, you'll get better and see the King and Queen.

So everyone at the inn knows our business.

Giovanni wanted to stay and take care of me. I sent him

away to the public room until after supper – I have ordered Gemma to stay away too.

For the last few days we have let our sons roam. They were spending most of their time at street theatricals and cockfights. I put my foot down about the cockfights, made Giovanni back me.

God knows what they are up to. Like all young, they tell only what they think parents want to hear.

God be with you, my dear Nurse. I hope you will go to Montebelluna, out of the heat of Venice.

Mathye

Tuesday after the third Sunday of Easter, under seal.

DIARII

The George, London
April 16, 1497

Decided to send Gemma and Guido overland. Giovanni says they will arrive in three or four days. They will prepare the house and garden.

Had to remind Gemma I've been to the Holy Land – know how to take care of myself.

Feast of Saint Magnus.

DIARII

The George, London
April 17, 1497

The Royal Court.

The King asked his guests if they had questions for Giovanni.

A few – of no consequence.

Then Gonsalez de Puebla, ambassador from Queen Isabella, insisted that according to the Treaty of Tordesillas the whole world, for the purpose of exploration, was divided by Pope Alexander VI between her several countries and Portugal.

De Puebla had a high whining voice – his French not perfect.

The King intervened, told the Ambassador the English court

recognises lands already discovered by every and any nation; but any land not yet discovered is as much the prize of the English as any other nation. The Letters Patent stated that.

The King did not wait for another question.

He rose, invited his guests to follow himself and his Queen into an adjoining room, where sweetmeats and wine – real wine – were laid out.

Giovanni told me he curtailed his answers when he saw the whining de Puebla.

Feast of Saint Innocent.

The George, near Powels Wharf, London
April 17, 1497

My dear Lodovico,

Your father has his Letters Patent.

We met the King and Queen on the Feast of Saint Magnus.

It was a brief ceremony. After the signing, the Archbishop invited your father to address the group. Your father explained the direction he intends to sail, how long it will take, the tunnage of the *Mathye*, the composition of the crew and any number of other details you and I have heard many times before.

There followed questions from various ambassadors.

The King then led us to an adjoining room for an informal gathering that included the Royal children.

When the Royal Family left, the Librarian invited me to see the scriptorium.

Your father was surrounded. I went off.

The King's scriptorium is quite large and clerks were working here and there on manuscripts.

There were only a student's collection of Latin manuscripts and many of these translated into French. There were a small number of books in Greek and none in any other language.

It is a scriptorium of mainly French-language manuscripts and books. When I raised this with the Librarian he told me both the King and Queen have French ancestry. The King spent many years in exile at the Burgundian Court and French is the language of the English Court.

He said the King and Queen speak perfectly good English.

I am not sure he would recognise good English: he too was from Burgundy – spoke to me in French.

I have worked hard perfecting my English. To date, only the servants speak that language with me.

A strange country.

We leave for Bristol Friday after the third Sunday of Easter.

May the Holy Spirit guard you, my dear son.

Your Mother

Feast of Saint Innocent.

The George, near Powels Wharf, London
April 17, 1497

Dear Isabetta,

We have been to the Royal Court. Giovanni received his Letters Patent. There were more people than I expected – ambassadors, nobles, the papal legate.

The Court was at Westminster. We were met by the Archbishop of Canterbury, who is the King's Chancellor. The Church plays a larger role in State matters here than at home.

While we were waiting for the Monarchs to arrive, the Archbishop introduced us to a priest from Brescia – Friar Pietro Carmeliano – who is the Latin Secretary to the King. He writes the Royal letters addressed to foreign courts; as well, he is one of the King's chaplains. The English Court, and the better educated of this society, affect Latin handwriting and this poor cleric, because of his talent, must stay on here, although he is pitiably homesick.

When the King and Queen arrived they went directly to elaborately decorated chairs set on a dais.

Queen Elizabeth of York is the rightful heir to the throne but it is the King who is ruling the country.

She wore a mulberry velvet dress with a square neck, and a square pendant of eight rubies, a larger one in the centre. On

254

her head she had a heavily embroidered gable hood of the same material; she wore two rather modest rings, a pearl and a ruby. The Queen is slender, has yellow hair, about our age.

The King looked austere; he is not above medium height but is straight-limbed.

He wore a cap of black with a large blue jewel on the left side. Over his loose-fitting violet robe he had a coat of embroidered black stuff. Around his neck, a jewelled chain with a horseshoe encrusted with the same blue stones.

There were no preliminary formalities. The Archbishop presented the Letters Patent to the King, who inscribed his siglum, dated the document, gave it to Giovanni. Giovanni was invited by the Archbishop to address the gathering.

After, the King, with his Queen, led us to an ante-room for a reception.

I spoke a while with the Queen.

Marco Polo reported one-legged creatures. But I doubt his account.

Madam, I will ask my husband to study any such phenomenon and to send a description to the Court.

The Navigator must return to the Court, describe them to us.

Yes, Madam.

I was wearing silk shoes. I brought them in my handbag, put them on in an outer room. The Queen admired them.

I believe the King and Queen are happy; I saw their eyes meet; they smiled.

We brought our sons with us. During the reception Sebastian led the young Prince of Wales to where the sphere was laid, picked it up, pointed out something to the Heir to the throne.

Always the young manage to be more natural.

May the Spirit of God surround you.

Mathye

Feast of Saint Innocent, under seal.

DIARII
Aboard the Mathye, London
April 18, 1497

The quay is full of people. They have come to look at the new caravel, its square rigging.

Everyone seems to know she is on sea trials – will go on a voyage of discovery.

I hear a man tell Giovanni:

That's a powerful-looking ship you got there, skipper.

I want to believe this.

They are loading casks of liver oil on deck – Giovanni, true to his dictum: every voyage a paying voyage.

Before we leave the Port of London, Giovanni calls us together, takes the name and village of each mariner.

I hear one man say:

Llanuilling Under the Hill.

Is that the name of your village?

The man spells it.

Giovanni writes it down.

He counts us, including myself, and himself:

We are thirteen.

A pall falls over the crew.

The Master can leave, I'm not leaving.

Is that really my voice?

Giovanni laughs.

The mariners laugh.

I have surprised myself. When did I become passionate?

Giovanni names the watches. I am on the first watch.

I hear one of the mariners say:

This ship carries no passengers.

All the men, including Sancio, sleep below. Giovanni will sleep there nights when I am not on watch.

The lines are cast off.

Giovanni is on the top deck. He gives orders so quietly I wonder how they are heard. He calls each mariner by his first name.

My husband orders the sails raised. Sebastian jumps to the foot of the great square sail. I watch him untie ropes, yellow hair bouncing.

Seven of the youngest men line up either side of him.

Sebastian starts a shanty:

One for love, two for sorrow.

Here today, gone tomorrow.

They give a mighty heave. I see Sebastian's heavy thighs go almost to the deck.

The great spar goes up three feet.

He starts the shanty again, his voice young, clear. Ten times they sing and heave, until that powerful spar has reached the top.

The men release the ropes, the great square sail clatters to the deck, catches the wind.

The caravel shoots forward.

The mariners move to the spritsail, the topsail, the lateen. The son of the Master is the hardest worker.

Sebastian grabs the rigging, is halfway up, swinging off in space; he worries some small piece of rope that doesn't seem to need fixing.

My heart stops. Only the tips of his boots are in the rigging. He is using both hands to work.

My God, my young son hanging in mid-air!

Giovanni is not on deck; the rest of the men are occupied coiling, tightening, laying ropes in intricate patterns. Only I, with my stopped heart, notice the child in the rigging, standing as if he were in the middle of the piazza.

I want to call: *Come down here this minute*.

I choke on my need to do it.

Sebastian ties the rope, runs down the rigging, jumps onto the deck – he doesn't look my way.

He goes below.

I go to the side of the ship, will myself not to be sick.

Friday after the third Sunday of Easter

DIARII
The Mathye
April 18, 1497
Making good time.

Giovanni has excellent portolano charts. Every harbour and rock has been charted.

We see six sails off to the south-east.

My husband says they may be out of Flanders – they are not galleys.

Friday after the third Sunday of Easter.

DIARII
The Mathye, off Sandwich Bay
April 19, 1497
Am roused for the dawn watch by half whispers. The night watch slips away.

We are already in the English Channel – the wind in our teeth.

I stand at the port side and stare over the sea. The sails are catching a rough breeze.

After an hour, Iugh, the watch leader, comes from the galley with hot drinks of mild ale. I do not like it. I drink it. The morning is warm, daylight not yet on the sky.

The men move about on deck checking ropes – they are shadows. Robert, a man from Bristol, is at the helm; yesterday he taught me to steer the ship. I take the helm. Within a quarter of an hour I give it back, the weight more than I can handle. I am surprised and disappointed.

No ship has been sighted since our watch. I look around, the other two mariners are nowhere to be seen. I am alone on deck. I hear the helmsman at the helm.

I have a sense, at this moment, I am the one keeping the ship safe.

I look up in the rigging, the great square sail fills and shivers. In the half-light, the ship takes on the loftiness of a cathedral. A peace I haven't known since I left Venice settles over me.

With its great sail, this ship will take Giovanni to the East and return.

In this moment all gloom of doubt vanishes.

Feast of Saint Alphege.

DIARII

The Mathye, off Selsey
April 20, 1497

The ship looks finished. Giovanni tells me it is two weeks behind schedule; I see this delay annoys him. Much of the finer work is yet to be done; he keeps the two shipwrights and the rest of the mariners hard at it.

There is a low hum of hammering, scraping, rattle of sails, slap of water. I am lulled.

Someone tips over a barrel of liver oil. The mate who told me earlier the ship was his – because he knew most about it, has been with her the longest – leaps across the deck and grabs the barrel before it hits. But the damage is done, the lovely new deck has gallons of oil racing toward the scuppers.

Buckets appear – mops, brushes, lye soap, every man is in his bare feet, the rush begins to halt the damage.

Giovanni is down among the mariners. He works at a furious pace. Four men are on bucket brigade, sea water is being poured on the black stain, the men scrub like demons, Sancio among them; their faces run with sweat. They don't halt until every ounce of oil has been washed away. The black stain remains.

The men put away their swabs, brushes, and buckets; they heave off on the deck.

I sit on a coil of rope. Giovanni joins me.

The stain – can it be removed?

Yes, at Bristol there are some of the best shipwrights.

The cook brings food.

We drink sack, chew bread, talk quietly.

The men are pleased with their work. They sprawl on deck.

I covertly watch Sancio trying to fit his body into the same posture. He doesn't get it right.

The ship settles back into the quiet rhythm of the voyage.
Fourth Sunday of Easter.

DIARII
The Mathye, off Portsmouth
April 20, 1497
Third day at sea.

At noon, there was a lull. Giovanni tells everyone to down tools.

He gathers us on the main deck.

He reads the Epistle and Gospel from the day's Mass.

We sing the Gloria, Credo, and Paternoster.

These English men throw back their heads – sing heartily.

All seem satisfied with themselves.

Including me.

I go to the chart room.

Giovanni is poring over a portolano chart. I see Southampton is just inside Portsmouth.

Giovanni sees me seeing it.

All the anger associated with the time of Piero's capture crowds my mind. I am ready to relive it.

Here. Now.

Whales!

What?

The helmsman is staring to starboard.

Whales.

I back out of the chart room. Go to the side of the ship – watch two great whales swimming northward.

I stay until they disappear.

A great fish has saved my husband the ignominy of his wife arguing with him in front of his mariners.
Fourth Sunday of Easter.

DIARII
The Mathye
April 22, 1497
Sebastian gives me the briefest greetings. Not once since I came aboard has he come near to talk.

I try not to watch him but I know my eyes follow him everywhere.

At home he is the only one of our sons who jests with his father. At sea he speaks to him only when spoken to.

Sancio is staying close to the shipwrights. He beams when they give him any small piece of work.
Feast of Saint Theodore.

DIARII
The Mathye
April 24, 1497
Seventh day at sea.
I am awakened.

I feel a change in the tides.

It is almost dawn.

I go on deck.

The ship rolls about.

I do not see Giovanni come from below.

He is there. I rest against him.

Where are we?

Off Lizard Point. We are out of soundings. You can feel the heave of the ocean sea.

It woke me.

By sunset we will round Land's End – the furthest to the west we can go and still be in England. Directly across the sea is the East – I know it.

I look out into the swells, into the distant emptiness.

My husband's arms about me, I almost persuade myself – out there in the deep blackness – all is benign.
Feast of Saint Fidelis.

DIARII
The Mathye, off The Scivies
April 25, 1497

Sunshine, seas calm, making good time – this north-tending coast is bleak.

Today on Piazza San Marco the place is alive with processions.

Every church has had a sung Mass – three – four.

Bells peal.

I am down-coast from Bristol.

Hove to near Kingroad, a few hours from Bristol. The tide is going out – running at a fierce rate.

We are anchored in the stream.

As the water recedes, boats near shore are high and dry in the sand, a desolate sight.

We will stay the night, be swept in on the morning tide.

Old Man Pill is coming.

I follow the helmsman's gaze.

A river boat is being rowed toward us at a punishing speed. A man stands in the bow – clothes blown against his skeletal body.

As the boat nears the *Mathye* I see that the one doing the rowing must be a son – they both have the merest covering of flesh, small heads, sharp noses, the rusty complexion of men who live on the water.

I am with Giovanni in the chart room.

Who is this man?

Old Man Pill, the river pilot. Only the Pills take ships up to Bristol.

But there are many ships.

The merchants recently tried to regulate the pilotage – Old Man Pill sent the first crew home without their ears. After that, the river was left to the Pills – his many sons, relatives.

Pill climbs the rope ladder with the agility of a cabin boy. In two leaps he is at Giovanni's side.

His voice like shots from a falconet.

Giovanni nods his head. Raises his hand in salute.

Pill is over the side again – being rowed away by his hungry-looking son.

He will come in the morning. Take us in on the tide.

You trust him?

As myself.

I look at my husband.

He is serious.

He is.

Feast of Saint Mark.

DIARII

The Mathye

April 26, 1497

On the run into Bristol.

People along the riverbank wave.

The keeper in the gunpowder shed gives us a three-gun salute. We answer.

Boats blow their horns.

We are sailing into the gorge of the Avon. The hills lean over us, breathe their cool leafiness on us.

I did not expect this sweet air.

This welcome.

Feast of Saint Marcellinus.

DIARII

Bristol

April 27, 1497

This is a small town; our house is smaller than I imagined; there are enough rooms but all are small. I couldn't keep my disappointment from Giovanni. He says it's the largest he could find.

He promises a palace when he returns with his shipload of spices.

I don't want a palace in this northern land – I have a home on the Grand Canal.

Fifth Sunday of Easter.

DIARII
Bristol
April 30, 1497
Gave Giovanni Michelangelo's painting of Saint Nicholas.

He says the torturous look on the good saint's face will frighten his mariners.

He will keep it in his cabin.

Feast of Saint Catherine of Siena.

Saint Nicholas Street, Bristol
May 4, 1497

My dear Lodovico,

Your father is working at a fierce pace to have the caravel ready for departure on Whit Thursday.

He has hand-picked every member of his crew. Every mariner has experience as a pilot including the astronomer, friar, and two shipwrights.

He has persuaded the merchants Robert Thorne and Hugh Elyot to go with him on this voyage. They each have taken a one-fifth share. With these two aboard, the mariners will be more confident.

Robert Thorne owns the caravel.

Sebastian is going through his dark days – he has to be back at Sagres by the first of September. Your father can't be persuaded to take him.

I would be disheartened if they were both sailing together into the unknown again this year.

May the Eyes of God be on you.

Your Mother

Sixth Sunday of Easter, under seal.

DIARII
Bristol
May 6, 1497
A wheedling letter from Paola – looking for a berth for her cousin Roberto.

Odd – he never showed interest before.
Tuesday of the Rogation Day.

Saint Nicholas Street, Bristol
May 11, 1497

Dear Paola,

You want to know if your cousin Roberto may secure a berth on the *Mathye*.

It is too late for this voyage.

Giovanni will write to him when he returns.

No, I am not unhappy in Bristol; not while I have my husband and sons with me.

It is a clean little city, the streets are paved, and the people are proud.

But I hope it will not be a long sojourn.

Blessings on you, Piero, your children.

Mathye
Sunday after the Ascension, under seal.

Saint Nicholas Street, Bristol
May 17, 1497

My dear Lodovico,

If you have received my last letter, you know your father will take a priest with him on this voyage. This will give some semblance of ordinary life, in that most extraordinary time.

His name is Giovanni Antonio de Carbonariis – short, sturdy and full of laughter. He plays numerous musical instruments. He's quite prepared to be a working member of the crew.

His English is correct, with what I believe to be a Gallic accent; he is not above making it thicker for effect, which gives an amusing twist to almost everything he says.

He is attached to the Benedictine House at St Albans. We met him at London. Friar de Carbonariis has some sailing experience: as a young man he worked aboard his grandfather's galleys trading out of Pisa, to France.

Your father has promised to name some headland after him when they arrive in the East. The Friar often presents himself to him as:

Headland Carbonar, reporting for duty, Master.

This Friar is not at all who he appears to be: Richard Americ told your father he was once employed by Henry VII as a Royal Messenger to the Duke of Milan.

Your father wonders if the good Friar is on the *Mathye* to hold Sunday service, report to the King of England, the Duke of Milan, or all three.

Yes, in England too, intrigue proceeds apace.

My blessing on you and Alessandra.

Your Mother

Vigil of Pentecost, under seal.

Saint Nicholas Street, Bristol
May 18, 1497

My dear Isabetta,

Bristol is an inland town. Two rivers run through it, conjoin, meet the sea some forty miles downstream; ships come into the middle of the town, as in Venice.

Their Common Council has been in existence only two hundred years, yet the people are proud of it, think it very ancient.

There is a great Festival of the Sea taking place here today.

First you must imagine a mile of ships, a great forest of spars, from all nations of the world. There is one from Riga, bearing the name of the patron saint of mariners: *Saint Nicolas*. This ship came last Autumn with a load of furs, sold them here, had to wait out the winter in this port because of ice.

The *Saint Nicolas* is designed like the *Mathye* but is much smaller. I went aboard, as everybody was doing; was satisfied if this small ship could make it from Riga, loaded, Giovanni has a much better chance with his larger one.

But the festival: there are – for it is still going on – five thousand people, at least, circulating around the narrow strip of waterfront. Everywhere you look there are tumblers, musicians, people hawking food and every other saleable item.

There is a veritable army of small boys ferrying people, for the price of a groat, from one side of the river to the other.

On the deck of one ship, I saw eight men doing a morris dance; they were dressed in red trousers and white shirts with bells on their shoes and legs. They snapped white handkerchiefs to the rhythm of their feet. The leader wore a red lanyard across his shoulder and chest, a black cocked hat with a feather. The dance was similar to our Il Matachino – a series of hops, turns and changing positions.

Dame Americ, who accompanies me on all these outings, said these morris dancers are seen all over England during the summer. They dance the boundaries of their villages.

On almost every ship there are mariners jigging to pipes. The mariners from Riga are the most spectacular – they seemed to dance on their knees, doing great backflips to a lute-like instrument which one of the mariners plays at a ferocious speed.

Children's choirs, clear and well-tuned, are positioned all along the riverbank. Singing is continuous. I did not expect these English to be such good singers.

At one moment I saw the mayor and his councillors being made way for; they went aboard one of the ships from Flanders, where a great banquet table was set up on deck.

They ate sumptuously.

Giovanni, Sebastian and Sancio are aboard the *Mathye*. People line up to go aboard. I am not skilled at being the jolly host to thousands. The men in my family seem to enjoy it.

I must stop here.

We are expected at Phillipa Americ's for supper.

God be with you and your family.

Mathye

Pentecost Sunday, under seal.

Saint Nicholas Street, Bristol
May 19, 1497

My dear Nurse,

This morning, Giovanni, Sebastian, Sancio and I attended Mass at the Church of Blessed Mary Redcliffe, the mariner's church; the floor was strewn with rushes.

A former mayor left a bequest to this Church to have three sermons preached before the Mayor and Council on the three days following Pentecost Sunday.

The Mayor and his Council, like everybody else, entered the Church carrying a nosegay of herbs against the smell, crush of people, pestilence. Giovanni and I carried one too, and had a clove of garlic tucked into it, an idea my husband picked up at Mecca; our sons scorned both the nosegay and the garlic.

The sermons are being preached by the Abbot of the Dominican Priory; he took his theme from the Epistle of Pentecost:

. . . your old men shall dream dreams, your young men shall see visions, your daughters shall prophesy.

After the sermon, the builders of the *Mathye* brought a model of the ship to the altar and placed it in the sanctuary. The presiding priest blessed it, asked for prayers from the congregation for safe return of the voyagers.

Giovanni was pleased; Sebastian was bursting the strings on his English jerkin; Sancio was indifferent; I was slightly embarrassed.

Dear Nurse, you must tell me all the news of my home, I long for it.

Bless you.

Mathye

Whit Monday, under seal.

My dear son Lodovico,

Tomorrow I leave for our voyage to the fabulous East.

I write to you at this time because I must meet all eventualities.

As my eldest son, with some experience of life, you will understand why a man sometimes must write such a letter, although with a father's heart, I hope it will never fall to you to carry out any of the provisions I speak of.

Sebastian will return to Sagres on or about the Feast of the Seven Dolours of Our Lady; your mother and Sancio will be alone in Bristol; I must be certain of their wellbeing.

My ship is victualled for three months. I shall make every effort to be back within that time, but you know how it is impossible to be exact about winds and storms. I have given your mother September as my return date.

Should it happen that the worst occurs, and God forbid that it should, I want you to come to Bristol to be with your mother and brother. Should it be necessary, and should your mother wish it, I want you to escort them back to Venice.

I want to express my concern about Sebastian's future: he has one more year's study at Sagres. I want him to return there and finish that work; it is the only place on the face of the earth where they prepare the whole man for the job of navigator, and as there is no doubt that Sebastian has the will and the ability to do this work, I want him to have the right formation. Already he is hinting he doesn't need to continue his studies; I have made it quite clear to him I will not consider it.

Sancio will not follow me and your brother on the sea. Your mother and I expect him to continue his classical studies at Padua. When he is finished, he should know what he intends to do with his life. I do not worry about Sancio – he is a serious young man and should do well.

I realise this is not an easy letter for you to read, but my heart is light. I fully intend to return.

However, I must tell you that my Will is made. You will find it in the Chart Room, in the cupboard above my desk, wrapped in white silk. Your mother has read it; it will not come as a surprise to her.

Pray for your father. I have a sturdy ship; I have a steadfast crew. I am off with the tide in the morning.

May the Spirit of God keep you, my son.

Your Father

Wednesday of the Pentecost Ember Week, under seal.

DIARII
Bristol
May 23, 1497

We went to bed early. I didn't sleep. Giovanni slept like the dead, his body giving off waves of heat.

On the stroke of five he rose like an arrow. In his nightshirt he did a barefoot dance, his feet hitting the cold floor in a rat-a-tat-tat.

Behold how fast a mariner dresses for the sea.

I watched him fling himself into his clothes with a certain crazed bliss. He swooped down on me.

A few seconds, he was out of the door.

I heard the toes of his boots tap down the stairs; I heard him close the outside door; I heard the iron cleats on his heels hit the cobblestones.

I was out of bed.

I saw sparks rise in the still dark night.

At the corner he stopped, looked to the window, took off his cap, swung it over his head, turned, was out of sight.

I heard each spiked footfall as he seemed to dance his way down to the quay. When they faded I lay on the floor.

Gemma woke me at noon with broth. I got into bed, drank greedily, went to sleep.

At suppertime I didn't eat the gruel she brought with such murmurings of tenderness.

At breakfast I read the note Giovanni wrote before he left the quay.

Friday of the Pentecost Ember Week.

> *Aboard the* Mathye, *Bristol*
> *May 22, 1497*

My darling wife,

Do not fret while I am away. I remember where my true home is.

Giovanni

Whit Thursday.

DIARII

Bristol

June 1, 1497

I take out my lute, play over and over the parts of the Jubilation Mass I had written before I left Venice.

Have written no new music.

With almost nothing to do, I do nothing.

Obviously it takes a sung Mass every day, three choir practices a week, four hours a week at Scuola di Sant'Orsola, ten hours overseeing the Fraterna and three commissions keeping my back to the wall – to inspire me.

It takes Venice!

Second Sunday after Pentecost.

My dear Nurse,

Our little house has three levels. The rooms are small. We are constantly running into the walls. I cannot get used to living on the ground floor – having few windows to open.

I hired extra servants to give the place a good scouring – it still smells of other people's lives. Sometimes my stomach rebels.

I have hired an English language tutor for Sebastian and Sancio; they work all morning.

In the afternoon Sancio goes to the Dominican Friars to continue his Greek and Latin studies.

Sebastian disappears to the quay. I see him again at supper.

Only in the evening, when there is a curfew, do we sit as a family.

Sometimes we sing.

Sometimes we speak English and dissolve into gales of laughter: Sebastian, I fear, is learning all the Anglo-Saxon street words.

Sebastian will leave for Sagres sometime after the Tenth Sunday after Pentecost; Sancio for Padua after the Sixteenth.

I promised Giovanni I will not set a day for my return until he is back at Bristol, which should be around Lady Day.

My dear Nurse, I bless you and miss you most grievously.
Mathye
Second Sunday after Pentecost, under seal.

Dear Isabetta,

I have a few friends who help me through, even in June, these not-so-warm days.

I spend most of my time in the company of Phillipa Americ,

the wife of Richard Americ, Sheriff of Bristol, and a partner in Giovanni's venture.

First, you must imagine a woman who comes to my shoulder, then you must bring to mind Adriana's shape – you have Phillipa.

Phillipa has a high colour and very black hair, a round, laughing, open face. When you sit at her table she interrogates you constantly with:

That's good?

She is proud of her cook. She calls her to the table after each meal and heaps praise and hugs upon her. The food is excellent but often arrives lukewarm, which these English seem not to mind.

Phillipa has nine children between the ages of fourteen and four, including two sets of twins. She sits them around her table, cheers them on when they eat heartily.

Before they leave, they must give her noisy kisses and hugs. I find this very touching, given my solitary upbringing, my few sons.

Every Saturday when the weather is fine, Phillipa packs two enormous baskets of food, gathers up all her children and two servants to bring the baskets, and heads off down Temple Street along the city wall to the Avon River. She sails ahead of us. The great expanse of her skirts gives the impression she is being propelled by a slight breeze.

She talks all the way, pointing out objects of interest, warning the nine-year-old twins she saw the rocks they flicked over that fence – it will cost them four kisses when they get to the picnic grounds. The while, she is greeting passers-by on all sides.

We may not be a Festival, but we could pass for strolling players.

When we arrive at the Avon, we are assailed by a mob of young boys who want to ferry us across in their coracles.

My dear Isabetta, you have never seen a coracle: a little round boat made of cowhide, about five feet in diameter, a draft of one and a half feet, a seat across the centre. The rower uses one paddle. If this sounds a frightfully delicate shell to be on the water in, it isn't; it is enormously stable and these boys are skilled in their business. However, they are not above giving the oar a twirl, which sets the little craft in a spin and makes the children squeal with delight.

Phillipa shares out her business among this clan of little boat owners, the same way she shares out her kisses.

No, William, as handsome as you are, you took us last week, I have to use poor old Harry this week.

Harry, take that basket.

Ah, Missus, you're nice.

This last from William, who has just lost a penny and the meal Phillipa serves at the picnic – for one of the baskets is a picnic for the boys.

We are each assigned a coracle for the five-minute row. We set off, a flotilla of twelve, my little ferryman chattering in an English I can't understand.

We troop ashore on the other side, the picnic now swollen by twelve boys.

Phillipa is in her glory.

Thomas, come here; show Dame Caboto your lovely curls.

The little ragamuffin who rowed me across, who hasn't had his hair washed since the last time he fell in the river, separates himself from the crowd of racing ball players and presents himself to her.

She praises his beautiful curls. She asks me to admire them. Sends him off fortified to remember for the rest of his life how, as a child, he had a head of admirable hair, and on a day on the banks of the Avon, Phillipa Americ called him to her side and told him so.

All this, on her part, is genuine; on a number of occasions she has said to me:

What I could do with those boys.

She sighs.

When the picnic starts, she sits everyone on the ground and urges us to eat more cheese, drink more milk, and wonders why with twenty-five people sitting around, there is cake left.

The cake gets divided among the coracle owners, while Phillipa preaches a sermon on the virtue of gathering up what is left over.

My dear Isabetta, may the Spirit of Pentecost be yours.

Mathye

Tuesday after the second Sunday after Pentecost, under seal.

DIARII
Bristol
June 15, 1497
Overheard Phillipa refer to me, in her not always restrained voice as:

Our exotic Venetian bird.

It was the 'our' I resented.

If Phillipa and the others refuse to wear jewellery or, worse – have none.

Well!

Fourth Sunday after Pentecost.

DIARII
Bristol
June 24, 1497
Supper at Thomas and Elizabeth Canynges.

One of the young Canynges men, down from Cambridge, amused me with tales of life at University – gambling, cockfighting.

I tried to imagine Lodovico, regaling a married woman with his gambling exploits. The scene would not form.

Maybe this is how mothers survive.

After dinner, this young man played the flageolet, an

instrument similar to our pipe, with two extra holes in the back. We sang English songs. Sebastian and Sancio seemed to know them all.

We were asked to sing. My sons agreed readily, put their bodies into it.

They are picking up English manners.

When we were ready to leave, Thomas Canynges arranged for an escort. At the door, he suggested Sebastian and Sancio return for dancing.

And don't worry about your sons, Dame Caboto. I will send the constable home with them.

I was astonished to have the decision, that my sons return for dancing, taken out of my hands.

In this foreign land, in this empty house – servants in bed or gone home – I feel abandoned.

I have never before felt this sense of being utterly alone. Never.

Feast of Saint John the Baptist.

DIARII
Bristol
June 25, 1497
Last night – blacker than I want to remember.

The Canynges eat with their servants, leave their children alone all night to revel.

Phillipa says if I have a supper party without my husband, none of the men will come.

What peculiar people I find myself among.

Feast of Saint William, abbot.

Saint Nicholas Street, Bristol
June 26, 1497

Dear Paola,

You are right. I ask myself twenty times a day what I am doing in this northern country, where the sun shines so feebly;

where the clothes I have brought never seem to keep me warm; where I have been ailing. The answer of course is – my husband invited me.

But all is not lost in sniffles; I have been making myself useful. They have here a hospital which administers to the sick and the poor. It is outside the gates – yes, here too they keep the poor outside the city gates.

It was founded by the de Gaunt family, Normans, and run by their descendants. Everything in this city, it seems, is run by the descendants of the Normans.

Each morning I go to this hospital, help wash and dress the smallest children. There is one little girl, about three, who has attached herself to me. As soon as I am seated she comes to me with news of her day.

This morning she laid her hands on my lap.

I going to the farm.

To see the cows?

No, the sorses.

Ah, to see the horses.

Yes, the sorses.

Her small mission accomplished, she toddled back across the room.

I now look forward to the little one. You see, I am lonely.

When I have washed and dressed the three children assigned me, I go next door to the Chapel of St Mark and the Blessed Virgin to hear Mass – they have a fine organ, a poor choir.

There are four chaplains living in the hospital, each one is a chantry priest. Every morning one of them says a Mass for Giovanni, Sebastian, and the crew of the *Mathye*.

The chapel of St Mark and the Blessed Virgin is Gothic, with very large windows through which the sun slashes, when it does shine. It illuminates a stained glass window of the Annunciation; the Blessed Virgin wears a black mantle, stands with her hands thrown out, as if to push away the weight of the news she has just heard.

I often sit and ponder that image.

There is another small task I perform for the hospital: I go down into the vaults, where they keep the offertory wine, draw off a jug, fill the cruets used at the four chantry Masses.

I have been know to take a rather good swallow.

May the Spirit of Pentecost be with you and your family.

Mathye

Feast of Saint Pelagius, under seal.

DIARII

Bristol

June 29, 1497

I take Gemma and Guido away from their work.

Yesterday, we walked to the Back where ships were unloading wine and firewood. We talked to Venetian mariners working there.

In the afternoon I forced myself to work an hour on the music for the Jubilation Mass.

I forced myself.

Vigil of Saints Peter and Paul.

DIARII

Bristol

July 16, 1497

I was walking down Saint Nicholas Street toward Saint Mary Redcliffe.

In a garden a number of women kneeling on the grass around a caged bird.

At a short distance – a trap made of fish net. Strings attached. The caged bird was being used to lure other birds.

One of the birds flying above the trap was lured in, a woman pulled a string: captured!

Phillipa says the women bring the birds indoors, keep them to amuse the family.

In Venice we buy birds on the Rialto.

Feast of Saint Helier.

DIARII
Bristol
July 27, 1497
Fog on the ground ten days.

It has muffled the music of the spheres.

Not a note sounds in my head.
Tenth Sunday after Pentecost.

DIARII
Bristol
August 1, 1497
Sebastian has left for Sagres. He so wanted to be here when his father arrived.

I am more lonely than ever.
Commemoration of Hagia Sophia.

DIARII
Bristol
August 3, 1497
As time winds down to the date of Giovanni's return, anxiety rents me.

I am awakened each morning by the sensation of a blow to my heart. The sick pain spreads.

How will I stand it if Giovanni finds a short route to the spices of the East and diverts the trade from Venice to Bristol?

Will the Collegio send their axemen after all of us?
Eleventh Sunday after Pentecost.

DIARII
Bristol
August 5, 1497
Giovanni has returned!

He has found land but not the short route to the wealth of the East!

Thank you God! I'll finish my Jubilation Mass.

I will.
Feast of the dedication of Our Lady of the Snows.

DIARII
Bristol
August 6, 1497
Giovanni jumped from the *Mathye*.

His mariners hoisted him to their shoulders, brought him through the streets to our little house.

Watching him bobbing along in mid-air, I tried to be modest. He would look around, find me in the crowd, snatch off his hat and wave it over his head.

Sancio kept leaping up and slapping him on the back.

Richard Americ brought a puncheon of ale, placed it by the front door. Within two hours it was empty.

All day, late into the evening, our house was full of people. Giovanni told the story of his discovery over and over.
Feast of Saint Sixtus.

DIARII
Bristol
August 7, 1497
Giovanni and Sancio up at dawn.

Are racing toward London and the King, the fastest horses from the post under them.
Feast of Saint Donatus.

Bristol
August 15, 1497

My dear son Sebastian,

I have just returned from the King.

I reported to him on the vast new land I discovered.

This land is found 1,800 miles west of Dursey Head.

If you take your dividers, place one leg on Dursey Head, the other at the opening of the River of Bordeaux, France, and draw two parallel lines to westward, you will know, approximately, where the new land is, in relation to Europe.

As planned, off Dursey Head, I set out into deep water and set my course for the sixtieth parallel.

Off Iceland, I picked up the prevailing winds from the east that I knew blew in that region and, with the helmsman keeping her straight, in fourteen days we were in a position where I expected land. I turned the prow of the *Mathye* southward and after four days of easy sailing we sighted it: a magnificent forested land, so vast that all the peoples of the world could take timber from it and there would still be an abundance.

On the Feast of Saint John the Baptist, I entered a sheltered harbour and planted the flag of Venice, the banners of King Henry and the Pope.

I found in that harbour so many codfish, my mariners gathered a quantal just by putting down baskets. These codfish are in such vast quantities England need never again buy Iceland stock.

This news is in every mouth in Bristol.

I had my mariners collect a few casks of water from a river that ran down to the sea.

I picked up from the beach a needle for knitting nets and a snare used, most likely, for trapping small animals. This convinced me the land was inhabited, but we saw no one.

We left almost immediately; we were a small landing party and were lightly armed. As we were leaving the harbour one of my mariners thought he saw figures running through the woods, but it could have been animals, although we saw none.

I sailed south along that coastline for thirty days and didn't reach the end of this great land.

The King has asked me to make another voyage next year, to continue to search for a short route to the East. You can be sure I will do that and you will be with me. I will leave you and your brothers a great heritage, I am sure of it.

I am sending this letter by my friend Gonsalez las Casas

who will deliver it to you. You have taken an oath of secrecy. You will know how to guard what I tell you.

However, I expect that within a month every ambassador in London will have sent the news of my find to his master, and every foreign mariner now in the port of Bristol will have carried it to the ends of the known world. And unlike the Portuguese, the English King has no love for secrecy.

Nevertheless, you have details I have given to none but your mother and the King.

God bless you, my son.

Your Father

Assumption of Our Lady into Heaven, under seal.

Bristol
August 20, 1497

My dear Sebastian,

I have spent the last two days making a copy of the chart your father brought back from that new land. I will hold it for you until you return in the Spring. To date, there is only one other copy – for the King of England.

Your father has been made a hero by these English; he is followed every time we go into the street. Men gather around our house all hours of the day and night. They all want to be part of the crew of the 1498 voyage. Your father has had to take public rooms at Thomas Canynges premises to deal with them.

My dear son, there does seem to be opening for you a very bright future. Next year you will be finished your studies and be ready to meet it. We are proud of you.

The Holy Spirit guide you.

Your Mother

Feast of Saint Bernard, under seal.

Dear Paola,

Giovanni has returned. He has a new land in his pocket.

It is a cold land.

He brought back news of a sea afloat with codfish, which these English like better than malmsey. He says there are enough in that sea to feed the world into the next millennium.

This new land is covered with a great forest.

My husband has written to Roberto, offered him a berth for the next voyage, but he must come to Bristol this Autumn.

Has he received the letter?

Blessings on you and your family.

Mathye

Feast of Saint Sabina, under seal.

Chapter Seven

Sagres
August 29, 1497

Dear Father,

Sir, I am sending this letter in the care of Thomas Canynges. I know you would not want Mother disturbed by its message.

We had a north wind at our backs all the way to Portugal. I arrived a week early. I came on to Sagres rather than take an inn in the town.

King Manuel was in residence. I was hardly pitched in my room when a chamberlain arrived with orders to appear before His Majesty.

I thought I might be in for some form of yellow-beaking. I put on my court clothes but left on my two-day-old socks, and had intentions for them, were I the object of a ruse.

No, Sir, it was the real thing.

This King wasn't interested in any niceties:

Did you have a good trip, Messer Caboto?

No Sir, nothing like that, but straight to it:

Tell me about your Summer voyage, Messer Caboto!

Sir, I was glad to be able to say I had not been on the voyage!

There is nothing that gets a man's back up like orders given in that tone, even when given by a king.

This monarch knew you had left from Bristol; knew the number in the crew; when you returned; what you had found. He knew a great deal more than he should have, but then that King you work for has no secrets.

He knew you will go on a voyage of discovery again next year.

And Sir, there is a rumour that Queen Isabella, on the advice of her Navigator, Christopher Columbus, is sending her military captain, Alonso de Ojeda, to clear the ocean seas of explorers found west of the Tordesillas Line.

This is not happy news, Sir.

I also hear Amerigo Vespucci will be a member of de Ojeda's crew.

I am your respectful son,

Sebastian

Feast of Saint Sabina, under seal.

Bristol
September 20, 1497

My dear son Sebastian,

I am grateful for your warning.

It is ever the Portuguese way to want the latest news from the ocean seas.

I do not fear Portugal.

I will not be exploring in waters claimed by that King.

And I do not expect to meet any of Queen Isabella's navy in the waters leading to the East.

While I plan to sail as far south as is necessary, I am not going unprepared. The King of England will outfit one of our five ships with armaments. We will be ready to meet the best that Queen Isabella and her navy can offer. I would, however, hope her country's guns are not aimed at her English friends.

I am not surprised to hear that Amerigo Vespucci has finally become a navigator. He has been in search of a voyage since 1492. Be assured, I do not expect trouble from so old a friend.

My dear son, this is your last year at Sagres. Follow your studies closely. Work hard and be assured you will be with me on the voyage next year.

I promise you.

God bless you in all you do.

Your Father

Saturday of the September Ember Week, under seal.

DIARII

Bristol

September 21, 1497

Still surrounded by young men and boys when we go out the door.

They trail us, begging Giovanni's story.

I get pointed at even when I am not with him.

It embarrasses me.

Eighteenth Sunday after Pentecost.

DIARII

Bristol

September 22, 1497

Giovanni has made a deal with the throng.

When he is with me, they are not to approach him.

I still see youngsters lurking in the ditches as we pass.

I hear his name everywhere.

When he goes out alone he is a kite with a very long tail.

Feast of Saint Maurice.

DIARII

Bristol

September 23, 1497

We have bought horses.

We ride outside the town every day the weather is fine.

Carry a picnic.

Sit in the fields.

Giovanni plays his flute.

I sing.

I feel like a new bride.

Feast of Saint Thecla.

DIARII
Bristol
September 28, 1497
This is what other women have – this everlasting contentment
– their husbands – day after day.
Nineteenth Sunday after Pentecost.

DIARII
Bristol
September 29, 1497
I never thought I would contemplate staying in Bristol.
    Giovanni here – I can't contemplate leaving.
    I am beguiled.
Feast of Raphael, archangel.

DIARII
Bristol
October 4, 1497
I used to pray for this benediction – seven months with my
husband.
    I thought it would be in Venice – the centre of the world.
    It's Bristol – the rim . . .
    A great price!
        Gemma, we will stay in Bristol until Spring.
        In this cold, Donna?
        In this cold.
        Then you will have to buy me new clothes.
        When did I deny you clothes, Gemma?
        But warm clothes, Donna.
    Poor Gemma. She never imagined herself in a northern
country.
    Nor did I!
    Neither Guido nor Gemma are happy.
    There is nothing to be done.
Feast of Saint Francis of Assisi.

My dear Lodovico,

Your father is putting together a small fleet of five ships. He will leave for a third voyage to the East in the Spring, sometime after the Feast of the Ascension.

I will stay with him at Bristol until he is ready to sail.

He will spend twelve months exploring.

This time he plans to follow that new coast southward.

Sebastian will go too.

He will be a full-fledged navigator after this year. He should be a great support on that long voyage. Your father is making him captain of the *Mathye*. He will tell him when he returns from Sagres.

Don't drop a word.

The King is supplying a ship with armaments for which, I hope, they will have no use. Your father, as master of the fleet, will take charge of it.

Your father promises he will leave the sea by 1500. I believe he means it.

Jesus and His Holy Mother be with you, my son.

Mother

Twentieth Sunday after Pentecost.

DIARII
Bristol
October 7, 1497

Have bought a portative organ – will sell before I leave.

Working on my Jubilation Mass – started another Gloria – more joyous.

Feast of Saint Justina, patron of Padua.

DIARII
Bristol
October 18, 1497

Giovanni takes care of all the accounts.

We have no arguments.

I see my husband would be happier with a poor wife.

Yet he wants to make me richer than I am.

I do not understand this contradiction in my husband.

Feast of Saint Luke, Apostle.

DIARII
Bristol
October 28, 1497

Our first supper for these English. Only eight – Giovanni's principal backers and their wives.

No dancing. The English turn more to serious conversation.

We talked of *The Travels of Marco Polo*, Cardinal Pierre d'Ailly's *Imagio Mundi*, Nicolas of Lynn's *De Inventio Fortunata*, all of which – I should have not been surprised – they had read.

Phillipa commanded the table, illuminated a point in contention, talked louder then she ought, lapsed into silence the rest of the evening.

After supper Giovanni brought out a piece of parchment, sketched a mappamundo, sailed his caravel to the west – drawing in little caravels as he went.

He drew the Tata River beyond Tana, situated the Tartars along it: a whole village appeared on the chart with a few strokes.

Further west he sketched in Alexander's Wall, positioned behind it the Gogs and the Magogs who, he said, are the lost tribes of Israel who followed the golden calf to the East, came up against the barrier thrown up by Alexander, settled down there – I doubt that, but it made a good story.

My husband does not use the words 'spices and silks' even with his backers.

Feast of Saint Jude.

DIARII
Bristol
November 25, 1497

The words of my new Gloria are dissolved in the music.

I am working at the top of my bent.

Feast of Saint Catherine of Alexandria, philosopher.

DIARII
Bristol
December 1, 1497
Giovanni said we would spend every afternoon and evening together.

Already he has been away two afternoons – in Venice I would not allow that.

Months ahead of us; time seems an everyday commodity – we can afford to spend recklessly.
Feast of Saint Eloi.

DIARII
Bristol
December 7, 1497
Giovanni heard from Roberto. He turned down the invitation for next year's voyage.

He's going to Jerusalem – third hand, on the Contarini galley.

Then what was Paola's begging letter about last year?
Second Sunday of Advent.

DIARII
Bristol
December 15, 1497
Another caravel from Riga, loaded with furs.

Bought a bear rug for our bed and one for Gemma and Guido's.

Like sleeping in an oven.
Monday after the third Sunday of Advent.

DIARII
Bristol
December 24, 1497
Sun – frost.

Icicles hang from the eaves of our home.
I didn't expect congealed water to be so exquisite.
Guido says they are hazardous.
Wants to knock them off.

I won't let him.

At noon, Guido followed the example of our neighbours – knocked off the icicles.

They were dripping down our necks.

Vigil of the Nativity.

DIARII

Bristol

December 25, 1497

Last night attended the Missa Solemnis at Saint Mary Redcliffe.

Giovanni's friends go there.

The choir was stirring.

At the end of Mass the congregation sang what Giovanni says is a carol: Salvi Sancta Parent.

Half in English, half in Latin.

They raised their faces to the ceiling as if they were singing directly to God.

When they swirled out into the snow that seemed to hang in the air, they greeted each other with the warmth of travellers. Many lingered in the churchyard exchanging news of the day.

Giovanni held my arm tightly, mixed among them, found more people to introduce me to.

Feast of the Nativity of the Lord.

DIARII

Bristol

December 26, 1497

My body feels different in this northern land – stiff.

All those heavy clothes!

And everybody smells like oat cakes.

Feast of Saint Stephen.

DIARII
Bristol
January 6, 1498
My Jubilation Mass – I am drawing down the music of the spheres – I am.

The work will be completed by Paschaltide – I know it.
Feast of the Epiphany.

DIARII
Bristol
January 7, 1498
Have written to Canon Leonardo.

Proposed my Mass as suitable for the consecration of a church. Does he know of one being built?

There are few theatricals in this town – the one or two great houses that could entertain wandering companies, don't.

Giovanni says there will be a cycle of Easter plays put on in the streets – by the guilds.

Thank God Easter is early.

In Venice, by this time in the Church year, we would have celebrated twenty-five saints' days: for every one a High Mass in Office; a procession across the Piazza to San Marco's.

Then there is theatre, singing, unveiling of paintings, lectures – on and on.

And the Grand Canal brings the wonders of the world to my door.

I would perish in Bristol – Giovanni knows it.
Feast of Saint Raymond.

Florence
January 11, 1498

My dear Mother,
I have sad news; even now it is difficult to write.

Both Alessandra's parents died in a wave of plague that hit Florence in August.

It happened like this:

A couple of people living on the other side of the Arno died suddenly. The alarm went out.

Those who had summer places began to leave immediately.

Alessandra and her maid went to the Mugello. Her father, who had business to transact, stayed on for a few days, her mother with him.

They did not arrive at the Mugello within the time expected. Alessandra went back to Florence only to be met with the yellow block nailed to their door with the word *Quarantine* stamped on it.

She and her servant went to Isabetta's house, although only a few servants were left there.

Within a day both her parents were dead.

When I received the news I rushed to Florence. I found Alessandra still at Isabetta's.

She was desolate.

At once I could see what turn our future would take.

The plague killed thousands. After it had run its course, Donna Isabetta and Messer Lorenzo advised me to wait another three months to give Alessandra time to get over the worst of her sorrow.

My dear Mother, I must tell you that on the Feast of Saint Basil, Alessandra and I married.

I have now decided I will not finish my arts degree at Pisa but will go to the University of Padua and begin my canon law studies. That move will enable me to earn a living within two years, and will give my wife some time away from Florence, which I hope will relieve the worst of the dreadful memories.

Alessandra believes there will be patrons for her paintings at Padua. I will introduce her to those in Venice who buy pictures.

We will be in Padua for the May term. With Sancio there,

we will make a small family. Alessandra has only second cousins left in Florence.

When you return, you will again have three young people to visit you, although Alessandra will still be troubled.

Dear Mother, I need extra money. Will you and Father kindly arrange that I receive the stipends you promised?

Alessandra has more money than she needs, and will make more from her painting, but you know how I will want to pay the daily expenses.

I am, dear Mother, your respectful and truly married son,
Lodovico
First Sunday after the Epiphany.

Bristol
February 10, 1498

My beloved son,

We have had a Requiem Mass sung for the repose of the souls of Alessandra's parents.

Alessandra's grief must be unbearable.

You made the right decision to marry. I only regret your family was not there to support you.

I am delighted you have decided to go to Padua.

Your father and I have both written to the Pisani and Tiepolo Bank, and arranged for you to be paid the extra money.

I look forward to the holidays you will spend at home.

My darling son, how we grieve for you both.

But there is joy too in your marriage.

The enclosed letter is for Alessandra.

God bless you both. Bless your life together.

Your Mother
Feast of Saint Scholastic, Benedictine nun, under seal.

DIARII
Bristol
February 12, 1498
My darling son – so melancholy – his marriage day.

How did Alessandra survive it?

Isabetta said she wore a black cloak over her wedding dress.
Feast of Saint Eulalia.

DIARII
Bristol
February 23, 1498
We are still subdued – Alessandra's parents were the same age
we are.
Feast of Saint Milburga, healer.

DIARII
Bristol
March 8, 1498
Letter from Canon Leonardo.

Ever cautious of his Parish dues – offered me a Venetian
deal:

. . . the chapel at the convent of the Sisters of the
Atonement will be finished by the Nativity, next; if you
will *give* the Mass to the nuns for that celebration – I will
pay you one hundred ducats when it is sung at Easter at
San Zan Degolla.

Not a bad deal.

I will direct the choir at both churches!

Yes, I will!

I long for 1500 Anno Domini.

I long for home.
Second Sunday in Lent.

My dear Lodovico,

Your father will leave Bristol on Easter Monday.

North of Ireland they will pick up prevailing winds westward.

I shall return on the family galley in April. Gemma, who has never liked Bristol, is jubilant.

I have bought a number of fur rugs from a caravel that comes loaded from Riga each Autumn. I am bringing one to you and Alessandra. In the coldest night you stay as warm as a May day in Venice. It's a miracle. Those English use them all winter. Both your father and Sebastian each will take one aboard ship.

How I long to see you, my dear son, and meet Alessandra!

First I must leave your father. You can now understand what that will cost my heart.

However, it will be just two years and he will stay in Venice for the rest of our days.

Jesus and His Mother be with you and Alessandra.

Your Mother

Feast of Saint Constantine.

DIARII
Bristol
March 17, 1498

My husband doesn't want to hear me speak of leaving.

We do the preparations when he is out of the house.

Gemma reminded me: at Venice I turned a blind eye to his preparations.

Feast of Saint Gertrude.

DIARII
Bristol
March 25, 1498

Our galley will leave from London on the Feast of Saint Isadore.

Venice! Gemma and Guido are ecstatic.

Giovanni will accompany us as far as London.

Couldn't give up my little organ. Giovanni has shipped it to London to go back on the galley with me.

I bring a new Mass to Venice!

Feast of the Annunciation.

DIARII
The Thames, the Contarini galley
April 4, 1498
Giovanni paled as we said farewell.

Staggered.

I had to comfort him.

Poor lamb, it is easier to leave than be left . . .

Feast of Saint Isidore.

The Thames
April 4, 1498

Beloved of my life,

Incline the ear of your heart.

We will resume our days in each other's arms.

You promised!

Go now in the hands of the Living God.

Mathye

DIARII
The Contarini galley, off Lisbon
April 12, 1498
The first time I am not laid low by parting with my husband.

On a copy of his chart of that ocean sea – that new land – I measure the distance they travel each day.

I give them clear skies. Fresh breezes.

When I arrive at Venice they will have reached that new shore – maybe before.

In two years there will be an end to it. I am filled with a sweet peace.

Easter Sunday.

DIARII
Venice
May 16, 1498
The splendour of being home!

I feel like a tree that has been dormant – I want to stretch and shake my leaves.

No sons.

As I stepped off the galley, I expected them – still young – to run to me.
Feast of Saint Margaret.

DIARII
Montebelluna
July 7, 1498
Seven months in a small house with my husband – sometimes I turn, expect him still at my side.

Yesterday morning, I thought I heard him singing – stopped – walked out through the cloisters.

Were you singing, Guido?

No, Donna Caboto.

Went to the second floor.

Was Luigi here, Gemma?

No, Donna.

Are all the peasants in the fields?

Yes, Donna.

All day, not even music could bring back a quiet state of mind.
Feast of Saint Palladius.

Bristol
July 19, 1498

My dear Mother,

The most cursed luck.

I am back in Bristol!

We ran into a violent wind and rainstorm off Dursey Head on the Feast of Saint Athanasius.

The *Mathye* had her side stove in. The *Gabriel* managed to get a rope aboard her. We were hauled into port.

When the storm cleared, we took account of the damage: the rest of the fleet needed only minor repairs but the *Mathye* required a thorough overhaul. She couldn't be made seaworthy under a month.

I wanted Father to wait, or at least send another captain to Bristol with the *Mathye*. He couldn't be persuaded – she was my ship, I had to stay with her.

Part of our provisions, those that weren't drenched, were shared among the other four caravels.

Father and the others left Dursey Head on the Feast of Saint Brendan.

We limped into Bristol on the Feast of Saint Thomas.

This is the second time I have been on a voyage that has ended in disappointment. I hope it is not an omen for my future.

Mother, I am an unhappy man.

As you would say, dear Mother: unhappy men get only unhappiness.

I have pulled up my socks and have a contract to take a load of cloths to the port of Huelva, Seville. I will be back at Bristol sometime after the twentieth Sunday after Pentecost.

I will work out of this place until Father returns next Spring.

I am, my dear Mother, your loving but disappointed son.

Sebastian

Feast of Saint Vladimir.

DIARII
Venice
August 18, 1498
My heart – when I saw Sebastian's handwriting.

All my sons are safe!

My husband has only strangers to his back.

It never ends.

Feast of Saint Helena.

Dear Lodovico,

Yes, I am back at Bristol. A storm caught the fleet off Dursey Head and the *Mathye* got the worst of it. It took almost a month to have the damage repaired.

Father wouldn't be persuaded and went on without me.

I am a very unhappy man!

I am working out of Bristol until Father returns in 1499.

I was at Mass at the Dominican Priory last Sunday and heard the presiding friar pray for the soul of your friend, Friar Savonarola. After Mass I spoke to the friar. He told me an awful tale of hanging and burning, and the Pope involved.

What did the poor man do to have brought on himself such a dastardly death?

My respects to your wife.

Sebastian

Feast of Saint Bernard, under seal.

My dear brother Lodovico,

It is my sad duty to tell you that Father and his ships are overdue.

Mother told me you and Alessandra were home on the Feast of Saint Theobald, so you know she is worried.

Father would have run out of victuals by June. I am hopeful, but already Father's backers are sombre.

I am sure Mother is wild with grief; it is barely concealed in her last letter.

I will stay at Bristol until the end of September, which is the last month we can reasonably expect him.

Can you, Alessandra and Sancio be in Venice by the Feast of Saint Jude?

I can face anything the ocean has to throw at me.

I cannot face our grieving mother.

I depend on you.

I have written to Sancio.

Your brother,

Sebastian

Feast of Saint Titus, under seal.

Venice
November 11, 1499

Dear Donna Isabetta,

We are worried about Mother.

She gets out of bed only for supper.

Adriana visits daily but can provide no respite.

On the rare feast-day Lodovico, Alessandra and Sancio are home, Mother manages to be up by dinnertime. After they leave, her grief seems more intense.

I thought if you would visit you might help her through this terrible anguish.

Nurse and I are concerned.

With respect,

Sebastian

Feast of Saint Clement, under seal.

DIARII

Venice

December 4, 1499

Isabetta here – every morning!

She makes me get dressed.

We walk in the Piazza.

Each day she insists we visit friends.

I abhor it.

Feast of Saint Barbara.

DIARII
Venice
December 31, 1499
Sixth hour of the night.

How is it I am washed with sorrow?
My tears run down like torrents.

How is it my strength is weakened?
I am unable to rise from my bed.

How is it I have found no rest?
My friends appear as enemies.

How is it I am desolate?
My sons cannot comfort me.

How is it my frolics are departed?
The evenings of my long feasts forgotten.

How is it my gold has dimmed?
The colours of my clothes as ashes.

How is it I have become a widow?
Weeping in the night – the tears on my cheeks.

Feast of Saint Silvester.

DIARII
Venice
January 1, 1500
Where, then, did his great heart stop?
  STOP!

Epilogue

Antwerp
November 16, 1548

Dear Lodovico,

This letter, coming to you from the Netherlands, will, no doubt, surprise you.

I have found it necessary to leave Seville.

You see, my dear brother, I have discovered how our father died.

He was betrayed by his friend Amerigo Vespucci.

Here is how I came by this sad news:

As Pilot Major, I was responsible for the Chart Room at the King's palace. In that room there are deposited hundreds of charts and logs, many the work of the earliest navigators.

I often used them in training my pilots.

On the Feast of Saint Mark, I was reading Amerigo Vespucci's log on his long ago 1499 voyage to Coquibaçoa, in South America, when I came upon this entry:

Met the English this day, the Feast of Saint Helena.

Followed the Queen's orders and engaged them.

I was transfixed.

In 1499 Father's would have been the only English expedition on that coast.

My mind wouldn't take in the significance of what was before me.

Confused, I went home to bed.

In the night it sank in.

In his 1498 voyage, Father must have sailed the length of the coast of North America and into the Caribbean Sea where, in 1499, he met Amerigo Vespucci's ships somewhere near Coquibaçoa. Vespucci *engaged them*, that is, *blew Father and his ships out of the sea*.

My dear brother, this conclusion horrified me.

I had to find further proof of this treachery.

I reread Vespucci's 1499 log.

Vespucci and his mariners had four heavily armed ships. They were sent out by Queen Isabella to make the seas safe for Christopher Columbus, who earlier had made discoveries in the Caribbean Sea, and continued to explore there.

Vespucci wrote a book about it; I read it when still a young man.

I reread it.

All along the Caribbean coast of South America, Vespucci and his crew killed and maimed the people living there.

Vespucci made no reference in his book to his meeting with the English.

Why was this meeting kept secret?

I began reading everything I could find on that period.

In the meantime, I began searching for the charts Vespucci used or had made during his voyage.

The Chart Room was full of charts; many were resting against the walls; most were stowed in cabinets.

I immediately ordered my scribes to make a record of each, and store them in good order.

On the Feast of Saint Thomas the Apostle, I went into the Chart Room in search of a chart I wanted to use in a lesson I was preparing for my class.

A few large charts were stacked against the wall.

One had fallen.

I picked it up and noticed something was rolled inside; I opened the large chart along the floor.

I found a smaller one, about two feet by one and a half.

It was drawn by Father!

He had fixed his siglum to it.

It was dated 1499, in the Year of Our Lord.

It was a mappamundo that included the coasts of North and South America starting at the Newfound lande Father discovered during his 1497 voyage.

A wave of light broke over me!

Father, as his chart shows, was the first to discover North America and realise it was a new continent.

He had drawn on his chart five English flags to mark the places where he had landed.

I looked down at the large map at my feet.

It was an exact copy of Father's smaller one!

It was drawn by Juan de la Cosa, Vespucci's cartographer.

My dear brother, it is common knowledge among mariners that Amerigo Vespucci did not go near the coast of North America in 1499.

Vespucci not only stole Father's chart, he stole Father's place in history. Father discovered America.

I immediately sent one of my scribes to the King's scriptorium for Vespucci's Letters Patent.

My scribe found nothing.

I then remembered it would have been the expedition leader, Alonso de Ojeda, Queen Isabella's military chief, who would have been given the Letters Patent.

So closely had Vespucci, through his writings, associated himself with their 1499 voyage, de Ojeda's name has almost passed out of history.

My scribe found no copy of the 1499 Letters Patent, but he did find the ones given to de Ojeda for his next voyage in 1500.

Here is what they say, in part:

Her Highness grants you a gift of six leagues of land on the island of Hispaniola . . . *for stopping the English . . . and for what you shall discover on the coast of the mainland.*

This is nice diplomatic language to confuse the fact that Ojeda/Vespucci had come upon Father and his English explorers and killed them. That he had stolen the chart of the coast of North America Father had explored and charted.

Then a part of the puzzle that had completely slipped my mind fell into place.

I had known about the Vespucci/de Ojeda proposed voyage. I had been told by one of my masters in 1497.

I had written to Father about it.

I had to find out more about Amerigo Vespucci and his activities.

There is a colony of Venetians living in Seville, as in almost every major city.

I found among them a lawyer I could trust and sent him on a mission to Venice, with enough money to buy any information.

My man was gone six months. He brought back a record book containing what I was looking for.

This book showed there had been traffic between Amerigo Vespucci and a Secret Committee of the Venetian Collegio for the whole period Father was working out of Bristol.

Amerigo Vespucci, Father's so-called friend, was a spy to the Republic of Venice, for Queen Isabella of Castile.

The Secret Committee had one meeting with Vespucci in each of 1492, 1493, 1495, 1496, 1497.

The record book also contained two letters from Queen Isabella: one telling of a report of a meeting of the Secret Committee of the Collegio, and one enclosing *Mother's letter to Paola*.

It was a great shock to see our valiant mother's letter in such reprehensible company.

I will deal with Mother's letter first.

It told about Father's return from the 1497 voyage, that he would go on another in 1498. Almost anyone in Bristol could have provided those facts.

How did Mother's letter end up in the hands of the Collegio?

It could have been intercepted. The Republic of Venice had, and has, the most efficient set of spies in Europe. And I have never done business with a postal service that didn't have its price.

It could have been stolen from Paola's home.

Or the unthinkable: Paola could have given it to them.

Didn't Paola have an uncle in the Collegio?

But now to the letters from Her Highness.

As both letters contain much the same material I will send you a copy of only one:

Seville
December 8, 1497

The Sovereign Queen of Castile sends greetings to the Doge and Senate of Venice.

Through these our letters, we have commissioned our well-beloved friend, Amerigo Vespucci, to bring our concerns regarding the invasion of our territorial seas to the rulers of the great Republic of Venice.

We have knowledge that a certain citizen of Venice, Giovanni Caboto by name, now in the employ of the King of England, is voyaging in our waters beyond Cape Verde Islands.

By the Treaty of Tordesillas negotiated with Portugal in 1494, a line was drawn from pole to pole, 370 leagues west of Cape Verde Islands; this line cut the sphere in two halves; all to the west of that line was ceded to our realm.

Always craving harmonious relations between our several States and that of the Christian State of Venice, we pray God that La Serenissima will respect our seas to the westward, as we respect the great trading routes through which Venice brings the wealth of the East to the Christian countries of the world.

We have requested that our friend Amerigo remain in Venice until an answer is prepared and then return in haste to our Court.

Yo la Regina

Monday after the second Sunday in Advent.

As to the records of the Collegio meetings: there was only one full set of notes. Where the others should have been, there was just a date, the titles of the three Venetian officials attending, and Amerigo Vespucci's name; the rest of the paper was blank, except for the phrase: *no record kept.*

Here is the one entry of the Collegio meeting:

Secret Meeting
Doge's rooms
Third hour of the night

Messer Vespucci came for the decision.

The Secret Committee, dealing with the threat to the State of Venice from one of our citizens, now in the service of the King of England, gave this reply to the Letter from Queen Isabella of Castile.

The Doge, on behalf of the Committee, confirmed that in 1496 the citizen in question made one voyage westward in search of a short route to the spices of the East. No route was found. He made a second voyage in 1497 and discovered land. It is understood this citizen plans a third voyage in 1498.

The Doge stated that if any such short route were discovered it would be to the destruction of the trade that our Illustrious Republic now carries on with the countries of the East, on which the wealth of our people depends.

The Doge further stated that the Republic would not take direct action against the said citizen as he was married into one of the oldest and noblest families of Venice and his citizenship gave him the status abroad of an ambassador; however, *neither would the Republic find cause to concern itself if Her Highness found it necessary to protect her territories from countries that sent ships into her seas.*

In coming to this decision, the Doge stated, the

Committee had taken into consideration the Treaty of Tordesillas signed between Her Highness and Portugal in 1494.

The Committee requested that Messer Vespucci take their decision to Her Highness under burden of the utmost secrecy.

A letter of greeting was handed to Messer Vespucci to deliver to Her Highness.

Signed:

The Doge, Agostino Barbarigo

Inquisitor, Antonio Loredan

Grand Chancellor, Zuane Dedo.

Third of the Ides of March, 1497.

My dear brother, after reading that document, I felt as if I had been tortured by the Inquisition.

I had no one to whom I could go with my grief. I was alone in my house with my servants.

One country against him, Father might have escaped – both Venice and Castile against him, he was doomed.

You can imagine, my dear brother, there were a number of people I wanted to send to God.

The first would have been Father's so-called friend, the spy and double agent, Amerigo Vespucci, followed by Alonso de Ojeda, Juan de la Cosa, and Her Highness, Queen Isabella.

All are dead.

I knew I could no longer live in Seville.

I decided to come to the Netherlands.

I brought Father's chart with me, sewn in the lining of my cloak. I have the record book containing the documents from Venice, and I brought the copy of de Ojeda's Letters Patent.

Father named the whole of the land mass, of what is now North America, after Richard Americ, his chief backer.

And is it not unbearably ironic, because of his writings, it is

Amerigo Vespucci who has been given the honour of having that vast land named after him?

Now I have to find my way to London, from where I will make these things known in the proper time.

I have no intention of returning to Seville. That country has the death of one Caboto on its conscience, it won't catch another.

Before I leave this world I will try to right those wrongs.

Mother, God rest her soul, would remind me vengeance belongs to God.

Your brother,

Sebastian

Feast of Saint Gertrude, under seal.

Glossary

Alb A loose-sleeved, floor-length linen garment worn by men of Eastern countries.

Albergo A small boardroom where the officers of the Scuola held their meetings.

Altana Wooden platform on the roof of a Venetian house.

Asper Small coin used by the Saracens of the Ottoman empire, approximately 120 to the English penny.

Aut vincamus aut vincamur! Let us either conquer or be conquered!

Avaunt! Be gone!

Bucintoro Large state galley used by the Doge for ceremonial purposes.

Calcio Football.

Calle A narrow roadway.

Campanile Red-brick tower at the south-east corner of the Piazza San Marco that served as a beacon tower and church belfry.

Campo A square. In Vencice, only the square in front of San Marco's was called a Piazza.

Caravel Sailing vessel. In the fifteenth century it was rigged with a topsail, spritsail, a lateen and a great square sail.

Carrack A merchant vessel used by Mediterranean countries in the fifteenth century.

Catholic Monarchs Title conferred by Pope Innocent VIII on Queen Isabella and King Ferdinand after they expelled the Muslims and Jews from Granada.

Cob Merchant ship that sat high in the water; it carried various sets of sails.

Collegio The executive committee of the Venetian Senate.

Condottieri Leaders of mercenary soldiers.

Dies Irae Day of Wrath, a hymn usually sung in plain chant during the Good Friday services.

Ducat In 1495 there were 124 soldi to the ducat. One ducat was equal to 55 English pence.

Ecce homo Behold the man.

Flageolet Whistle flute with four holes in the front, two at the back.

Fraterna Family trust. The bulk of family wealth was vested in the Fraterna; it was generally entailed on male heirs.

Frottola A simple song with the melody sung in the highest voice, all other voices weaving the harmony underneath.

Greek Master Term used to designate the architect in the medieval period.

Haec igitur regio, magni paine ultima mundi Such then is that region, almost the furthest in the vast world.

Holy See The Roman Catholic bishopric of Rome.

Istoria Large-scale pictorial narratives on walls of Scuole and other public buildings in Venice.

Kyrie Eleison Greek for 'Lord have mercy', intoned six times in the second part of the Mass.

Loggia A gallery open to the air on one or more sides.

Mappamundo Map of the medieval world.

Mind's Mass A Mass said thirty days after death to ensure the mind of the deceased was at rest.

Narthex A vestibule between the church porch and the nave.

Natural son Illegitimate son.

Portative organ Medieval instrument small enough to be carried; it had a single rank of pipes; the keys were played by the right hand while the left worked the bellows.

Portolano charts Practical charts of shorelines drawn by ships' masters to indicate wind directions, bays, headlines, islands.

Provveditore Commissioner for the fleet.

Provveditore di Comun Commissioner responsible for streets, bridges and public wells.

Quadriga Four bronze horses that surmounted the central portal of San Marco's in the fifteenth century.

Ri Small canal.

Saltarello A dance of hops and turns which people danced in groups of twos and threes; it was accompanied by pipes and drums.

Salvi sancta parent Hail holy parent.

San Petro ad Vincula Saint Peter in Chains.

San Zan Degolla Saint John with his throat cut.

Savi de Terraferma Members of the Collegio who had expert knowledge of the towns and other lands Venice possessed on the mainland of the Peninsula.

Scuola Religious confraternity.

Signoria Government of Florence.

Soldo Venetian coin. Two soldi was equal to approximately one English penny.

Tempus fugit Time flies.

Thirteen crew members There were thirteen in the first band of followers of Jesus, including Himself. One of them betrayed him.

Tow Material made of flax, hemp or jute.

Yaffel An armful (of wood, for example).

Yo la Regina I am the Queen.

Playing Madame Mao
by Lau Siew Mei

£7.99 • paperback • 1 84024 211 6 • 129 x 198 mm/320 pp

A potent weave of political intrigue and self-discovery.

'I play Madame Mao. Death is my familiar. On opera nights, I paint my face a ghastly white, and stretch my eyes with black grease till they touch the outermost limits of my face. I screech my killings.'

Contemporary Singapore: jangling to the clamour of its past struggles and the realisation of its new. The country's story is also that of an actress, Chiang Ching, who performs Madame Mao Tse-Tung on stage while her scholar husband is accused of Communist conspiracy, arrested and detained without trial. Struggling to understand her own role, her origins as a prostitute's daughter, her country's cultural and political history and, as was her alter-ego, increasingly delusional, the lines of Ching's world – the real, mythical and imagined – become blurred.

Lau Siew Mei was born in Singapore in 1968. She emigrated to Australia in 1994 where she now works as a journalist. *Playing Madame Mao* was nominated for the Queensland Premier's Literary Award and was one of only six books shortlisted for the NSW Premiers' Literary Award for Best Work of Fiction. *Playing Madame Mao* is Siew Mei's first novel.

Salar Jang's Passion
by Musharraf Farooqi

£7.99 • paperback • 1 84024 224 8 • 129 x 198 mm/320 pp

High farce and the spice of conflicting passions in Pakistan.

'Farooqi combines Desani's eye for absurdity, Rushdie's delight in wordplay, the gently wicked humour of Dickens and George Eliot's ability to find the right word for everything.' *Mitali Saran*

The sleepy town of Purana Shehr is happy to trundle along in a round of petty arguments over tea and frustrated fantasies. Until, that is, the arrival of the termites. In the narrow lanes and grubby markets of the Topee Mohalla neighbourhood, and against a backdrop of destruction, passions stir as the residents begin to come to life. A royal chaos ensues as boundaries are broken, old fools are made, and overhand plots are hatched. And at the eye of the storm, Salar Jang, an eccentric septuagenarian with a fortune to bequeath, embarks upon an increasingly bizarre courtship, much to the dismay of his only heir and daughter.

Musharraf Farooqi was born in 1968 in Hyderabad, Pakistan. He worked as a journalist and editor in Karachi and has since translated many Urdu classics. *Salar Jang's Passion* is Musharraf's first novel.

House of the Winds
by Mia Yun

£7.99 • paperback • 1 84024 212 4 • 129 x 198 mm/256 pp

At this world's heart are Korean women . . . laughing, wailing, spirit-cajoling, bosom-bracing, fire-breathing.

Korea, 1960s. A girl stands in the middle of a sunny cabbage patch with her mother. The air is full of butterflies (the souls of children in afternoon naps) and secrets (although they were not secrets at the time). War, Japanese rule and loss are bleeding wounds in living memory, and sadness springs in the heart of this Korean family. As a child, Youngest Daughter believed that her mother was happy with nothing but her children; as an adult, she unravels her memories and finds the threads of her past – of brutality and tenderness, of magic, of the ghosts of ancestors, of words unspoken – that weave themselves into the fabric of all their lives.

Mia Yun was born in Seoul, Korea in 1956. She now lives in New York and has worked as a reporter, translator and freelance writer. *House of the Winds* is Mia's first novel.

For a current catalogue and a full listing of Summersdale books, visit our website:

www.summersdale.com